THE PERILOUS CHALLENGE

Book 3 of the Max Series

David W. Walker

The Max Series

Book 1 – The Witch's Tower
Book 2 – The Clouds of Izmah
Book 3 – The Perilous Challenge
Book 4 – The Return of Fears (coming soon)

COPYRIGHT

Copyright 2023
David W. Walker

Fanzig House
1904 Evergreen Lane
Hattiesburg, Mississippi 39401
United States

Library of Congress Control Number: 2023901106

VNo V A18/2023

DEDICATION

I wish to dedicate this work and all stories of *Gaspaar* to those writers who first moved me in my love of children's fantasy and young adult writing and as guides to a richer deeper world behind the illusion of the mundane: C.S. Lewis, Lewis Carroll and Madeleine L'Engle.

I also happily dedicate this third tale to two friends whose influence continues decades beyond our summer staffing a student coffeehouse in Lake Geneva Wisconsin way back in 1970. Scott Davis and his brother Keith were soulmates of mine on that long ago mission. In a random conversation these two decided I must read C.S. Lewis (I apparently had no say in the matter) and thus enter the path of fantasy and spiritual imagination. I can never thank either of them enough.

David W. Walker

INTRODUCTION

Dear Reader,

The Tales of Gaspaar are told of a long-forgotten time at the edge of a legend whose retellings have grown wide and wild. Time and tongue have added and lost many of those things we look to set in the world around us. Mountains and rivers and lords and ladies change names and places. Yet the stories live because the dragons and wizards even of our day are only reflections; shadows of something out of all time together. May this telling of such tales inspire those best dreams in the reader and encourage the living of a quest in us all. May you journey with hope no matter the darkness and find light on that way. There are good friends to be found in the strangest places and behind all manner of faces. There is much good...and more.

--your honored scribe--

CHAPTER 1

THE INVITATION

The summer after King Randrew's grave illness and his near miraculous recovery was a time when the kingdoms stirred with whisperings of evil deeds and secret plans. Fear stole its way among the people, both noble and peasant alike. Many felt the days of peace were falling away and a time of war was approaching. And so it was with great relief and high hopes that the kingdom of Gaspaar welcomed the invitation to the great tournament at Leorna.

"What's a *list* anyway, Prince Max? I thought it was a way of writin' things." Boxen stood beside the prince on the south lawn of the palace. The boy waited impatiently for the noble to shoot his final arrow. He had watched Max empty his quiver into the target at the end of the green. He had already gathered the arrows three times and was bored with his chore. Being nine years old, Boxen was four years younger than the prince. It was a struggle for him to concentrate on any task for very long at a time.

Max felt a kinship with the young page. He knew what it was to be the youngest of three brothers. He remembered being dismissed as unreliable and inattentive. The prince balanced the last arrow on his finger as he answered Boxen's question. "A list is a tournament of knights and men at arms. It is a great test of skill and courage." He slipped the arrow into place and raised his bow to sight the target. Max took a long breath as he pulled the string further then breathed out slowly. Jippit Jumpjilter had taught him in the elf fashion of archery. He tried to see the arc the arrow must travel in his mind's eye.

"How?" When Boxen had a question he always asked it.

The question broke Max's concentration and he loosened his pull on the bowstring. "How what?"

"How is it a test of courage?"

Max grunted. "The best knights ride against each other with their lances. They battle for a prize and glory. It is a battle of peace, not war." This time he waited before attempting another shot but again Boxen interrupted as he lifted the bow.

"But this one's in Leorna, ain't it?"

"Yes."

"My dad says they're bad folks. He says one day we're like as not to be at war with them."

"Many say that. That's why it's good news that King Lull has invited our knights to the lists. It is a sign of friendship for us to be included in the games. We haven't been to a tournament in Leorna in years and years."

Max looked at the nodding Boxen and slowly raised his bow hoping to shoot the final arrow, but the page spoke again.

"Have you ever been to one of them lists, Prince Max?"

"No, but Derek told me all about them. He's been in tournaments in Averon, even one in Camelot. It's a great thing to see, Boxen. All the knights in shining armor and the ladies in finery, bright tents, banners—"

"And horses? Lots of fighting horses?"

"Horses like you've never seen, except for Derek's

Moonstone. Horses with armor all over and battle skirts. Horses that could pull a castle down. And all that strength to rush two knights, with all their might, to strike lances."

Boxen laughed. "It must be a great crash!"

"Like mountains falling on each other. Derek says, the ground shakes, the air splits, and one rider is thrown down like a thunderbolt."

"You mean killed dead?"

Max had been imagining the tournament but turned back at Boxen's question. "Well — it has happened — but not often. Knights are very strong, and their armor is a help, of course. They put a ball on the end of the lance so it can't punch through the shield or armor. But still, broken bones and lots of bleeding. It's no sport for a weak man. Two years ago Derek broke his leg at Averon."

Boxen grinned. "I heard it was Sir Galen broke it for him."

Max reached out and twisted the boy's nose. "His horse stumbled, you rat! Now be quiet and let me shoot or I'll put an apple on your head for a target."

Boxen pulled away laughing and watched as his young liege set the arrow whistling high through the air. The shaft angled down onto the far target at the end of the lawn. The prince might not be a knight, but only the king's archers could best him and his elf's bow.

***

The Throne Room

Queen Maeve, sitting on her throne, turned to look at her oldest son. "I'm not at all certain what to make of this tournament, Derek. King Lull has shown little kindness to this court. It is hard to imagine his turning around so completely. But perhaps I am judging too harshly. If there is to be peace, surely there must be trust."

Prince Derek crossed his arms. "It's times like this I wish Gerald were still here. One thing he knows are tricks and traps. He'd see what's to see in this business, I suppose."

3

The queen frowned. "You must not speak ill of your brother, Derek. Craft is not always an evil. If Gerald ever opens his heart, it will be as full as his great mind. And he is your brother, wherever he has journeyed and for whatever cause. You must never forget that."

Derek nodded. "Yes, Mother."

They turned as the door of the chamber opened and watched the entrance of the king. Randrew trod into the room evidencing only the slightest use of his polished walking staff.

"Your Majesty," the queen said rising.

"Please, dear, do not rise. Everyone from the street urchins to the bailiff has treated me with so much courtliness since my illness that it wears my nerves. If you want unswerving loyalty and admiration, then become deathly ill. That is my advice to monarchs!"

"How do you feel today, Father?" Derek asked.

"I am using this cursed stick less and less. It is more habit than need. I think riding in the afternoons has been a better medicine than anything the physician mashes up in his pot."

Maeve nodded. "I will join you this afternoon. The weather is too fine for even our widest balconies to enjoy."

"I heard what you were saying about Gerald," Randrew said as he lowered himself onto the throne. "I share your prayers for his hardened heart, my dear. Yet like Derek, I also wish he were here to un-riddle this proclamation from Leorna. I am not so certain of King Lull's new-found love for us."

The queen tapped her chin. "Yet it *is* true that Max risked great peril for his daughter's rescue last year."

Randrew frowned. "And for the courage of our youngest son are we invited to perhaps an *equal* risk? Peace is a fragile bridge and this one has had little weight upon it for a long time."

"Whatever the purpose," Derek said, "we *must* attend this tournament. If we do not, then we insult Leorna openly. King Lull might gain allies from other lands who would think badly of our refusing such friendship."

"That is true enough," said the queen. "Besides, we

might learn much from those who attend. Our knights shall see what strength Leorna commands and might sound out the true leanings of other lands towards both Leorna and ourselves."

Derek grinned. "And a show of strength would do us no harm. Unhorsing Leorna's best knights would make them consider long before marching against Gaspaar."

King Randrew leaned back in his regal chair. "It is settled then. Derek, you shall gather the best of our knights. A company of no more than ten is allowed from each kingdom, and these must be our ten best. You will be captain of this band and must ride for the honor of Gaspaar. Be ready within the week, the tournament is near upon us."

***

Max

Boxen had run on ahead with the arrows and Max was walking to the palace when an apple landed at his feet. Jerking back, he looked up to meet the gaze of Jippit Jumpjilter in the fork of the tree.

"Not much good an elf bow will give you if you keep your head down and your eyes closed, young prince," the elf taunted.

Max laughed. "I'm afraid I would lose a war with apples, master Jippit. But I have no enemies in Gaspaar except maybe an elf who makes me afraid to walk beneath the trees."

The small man gripped a branch and began a swift descent. "You may laugh now, master Max, but you'll not always have Jumpjilter to be your eyes and ears. The time comes when I go on to Elfenland alone. Ready or not, you must stand upon your own — quick-thinking and full-witted as your friend would teach you, but alone, whatever."

"But you can't leave yet, Jippit. You must come to the lists with me and Derek. It will be a grand adventure."

"Adventure, ha! I'd think you'd have had your fill of that by now. Do you not remember hanging above the giant's fire with only a riddle to save you, or racing the wolves on the

5

Lumbadil with but a blade between us and death? But I suppose dangers pass out of your memory as fast as they happen. And what do you mean *you* and Derek? Do you think your father will allow you to go to the tournament, if indeed he lets anyone go? It's all a smelly packet of fish if you want an elf's opinion, and who would not?"

Max shook his head. "Derek will go, you can bet your cap's feather on that. He promised me months ago that I could go to the next tournament as his squire."

"That was before he knew it would be in Leorna, no doubt. Besides, it's not really up to Derek if you go or not."

"When you and I left to find the great wizard at the world's edge, we didn't have permission either."

Jippit dropped deftly to the lawn and glowered at the young prince who had already grown two inches taller than his older friend in the year since they had first met on Max's quest. "Don't think you'll be trying *that* trick on me again. There was a powerful reason for that journey, and it could not be avoided. This would be a selfish prank and a childish one indeed. I'd have the king onto you before you reached the Lumbadil."

Max frowned. "But, Jippit, this is to be the greatest tournament of them all."

"Don't waste your words on me. The king's the one to make your plea to and I doubt he'll think it any wiser than I do. King Randrew's near shrewd as an elf, but don't tell him I said so."

***

The Throne Room

Yet when Max finally did go to his father to make his plea, he was much surprised at the king's words.

"That is the very matter I am trying to decide, my son. You see, just this morning we have received another pair of messages from Leorna. King Lull has asked especially for you to attend the tournament as an honored guest. It seems his daughter asks to see you again. The king wishes to reward you personally for your brave effort in rescuing her. What think you of that?"

Max fought to keep his excitement in check. "I would be honored to see Rhe — I mean — to be the *king's* guest, of course."

Derek smiled at his youngest brother. "How about seeing the young princess again, Max? Does that not appeal to you as well?"

Max coughed. "Oh, well, Princess Rhena isn't like a lot of girls around here. She's not silly at all. Really quite agreeable — for a girl."

Derek laughed.

The queen turned to look out the chamber window. "Perhaps this is indeed the reason for Lull's new manner. If his daughter had risked her life to save *our* child, I am certain we would be deeply grateful. Perhaps we have grown too cynical of the human heart, even in an old foe."

The king nodded. "The princess has added her own message for you, Max." He handed a parchment to the prince who brought it up to read.

Max saw the princess' handwriting and was reminded it was more practiced than his own.

> *Come and let us see if your brother is the knight*
> *you say he is. Perhaps he can teach Sir Warren*
> *a lesson for not coming to rescue me as you did!*
> *-- Rhena*

Derek laughed. "The princess speaks treason for her knights. I'll do all in my power to teach poor Warren his lesson for the little maid's sake."

Max looked at his father. "Rhena would have nothing to do with a trick against us, Father. She would never have signed the letter if it were not truthful."

"I believe Max speaks rightly of the young maid," Queen Maeve said. "She appeared a true and noble princess when she visited our court. There could be no falseness, to her knowing, if she wrote such a note."

"Then I can go?" Max waited as the king and queen looked to each other.

"The hand of friendship is extended; we dare not slap it away. Yet, I do not like it. Our kingdoms have been rivals in bitter struggles in the memory of many still living."

Max took a breath before speaking. "What point were those wars if true peace has not followed, Father?"

King Randrew nodded. "If you go, Max, you must be certain to obey Derek at all times. Do not go anywhere or do anything without his instruction."

"As you command, sire!" Max was happy to follow his brother's lead for this was a knight's journey and his brother was the foremost jouster in Gaspaar.

The king continued. "And the elf, Jumpjilter, will accompany you. He may be a sour fellow in some respects but would face a lion before surrendering you to harm. He is quick-witted and sees and hears much that escapes others. He might serve well in this."

Max frowned. "Father, Jippit was once a jester in King Lull's court and I'm not sure if he had actually been granted *permission* to leave. He might not be *welcome* in Leorna, even if he chose to come."

Derek raised his eyebrows. "*So,* we've been harboring a fugitive all this time. A man of surprises is Jumpjilter."

"Elves do not belong to any country but their own," Max said. "We can't give him up to King Lull."

"I have no intention of delivering my son's stout protector into anyone's captivity, Max. But this does make it more difficult for the moment. I would be much relieved to have the elf accompany you on your journey."

Derek scratched his neck. "I think I know a way he might go. A jester's known more by his clothes and bounce than by his face. Let Jippit wear a disguise and act as a squire or page. He's short enough to be a boy. He'd have no need to come near the king if he tends the horses."

The queen smiled. "Few boys wear such beards as the elf's. I do not think he will part with that."

"Well, he can wear a hood and be a groom. Maybe a

false stomach would hide his shape," Max suggested.

King Randrew leaned back on his throne. "Send for the elf. I'll ask him myself." The king chuckled. "Mark you, this fellow will go in all good will, but he'll not show it, if I know him. Following a king's command is as foreign to his nature as flying. Heeding our request must be seen as a hard favor. He will make known it is against his better judgment and followed only with great courage."

CHAPTER 2

SCHEMES AND SCHEMERS

On the very day that Derek began assembling his knights in Gaspaar, King Lull of Leorna sat in private council. His most influential advisor always wore a hooded cloak which overshadowed his face and also added height to his tall frame. The king knew not the true name of his mysterious councilor, who he addressed only as *Darkcloak*. This unusual fellow had arrived at Leorna's palace many months before as a traveling magician, performing for the royal court. His feats included the usual vanishing rabbits and appearing pigeons, yet his astonishing ability to read the thoughts of those he called upon were what had drawn Lull's pointed interest. The king sensed something quite different from mere trickery in this traveling conjurer. Something dark and powerful. Lull considered that this Darkcloak might serve as a useful tool for his own secret

11

ambitions. It was apparent to the king that the stranger clearly understood his thoughts well enough. Day by day, Lull had come to rely upon the magician's words and schemes as the winter passed into spring and then to summer. In time the king was hard-pressed to decide which of his growing schemes were first plantings of his own thought or offshoots of his counselor's imaginings. The magician's words seemed somehow to mirror Lull's wishes almost before the king shared them.

Lull studied his counselor with a curious eye. "It seems peculiar to me, Darkcloak, that you should know so well the thinking of Gaspaar's leaders. The manner in which you sent the second message requesting the presence of the younger prince seems odd. The even more peculiar youthful greeting from my daughter you include, seems stranger still. From the beginning it has been your intention to draw both princes to our castle. This appears a shamble of loose planning to me."

Darkcloak sat still as he answered with a dry, tired, voice. "A shamble seems harmless where a polished lie is suspected for its smoothness. The *afterthought* of inviting the young prince will make the previous invitation seem well-intended and straight forward. The message from the princess performs an even greater help. The court of Gaspaar know her already as a true and upright child with affection for Max, her rescuer. Gaspaar's sovereigns value their own children very highly. They will think how such a rescue would move them to friendship, even if the rescuer were the very devil's cousin."

King Lull squinted. "You are not saying I do not hold equal value of my own child, are you, counselor? Let me assure you that such opinion runs dangerously close to treason. No one, no matter how close he sits to my throne, may make light of that charge."

Darkcloak sighed in a bored manner. "No, Your Highness, I only state that you, the king of Leorna, let no emotion color your intelligence. You are not unduly charmed by the adventurous pranks of the young prince. Chance alone led him to accidentally rescue your daughter. It was not the intent of his quest. In truth, turning the unreasoning deeds of your enemy to your advantage is a mark of your superior ability. It proves your right to rule in the place of such foolish and impractical monarchs. A great empire will require a great leader. He must maintain strict rule without the confusion of emotions and sympathy. The rulers of Gaspaar chose a future king *because* of his unthinking misadventures. They ignored the high qualities of others who would rule to much better advantage. This proves the unworthiness of that family to rule their land.”

The king grinned. “That is quite a spirited speech from you, Darkcloak. You have little love for the royals of Gaspaar. I wonder where this resentment was born, but I’ll not question it. I shall only accept the good it does my ambitions. Now, let us hope your clever invitation will also be accepted.”

Darkcloak paused before answering in a weary voice. “They will come. Prince Derek cannot resist a challenge of chivalry. Princess Rhena’s innocent request will open the path for Max as no soothing words of our own could do.”

King Lull turned to look at the large map of the kingdoms on the wall before him. “Let us hope your assurance in the pious virtues of Gaspaar are warranted.”

*****

Max

It was a deep, gray dawn. The moon was still in the sky and the sun had yet to break the horizon. No one stirred in the streets of the city as the dogs stretched themselves at their passing and the roosters had not yet crowed. Not a cheer or a shout met the company of mounted knights as they rode over the empty cobblestone streets of Gaspaar. The clopping of hooves echoed from the walls of the houses and shops. Max wondered if his friends turned in their sleep as the heavy horses rode by outside their closed windows. For a moment, he saw himself likewise in bed and these riders as a dream. “And how like a dream it *does* seem,” he whispered to himself, as they rode slowly out of the city gates onto the main road.

"A dream I am living." With this thought the prince departed with the morning mists as his friends woke to the new day.

***

Rhena

Rhena, the daughter of King Lull of Leorna, greeted the morning with a wide yawn. It had been a long night and little sleep for the princess. For several minutes she weighed the choice of getting up or closing her eyes again. Then her special project came to mind and she pulled herself upright and stretched. Another final, comfortable, yawn and then out of bed.

Remembering the last evening's ball, Rhena admitted that hosting the prince of Averon's party made for wonderful banquets. However, having to listen to the boasts of court champions was more than boring. "I shall be glad when Max arrives for the tournament," she thought, "At least then I'll have someone to be bored along with me." Of course, the tournament itself would be different.

"That's where 'bravery *talks* and braggarts *balk*,'" she repeated, remembering her uncle Leon's adage. She wondered again, as she often did, about her wandering uncle Leo and where he might be now. It had been almost six years — Rhena had been a mere child of nine — since he had left the court as a paladin or free knight. The princess sighed. "And all for un-requited love!" She had only gathered bits of the tale from gossips of the court and knew to put little trust in such talk. Sometimes Rhena felt as if she were about to remember something important about those days. She could almost see the face of the one whom Leon had pledged his love to and had lost through some terrible fortune. Her uncle's name was seldom spoken since the death of her mother, Queen Lynette. It seemed none would speak of Leon's story. It was her mother's sister Caroline whose image Rhena sometimes imagined through a fog of years. She had married a king far away and the tale ended with Leon becoming a *paladin*, pledging to travel alone and to battle evil at all times.

Rhena's uncle had scarcely visited the court since that time. The last she remembered was of a Christmas three years ago when she was twelve. Most of Rhena's impressions of him stemmed from that visit.

"Wouldn't it be something if Leon came to this tournament," she thought. But there was no sense in building false hopes and she should be happy enough that Max was coming. It seemed funny to think about the youngest prince of Gaspaar now. It had been a year since she had seen him last. Certainly, they had quarreled enough then, but Max was fun and brave, and he did things. Her friends all seemed to think the next ball or pageant was the highest thrill in living. Rhena shook her head. Since her taste of adventure in the Runruggel Mountains, she sometimes longed for exciting things to really happen again.

"Now to work on Max's surprise," she chided herself and pulled open the fabric chest, hunting for her needle. She held up the tunic she was finishing with the colors of both Gaspaar and Leorna sewn into it. "It will be fun to see the look on Malvern's face when Max wears this in the archery tournament."

Malvern was a year older than Rhena and she thought him quite taken with himself. The princess could scarce bear his company or the attention he seemed determined to demand. She knew he boasted to his friends that he would marry her one day and become king. "'*Who else* would she choose?'" Rhena mocked his question. "'Am *I* not the best of all the lads of Leorna?'" She shook her head. "But Leorna is not *all* the world, Malvern."

***

Max

As Gaspaar's knights plodded across the stones of the Lumbadil bridge and past the Red Lion Inn that afternoon, a small band of country folk gathered to watch their passing. Twice before, Max had set out for adventure past this inn and now he saw old friends among those clustered about the door.

15

He waved to Joel and Maude, the innkeeper and his wife. There was Lund, the potter who had lent the prince his horse on his quest of the great wizard. They cheered the knights each in turn and the riders raised their lances in formal salute. The squires straightened in their saddles as they rode by. Cheers rose especially for the champions: Sir Quinn of the Raven and Derek of the Lion's Mane, as each shield displayed the crest of its rider. Lund recognized Max and raised his tankard of ale, and all the patrons did likewise in honor of their crown prince. Max's heart swelled with pride and he blushed when Maude threw a bouquet of flowers clutched from a table centerpiece to the princely squire. A trio of children rushed from the stables with a collection of dogs and pigs. Shouts, barks, and squeals followed the glittering parade for some distance down the road.

When the inn had been left behind and the children had dropped back, Jippit Jumpjilter rode near to Max. The elf shook his head. "Come Max, relax your stance. To sit so stiffly and smile so tightly will break your back and face. The applause was not *all* in your honor. Most adventures start well enough. Let's see how high we hold our lances after the tournament, if you catch my meaning."

Max laughed. "True, Jippit! But didn't your own back straighten as we passed the inn? Besides, is this not the best company of knights in all the lands?"

"I'm sure they'd each agree with you, but that isn't the point. We may be in for more than a pretty tournament. Ten of the best would have a hard time facing a hundred of the worst." A glint shown in Jippit's eye, "And besides . . . you forget that I was at Lull's court for some time. There has been a knight or two of that table who might prove more than a match for Sir Gwen of the Blackbird."

"That's Sir *Quinn* of the *Raven*!" Max said, rising to the bait.

"What's that, squire?" Derek turned to look back at Max and the elf as Jippit chuckled.

That night the company camped in a vale bordered by a brook on one side and an apple orchard on the other. The campfire was warm, and the night sky sparkled with stars as the knights and squires shared their suppers and tales of glory. Max was eager to listen to the stories but marked the quiet manner of the older veterans. Where Sir Brian or Sir Clive would go on long and loud concerning a brave adventure, Sir Quinn or Sir Claire merely smiled, never referring to their own legendary deeds and Claire had once been of the Round Table itself.

Jippit noticed Max observing the behaviors round the fire and leaned close to speak. "So, you've noted the way the band plays? As you've seen, it's an established sign of rank, this informal campfire court. The greater the knight, the less he speaks. Whether this is considered or if it happens naturally, I am not certain. Yet never have I heard a great knight who spoke too loudly of his own merits. An over-bold tongue is an offense to chivalry. It is good to see that we have a few 'silent ones' in our company."

Max nodded. He was also proud to see that Derek was among the quieter participants. Still, at least once he made mention of *Gorackle*, the fierce dragon of far Empt he had slain. Max felt somewhat responsible for this. The squires of the great knights more often argued their master's merits while he, being himself the crown prince, felt awkward doing so for his own brother.

While the moon still hung in the early morning sky, Max woke from a dream. In the middle of this band of champions he felt oddly alone in the stillness and a sense of helplessness weighed upon him. He could not recall his dream, yet he felt an unnamed grief he could not relieve. All the strength of all the armies of the world could not resist the powers of dreams, he decided. "If our mission ends in some terrible disaster," he thought, "it may hang upon strengths greater than sword or lance. I would trade five of our knights for Father Reynard in this." He shuddered and reminded himself that this was a devout company of good heart. Father Reynard himself had said that it was a man's heart and not his armor that served him best in the eyes of heaven.

Max studied the polished shields hung on the braced lances ringing the camp. There was the pale blue field of Sir Claire with the small white tree, the red and black bands of Sir Trevor's shield, Clive's horse head, Derek's red lion prancing on a yellow field, Gavin's black stag . . . In the early light these polished heralds were dull; their bold creatures and high symbols seemed lifeless tokens in the cool stillness. "*Their powers sleep with their masters*," Max thought, "*and live only at the whim of fate.*" The nameless anxious dread settled over his heart and he turned to watch the sun's approach in the orchard. There he saw a single figure kneeling in the wood bowed before the rising light.

Something stirred in Max's heart and he woke the young squire next to him to ask the name of the knight in the orchard. The squire protested but at last rose upon an elbow and turned to look where Max pointed. "Oh," he mumbled, "it is only Sir Claire praying for the souls of the enemies he has dispatched. He does that." Saying this, the squire yawned, flopping back on his pallet to resume his sleep. Max studied the bowed silhouette in the wood and felt his fear dissolving with the growing light.

*****

Lull

The man known to King Lull only as Darkcloak strode with purpose into the royal chamber. The king was looking over a polished suit of chain mail that the anxious armorer and his assistant were holding up for his inspection. Lull was known for his moods. Fortunately for the armorer this seemed a lighter one.

"Yes, yes, I think this should do nicely, my good man. Just the thing for the tournament!" Lull turned to the scowling hooded figure. "Ah! Darkcloak, what has brought you to us in such an agitated state?"

The hooded counsel held out a torn poster. "This, Your Highness — and it is *you* who should be agitated. It was nailed to the church doors this morning."

The king took the document and read aloud:

The king laughed. "Is this what has you so upset, Darkcloak? This is no new thing. This *Catterline* fellow makes great noise but is only a fly on a horse's behind. A few nobles have been robbed and tax collectors chased home empty handed. Hardly a pressing matter. And besides, blessed few of our people read, so such a letter is wasted on the unwashed."

Darkcloak did not rest his hooded stare. "You laugh, highness, but such flies as this may carry sickness that will bring your high horse to its knees."

The king motioned the armorer and his assistant to leave. "Nice poetry, dark one, but really, this peasant leads a band of a few dozen men and boys with little more than hunting bows. From all accounts, they live like beggars, barely surviving. Such a troop might be hard to hunt down, but they are hardly to be feared."

Darkcloak snorted. "Not feared for the numbers of men they command, but for the ideas they hold before the people, excellency. These rebels defy the tax and the army and they are growing. The taxes are not being gathered so easily. There is no room in an empire for even feeble opposition."

Lull nodded. "Yes, yes, I suppose you are right. Well, if it will ease your worry, I'll send a column or two of soldiers after this Catterline — whoever he is. That should put an end to it."

Darkcloak shook his head. "No, you must not give him such importance as to make a show of hunting him down. It might even raise sympathy in the minds of the people and a reward might have the same effect."

"What then?"

"A man of craft and cunning should join Catterline's band. A spy, who for silent reward, would speak brotherhood while sliding home a dagger of deceit."

"Ah, Darkcloak, you must be a mathematician! You always see the most efficient way. Perhaps you have a man we can trust such a mission to? He cannot be known as my assassin, or close to me in any way."

"Wisely spoken, sire. I can provide the man we need, but he will require no small reward."

The king's smile stretched wide. "Oh, he shall have his reward. Do not fret about that, my shrewd friend."

***

Rhena

If there was a cloud on Rhena's happiness as she sewed the tunic for Max, it was the strange distance that had grown between her and her father the king. She could only just remember the happy times before her mother had died. Indeed, they seemed more like dreams of a fairy tale that she had been told over and over than memories of her real life. As she worked, the princess' gaze rested on a painting of her mother. The portrait had long been moved to her rooms from the great hall. Now the picture was growing darker as the sunlight died. Rhena thought of how her father's laughter had died long ago, and their times together had given way to gifts.

The king would obtain anything for her that she named, but no longer gave his laughter. And then it had returned — not as she remembered — but of a different kind. It was no longer a sound of joy, but a bitter mockery. Sometimes Lull's jesters might pull a laugh from him with twists at their foolishness, but never at himself or of happy surprise. And now he laughed sometimes at nothing. This was the most chilling of all, for it was the voice of a stranger. When Rhena had returned from the witch's tower after her escape with Max, her father had shown more feeling than he had in long days. Yet this had not lasted, and a year later he seemed further from her than he had even while she was imprisoned in the cold tower at the top of Tarrand Kittil. Yet Princess Rhena loved her father still and longed for him to open his heart to her again. She held onto that hope with the strength that only children may hold.

Rhena's eyes blurred and she wiped them. The more she let her mind set on this, the sadder she became. She knew it did no good to cry about it. She had done plenty of crying before and it hadn't helped a bit. A sharp pain in her thumb stopped her thoughts. Angry at pricking herself with the sewing needle, she paused to suck her thumb. In that moment she sensed someone pass in the hallway outside her room. Something in the near silent tread disturbed her. She rushed to the door. Looking down the passage she just caught sight a of a hooded figure descending the stairs.   Passing   a corner tower of the keep that merged with the outer wall, she saw the tip of Darkcloak's cape swing through the unlit passage and to the tight staircase that wound down beyond it. She knew these stairs well, the little-used turret was small, and the steps were narrow and steep, making a fast way to the bottom level of the outer wall. There waited a heavy iron door that was to be used only in great emergencies, she had been told by the captain of the guard. In all the years of the castle's defense it had never been used for escape. She often hid in the darkness of the stairs when she wished to avoid flute lessons or arithmetic drills. The ladies of the court never imagined a young girl would be at home in a dank, dark, tower. Rhena was following so fast now she was afraid she might overrun Darkcloak, and that thought brought her to a stop. She resumed her slow downward journey when she was certain she heard only a tiny echo from the bottom of the turret. Rhena waited for her eyes to befriend the darkness as Jumpjilter had taught her. Even elves saw better with a moment of waiting in darkness. Now, as Rhena began to step downward again, she noted a glow from below. Darkcloak had a candle. Of course. He was not so familiar with the turret as she. There came next a scraping sound, a pause, then another scrape. Knowing that there was only one more turn of the spiraled stairs between her and the bottom of the turret, Rhena stopped again. On her hands and knees she peered around the angled steps below her.

Darkcloak stood just inside the iron doorway peering out a small square of twilight. A single metal slot in the door was open. Rhena was certain this had caused the scraping sound she had heard. A key stood in a lock next to the open frame of dusk. No doubt this would have been used to check that the way was clear for those escaping to the moat. Her father's counselor held the candle up and Rhena almost cried out as a face appeared to block the moonlight. The candle flame showed up a cruel scar that ran from the edge of the man's left eye to the corner of his mouth. Darkcloak said something and the scarred face nodded, then said something which brought the counselor's hand up near the opening. The man seemed to stiffen but nodded and lifted his own hand into the window, palm upward and Darkcloak dropped three coins into it. Then the hooded one closed the metal shutter and locked it back in place.

A moment later the candle was smothered, but not before Rhena had begun to retrace her steps up the old turret. What had she seen? An outlaw? A guard? Alms for a peasant? How came the man to be standing at the base of the wall? The drawbridge was down of course. Perhaps this fellow was a soldier or a worker, one of those who worked at the repairs to the parapets but slept outside the gates at night.

Reaching the hallway before Darkcloak, Rhena rushed, grateful for the quiet carpet, toward the forward chambers of the keep. Her thoughts were a jumble. Should she speak to her father? No, for what would she tell him? She had seen Darkcloak do no evil — perhaps even charity. Instead of going to her father's rooms, she moved to a balcony and leaned out to watch the drawbridge as the sentries checked off the workers leaving for the day. She saw the men climbing up from the near side of the bridge where the old timbers were being repaired and repainted. She noted a straggler joining them. Was it her scar-faced stranger? From this distance, she could not tell. She must know more of Darkcloak's secrets before she spoke of them to her father. If the fellow were as dark at heart as in his manner and dress, then she must not catch his attention in any way. She must be certain and ready to make a clear case to the king if indeed there were danger here at court.

CHAPTER 3

THE QUEEN OF THE ORCHARD

Max turned to Jippit as the party of knights rode round the long shoulder of a hill that cast their path in shadow. "This is new land to me, Jippit. Since the last turning I know no mark. We must be nearing Leorna."

"I wish it were new ground to me as well," Jippit answered. "I was much happier on this road the last time I saw it."

"Why is that, Jippit?"

"I was traveling the other way."

"Well then, you must think of your return as triumphant. You come back with a column of royal knights and two princes of Gaspaar. What have you to dread?"

"If I knew what I dreaded, Max, I should be less worried. I'd trade these fine knights for one of the great wizard's spells right now. The evil that waits for us is prepared for knights and armor. That worries me more than somewhat."

Max rolled his eyes. "You will worry yourself to death, Jippit."

"More die foolish than worried."

Max stood up in his stirrups to look further down the road. "How far now until we reach Leorna?"

Jippit looked down the line of Knights as he answered. "Today and a bit of tomorrow at this easy pace will have us there . . . if we arrive at all."

***

Leorna's Forest

The man in the green mantle looked up sharply at the sound of approaching hoof-beats. He rose from his position in the brush and pulled an arrow from his quiver. Stepping into his longbow to string it and set his arrow, he eyed the roadway that twisted through the heavy forest. A sway-backed horse appeared, and the archer relaxed. He called to the rider astride the aging mount.

"How is it in the town, old Fred?"

The elder serf looked to the woodsman with no surprise as he drew his mare to a halt. "The knights come from near and far to join the lists, Corrin. The inns are filled with lords and squires. There is not a room to be had inside the town."

"And what of Catterline's message? Have his posted letters been read? What say the people of the town?"

Fred snorted. "The king's soldiers tear down the letters in little enough time. Besides, those who can read are nobles themselves and, like as not, friends of the king. There will be little support while Leorna is filled with so many soldiers."

"But they do not all belong to Leorna."

"No, but powerful men in armor attending at the king's request are frightening enough."

The archer shook his head. "Evil days, old one, evil days. Even this morning two more families have joined us. Their sons had been taken in the army and their goods taxed

26

too hard. They left their farm to come and plead for our aid. Soon we'll have an army of women, children, and old men."

Fred jerked the reins of his horse. "Do not speak lightly of old men. I fought with the king at the rout of Bundara when you were a baby!"

Corrin bowed. "True, old father, and would that both you and the king were now as you were then."

Fred patted the mane of his horse. "I would see Catterline. Is he at the camp?"

"So, I think, but one is never certain for he travels like a ghost."

"That is well. If we are not certain of his whereabouts, then that much harder for the king, eh?"

***

Rhena

Rhena had gone down to the orchard beyond the moat to escape her harp lesson. Resting against a tree trunk the princess tossed stones to the water. She liked the quiet in the corridors of arching limbs, though her conscience scolded her for going beyond the palace walls. "The moat is to keep strangers out, highness," the sergeant-at-arms had warned her. "You should stay on this side of it." But Rhena preferred the far bank, the quiet bank, she called it. It was the place she came to be alone and think. There was much to think about. Even with the tournament and all the extra tents and visitors outside the city walls, she felt more secure here than anywhere else. Then, as she threw another pebble into the water, she heard an unexpected voice behind her.

"A coin for your thoughts, young mistress."

Rhena turned sharply to face a woman in a dark green robe standing close to her. She didn't recognize her from the court, yet sensed she was of noble bearing.

"I didn't hear you approach," the princess said, eyeing the stranger cautiously.

"I move quietly. It is often best, don't you think?" The woman's face had drawn into a knowing smile.

Rhena felt herself smiling back. "I sometimes move quietly also . . . I learned from an elf."

"Ah! Then you are a rare young woman. Elves are seldom teachers." The woman knelt to settle next to Rhena. "What might be your name, young mistress?"

"It might be anything," Rhena said. "But you may know me as the queen of this orchard. I have declared it a place without names or ages. Here we are simply who we are . . . and not what others make of us."

"I see," the woman said. "I like your wood, my queen."

Rhena watched the ripples on the water. "And if you would claim a title, what would it be?" she asked, following her own rules.

The lady considered before answering. "I would be . . . the queen of last hopes and lost friends."

"That is a strange title. Strange and sad." Rhena stared at the woman. "I have unusual feelings about you, my dear Queen of Last Hopes. You seem like someone I should know."

"Everyone knows last hopes and has lost friends," the lady replied. "That is why I seem familiar."

Rhena nodded. "You are right . . . we all lose things and people that matter to us." She thought of her father as she spoke.

"It's only the people that matter," the lady answered. "Have you lost some young beau, my queen?" The lady's eyes never left her as she spoke.

Rhena was dismayed at this question for she did not like for anyone to mention her feelings for such things. Yet the smile on the lady's face was no taunt and she felt an unexpected desire to answer. "Oh . . . not really. There is one boy I'm fond of — for a friend. He's not at all like the others here. But I shall see him soon. He comes to the tournament, I hope."

"Then you should be happy. Yet you have lost someone?" The lady asked, her smile turning to a frown of concern.

Rhena considered. "Yes. Someone I've known all my life." It seemed so natural to share her thoughts with this lady.

She really had no one else to hear them. "I've loved Father always, yet he has changed . . . as if he's gone away and now there is a stranger in his place."

The lady was silent at this and when she spoke again, it seemed as much to herself as to the princess. "There is a hope, so long as there is life. Even the hardest . . . the coldest heart may return . . . if it will face the journey." She looked deep into Rhena's eyes. "You must pray for your father and you must love him. You must not let the coldness command your heart." She stood. "My queen, you have my prayers. Now I must go."

Rhena felt overcome with a sudden fear of the lady's departure. She reached out and grasped the woman's sleeve, rising with her. She was surprised at the strength of the arm she felt beneath the velvet cover. "My dear queen, you must not go so soon. If you must . . . I give you leave, yet only if you promise to come again."

The woman in green peered down at Rhena's anxious face. "I am your servant," she bowed. "A servant does as she is bid. I will return when time permits. But should you see me in the court, or passing in the crowd, you must not speak to me or of me. You must pass by as if we know not that we are queens. But then look for me here when first you may, when the sun sets as now on the horizon." With a final bow the green-clad lady moved away and was gone.

CHAPTER 4

THE WEIGHT OF WARS

Darkcloak unwound a long parchment onto the table and set a heavy brass candle stick on the edge to hold it flat. The king squinted at the map in the late-night lamplight. The two men were alone in the king's chamber and only a drifting sentry's watch-call marred the quiet of the room.

Lull tapped his lip. "So, this is your master plan. I trust it is the only copy. If such a paper were found, more than one head would roll, my plotting friend."

"There is no other and this one is as safe with me as your very life, sire."

Lull snorted but said nothing as his counselor continued.

"Here you see the lists as they are drawn. Here will be the knights of Averon and their Prince Galen. And here will be the knights of Wotterham and their Prince Linus. Your Eminence's royal box will, of course, be here, directly at the midpoint of the jousting range. And here," Darkcloak said, moving a finger across the lines, "will be the knights of Gaspaar and Prince Derek and Prince Max." He looked up. "They must both come."

Lull grunted. "Go on. I'm not keen on grappling with children in all this, but King Randrew made his choice. It is his fault really."

The hooded counsel nodded. "And here are the squire pits and the service racks for the lances. It is here that the change must be made. It must be subtle. We will stage a diversion to take everyone's eyes away long enough for the change." He looked up for an instant to make his point more certain. "The false lance tip cover will be thin and brittle, the hardened steel point will unhorse, and perhaps dispatch Galen. If it does nothing more than hit the shield a blow, we shall have cries of treachery against Gaspaar. If it kills Galen outright — we shall have war. Averon and Leorna will avenge Galen against Gaspaar. Wotterham and the other smaller kingdoms will follow. So much may be gathered up in a time of turmoil. Such times demand severe measures. Alliances profit well those who plan them in advance. Though it is best if we have both princes accusing each other, it would not ruin our purpose if Galen is killed. In this plan I craft another device. A false copy of Galen's shield. A brittle fake to shatter on impact with the steel lance point. Yes, you shall have your ally in Averon. Averon must avenge their favorite son, Galen, and we shall embrace their cause. We shall imprison the two princes of Gaspaar and their best knights. The high court of Leorna will decide their fate. King Lull will be seen as the preserver of law among the lands. King Randrew will bow in submission in order to ransom the life of his sons. Leorna's power is doubled, perhaps tripled, at a single blow."

Lull shook his head. "You are certain of this, Darkcloak?"

"Yes, of this I am certain. Though a war might achieve more for us than brokered peace."

***

Max

Somewhere near the noon of this second day of the march, when the shadows were underfoot, Max felt a gnawing discomfort. It was as if the trees had no life here. Indeed, no birds or forest creatures were seen in this dry, hot borderland between the kingdoms of Gaspaar and Leorna. This had been long contested land. Battles fought here left the bones and weapons of armies past littered beneath the shallow earth. Pride and anger had claimed the lives of past generations on these patchy reaches. Only since the days of King Todd, Max's great grandfather, had peace held an uneasy grip on these forests and vales. Silence lay thick here. The hoof beats of the horses were muffled. Not even the shrill buzz of the horseflies seemed to cut the quiet that hung over them like a gray dream. "Surely this is a dark place," Max whispered. "Not since Tarrand Kittil have I felt more certain of approaching evil."

Jippit Jumpjilter, who rode beside him, answered. "This place holds the smell of battles fought and lost."

"And won," Sir Brian added from behind them. "Every defeat was a victory as well, squire elf."

Jippit turned to look back at the young knight. "Have you fought in a war, Sir Brian?"

Brian colored. "Nay, I have not had the honor of that challenge. Thus far my fights have all been against villains and rogues. Yet, I can think of nothing more worthy of a knight than riding for his country on a field of battle."

Jippit looked back to Max. "Wars end. That is their only virtue."

Max gazed across the open field they crossed. He imagined rows of men marching into it from both sides. Death

33

and blood waited invisible before them. "But some wars had to be fought, Jippit. Sometimes . . . good people fight them. *Something* must have been worth the fighting."

"That is a question for priests and poets. I am neither."

Max stared at Jippit, but the elf spoke no more. The prince could see the brooding silence here rode on his friend's heart, heavy as his own. Passing the shadowy ruins of a tower, Max caught a movement in the corner of his eye. When he turned to look more directly into the broken walls, he saw no more. Vermin? Ghosts? Max knew the feeling of being watched. Was this real or imagined, he could not guess, nor did he wish to.

***

Maude

Mistress Maude, hostess of the Red Lion, was wiping out the copper mugs behind the counter. The sunset's shadows brightened the candles in the common room. There were no new boarders tonight and Maude sighed at the thought of the passing band of knights from Gaspaar. Such a party spending even one evening under the roof of the Lion would have spent coins on ale and mutton. It needed a great night's profit to make up for such times as these. She had fondness for young Prince Max as well, for he had shown courage and kindness the summer before. It was rare compassion in a noble to take poor Dimbarell's flock for their journey to the mountains. It was told that journey had turned the quest for a crown prince upside down. That honor had indeed come to the lad's shoulders, though surely they were not yet ready for such a burden. Lost in her thoughts of Max, Maude was surprised at the entrance of the stranger. Inside stepped a tall man, draped in black and gray. He looked to be one of the king's wardens though he wore no chain as sign of rank. His beard was short but untrimmed as was his hair. It was obvious from the dust on his cloak that he had ridden a long way. His face was firm, lined with care, not age.

"Is there lodging for the night, good woman?" The

34

man's voice was tired but courteous.

"Tonight, you may choose your room, sir," Maude replied. "And if you can wait an hour, there will be dinner, though it will be only rabbit stew, I fear."

"A rabbit *I* do not have to hunt makes a fine meal," the traveler sighed. "I have put my horse in your stable. Is there a boy to brush him down? I have no squire."

"My husband will be here quite soon. He will attend your mount."

"Nay, I'll manage that. I am not so tired as my faithful horse."

"As you wish, sir."

"Another word, mistress. Have perchance you boarded a party of knights from Gaspaar in these last days?"

Maude wondered if such news were something she should share with just anyone who chanced by her door. She deemed Prince Max as her prince, at least to watch out for. Still, this kind spoken single visitor could offer no threat to such a brave band of knights.

"Two days ago the party you seek passed over the bridge. They did not stay here, for they were hard on their way to Leorna. They were pressed to make the start of the tournament." She smiled at the memory. "Ten brave champions and each with a trusty squire, Prince Max serving as Prince Derek's."

"And others? Mounted men of war who have been on their way to Leorna as well?"

Maude stared at the stranger wondering at his question. "In the last weeks there have been more such men along this way. Few spend their money to sleep here, though they have drunk ale enough to keep us running dry. I will say that we do not serve just any who would use our inn. There are tongues too loud for comfort, as my husband says."

"That is wise," the stranger nodded. "I am surprised your husband leaves you here alone with such goings on."

Maude stiffened and her hand slid below the wooden counter. "Alone I may or may not be, but unarmed, you must decide for yourself."

The man lifted his eyebrows and open hands. "Please, good mistress, do not distress yourself over me. I do not wish to see the sword or crossbow or whatever weapon you grasp. No woman manages such a hall without confidence in more than the good nature of strangers."

Maude smiled. "I trust a man who combs his horse after a hard ride to be a man with rightful regard for ladies and proper conduct."

The stranger brought out a leather pouch and laid three coins on the counter. "One for the stable, one for my room and board, and one for anyone who will polish my armor before dawn."

Cartwheels rattled outside and Maude looked to the window. "My husband is returned with new ale. He will make your shield and helm glisten for such a price! He will see to your horse as well."

The stranger shook his head. "I think bringing in his barrel of ale will be task enough for him now. I'll see to my horse. And I shall be glad to share the rabbits with you both in an hour."

Maude grinned as the man bowed and turned back out the door. If more nobles behaved as this nameless one, then the roads would soon be safe again, she thought. She slipped the gold coins into her purse and went to the yard to help Joel unload the barrels from Gaspaar.

.

***

Max

Max was tired and almost ready to turn in for the night but felt the call of nature after supper and the last drafts of water. He moved downstream alongside the little creek that bordered the knights' camp to relieve himself before seeking his blanket. He started back through a stand of trees when a familiar voice spoke from behind him.

"Greetings Prince of Gaspaar. It seems for once you travel with enough guards to see you through the lands without the aid of old friends."

"Fanzig." Max almost shouted. "It was you at the tower."

"I apologize for hiding in the shadows, my prince. I am afraid there are a number of your party who would see me first as game and too late as a friend."

"How did you know of my journey?" Max whispered. Even if he could explain the nature of the speaking fox prince of Dumbwillow Forest, the others would press upon them both with questions. At best, it would make their visit awkward and perhaps lose any chance at learning much from their time together.

Fanzig sat on his haunches. "Word travels quickly of tournaments. Even posters fastened to trees proclaimed this event. I wasn't sure if I could trust the young squirrel that carried the word from the Lumbadil to my forest. It was clear that he'd never seen such an array of knights . . . though not the hundred he imagined, I'm afraid. Still, one must make allowances for youth. And young squirrels chatter so swiftly they are hard to understand."

Max was grinning. "You mean there are *new* speaking beasts born?"

"Oh yes, though still no more than we lose from season to season. I'm afraid old Gnawt the beaver has left us without an heir. I was sad to see his pelt taken."

"And what of your cubs?"

The Fox rolled out his tongue. "One mumbles . . . he might speak yet, if that be Heaven's will."

"What of Knipper, the shepherd's dog? I often think of him and our adventure together."

"He speaks of you as well. I saw him a month ago working the flock in the lower pastures. Dimbarrel is quite himself again and the flock has grown."

Max had not felt so good all day. "Fanzig, I have looked so forward to this great tournament, yet today I felt a cold dread in the hot sun. The place we passed brought the wars to mind as strong as a memory though it was before my time. I cannot say why my heart was so sad. Grass has grown over the land. The ruins are old. What is this grief?"

The fox shook his head. "That is why I have come to trail you, young master. You have some of the gift your great grandfather was given. You sense more than a memory, but the approach of coming things as well. War waits. We feel it like we sense a coiled snake. We don't know how, but this tournament is like a whirlpool bringing things together for good or bad. It draws in the jealousy and pride that build together before a war can come."

"Then you say we should not go? That we should turn back?"

The fox raised his eyes to Max. "That, I cannot say. I do not think it would end the danger, and what may be done, may be best done where you are going. It is not for me to see. I know that there is a stirring among all the speaking beasts. Even old Fletcher is on the wing. We spoke this morning. He is drawn west. Birds are moved more by blood than even we four-pawed ones."

"If only there were an army of you beasts."

Fanzig raised his amber eyes. "Do not be fooled by tooth and claw, Max. Man has long outstripped the children of the forests in force and fierceness. The bear must be made angry to strike. He does not plot or plan. But you have us few to serve you and that is what I bring to you now. I shall watch for you beyond the walls of the city. I shall wait with what little good can be offered. One never knows the worth of anything, until it is needed."

Max had been overjoyed to meet his old friend again, but now he felt his sadness return. "I hope never to lose my friends of the forest, Fanzig. Not while I am prince."

Fanzig grinned. "Or king."

With that the fox turned and was gone before Max could speak again.

He would tell Jippit in the morning of his visit. For tonight he kept it to himself and mused long on the words of the fox before he fell to sleep.

CHAPTER 5

CATTERLINE

The knights of Gaspaar began their third day on the road, their second since crossing the Lumbadil and passing into Leorna. Their path had taken them deep into the forested hills that stood between the lowlands and the walled town itself. The final twist of road crested a tall rise that unveiled their first view of the castle and the town spreading out from it. Derek and Quinn stopped their mounts to view the land below and stretched their backs and legs. In that moment, the two knights were jolted by a familiar whistling each knew announced the passage of an arrow. Crying a warning to the troop behind them, they ducked low over their saddles. At the end of that instant, there sounded a solid *thwack!* Derek marked the shaft quivering at head height in the trunk of the tree beside him.

The riders grabbed their swords and twisted around, looking in all directions for ambush. No attack followed. Sir Quinn shrugged. "It seems a single outlaw has missed his mark, Prince Derek, and run for his life."

Derek reached over and tugged the arrow from the tree. "Alone he may have been, but he has not missed his mark. There is a note tied round this shaft."

Max had hurried Blueberry to the front of the column. "What does it say, Derek?" Max was frightened, imagining how close the arrow had passed his brother's head.

Derek unrolled the parchment and studied it before answering. "Well, it's nicely writ, though the warning is dire enough."

Jippit had reached them. "A warning or a threat?"

Quinn coughed. "May we hear it, sire?"

Derek nodded. "*Knights of other lands, The king of Leorna plots evil behind his welcome. Beware his hospitality. If you be true knights of chivalry, turn back and leave Leorna to its people.*" The prince looked up. "It is signed, '*Catterline.*'"

Max noticed Jippit's look of surprise. "An odd name, Jippit. Do you know this man?"

The elf thought before answering. "I am not certain, but there is a memory somewhere that echoes the name."

Derek rolled the notice up and handed it to Jippit. "Then you may keep the note, until you remember. What do you make of its message?"

The elf looked at the arrow handed him as well. "That King Lull has a dark heart I knew already. This arrow could have taken you easily if this 'Catterline' had wished. That's two points to favor."

Sir Brian had come forward on his mount as Derek read the note. He snorted at Jippit's comment. "I don't care to be ordered about by strangers, no matter who they are. True knights don't turn back at the first rock thrown at them."

Derek turned to Sir Quinn. "What say you, Quinn?"

The elder knight crossed his arms over his chest. "It pains me to agree with young Brian. Yet I do not see that we can take a warning from an unknown stranger as a sign to heed. We are following King Randrew's command as we ride."

"Yes," Derek said, "but we now ride with our eyes open and . . ." he turned to face the others, "in the tents of Leorna we will keep our ears open and our tongues sober. If I have a man or boy run loose or drink unwisely in revelry — I shall take it as treachery and have him in chains."

There was a murmur at this, but Sir Claire agreed, speaking up so that all the young charges could hear him. All listened when Claire spoke, for he seldom did so. "This is no May Fair we attend, gentlemen. A tournament of wits has begun already. I intend to sleep with one eye open until we are far from Leorna again."

***

Rhena

Rhena could scarce stand her excitement as she watched the banners of Gaspaar fluttering above the column of knights entering the town. Scanning the riders eagerly, she shouted with joy as she recognized Max and Derek, as the column crossed the drawbridge and beneath the portcullis. Breaking free of the royal maid who escorted her outside the palace keep, she was the first to stand before the knight's horses as they halted in the cobblestone square.

"Princess Rhena," Derek said, bowing from his saddle. "You do us honor."

"You are welcome, noble Prince Derek," she replied with a curtsy and glancing up at Max, smiled. "As are you, Prince Max, and all your bold company."

Max grinned. Rhena was taller than he remembered. He hadn't quite caught up to her yet. "Your servants, Princess Rhena," he replied, bowing as had Derek. He longed to get off from the others so they could talk without titles. Rhena was

41

the only girl he knew he could really talk with.

At that moment, Rhena noticed Jippit in his hooded squire's cape. She grinned. "My prince, you must instruct your fellow squire. Has this bumpkin no knowledge of courtly manners?"

Jippit fumed beneath his disguise but, with all eyes upon him, bowed, biting his tongue. Max whispered to his elf friend. "Be glad Rhena does not reveal your identity, Jippit. Her sport is a small price to pay."

The company dismounted and were led to the great hall by Rhena and the royal pages. As they entered, Max saw the king of Leorna sitting on a throne at the furthest end of the long room. Knights of Leorna, Averon and Wotterham, rose from the great table in respect as Derek led the knights of Gaspaar to stand before the throne.

Lull stood and raised a hand in greeting. "I bid you welcome, noble princes of Gaspaar, and your chivalrous knights, to the peace of Leorna. We are honored for your presence at our table." Lull took a golden cup from a servant. "To Gaspaar, old neighbor of Leorna, we raise a toast. And most especially to the brave and noble Crown Prince Max who brought our own daughter safe home from the clutches of the sorceress at the risk of life and fortune! His selfless gallantry has opened the gates to long abandoned friendships among the noble houses." The assembled knights cheered, and Max felt embarrassed at his nagging mistrust of the king.

After the formal feast of the assembled knights and lords, Max was shown to his room by Rhena. The two friends at last were able to really talk without all the burdensome manners of the court.

"What do you think of Leorna?" Rhena leaned against the carved writing table near the window of the room. "Is it not as grand a kingdom as I had said?"

Max turned a chair around and straddled it, crossing his arms over the back. "It is as you said, a beautiful country. This castle is far the largest I have seen. It is three times the size of ours at home. I am glad you wrote for me to come. I could never have talked Father into it without your letter."

The princess laughed. "I was just hoping for an adventure. One thing about you, Max, wherever you go, somehow things seem to happen!"

Max shook his head. "Once you've been out in the wild lands, nothing seems the same. Being back in a court and treated like a child gets boring soon enough, all right. Dangerous or not, our battle with the witch of the Runruggel Mountains was anything but boring."

"Do you remember how the tower cracked and fell?" Rhena beamed at the memory.

"And how the witch's 'nightmare' fell from the sky?" Max added.

"I heard that you journeyed to the edge of the world and brought back the wizard of Doonadim himself. You must tell me everything — you're a whole adventure ahead of me now!" Rhena threw a cushion at the prince.

Max dodged the pillow. "I'd have been happy to have traded places with you most of that winter trip I'm afraid. With hungry wolves and treacherous enemies plotting against us, it was all Jippit and I could do to come back alive."

Rhena rolled her eyes in mockery. "And now I remember the way you tell a story. I shall hear it even better than it was, no doubt."

"And I had forgotten why we always argued so much."

"Too bad Jippit can't be here to tell the truth of things." Rhena said. "He speaks plainly enough, with no regard for anyone's pride."

Max agreed. "I only wish he could have stayed in the palace as Derek and I shall."

"With so many nobles there is only room for the princes and their squires," Rhena answered. "Besides, you know if Jippit were this close, someone besides me would likely recognize him. His disguise is not too difficult."

"I suppose you are right. Well, tell me of this tournament of your father's." Max rubbed his nose. "I'm not certain in what ways it may differ from others I have known."

The princess smirked. "Yes, it might differ from all the *others* you have known . . ."

"All right, it's my first tournament," Max admitted. "Go ahead and laugh. Every knight had to have a first one."

"Agreed. Very well, tomorrow will be the opening festivities. There'll be a peasant's fair to be opened by Father. Then a grand parade of the companies of the four kingdoms. Then an open archery contest as well as riding and racing by the squires. The next day will be the lists. The knights will joust for the champion of the day. The champion's kingdom will carry that honor until the next year's tournament."

"It sounds like great fun."

"It is, but the joust can be quite terrible. One year a knight was killed."

"How did it happen?"

"They say the lance struck his helmet square and his brains were knocked loose in his head. He never stirred. It was horrible." She looked at Max and added, "Tell Derek to use his shield well."

"Don't they use the rounded tips?" Max's mouth felt dry.

"Yes, but accidents happen."

The prince knew what Jippit would say, *There are no accidents in an enemy's house,* but Max could not say such a thing to his friend. Nor could he speak of the fears that gnawed at him as he remembered the message from the mysterious Catterline.

CHAPTER 6

THE SPY

Jippit Jumpjilter sat scowling before the fire in the camp of Gaspaar's knights just outside the town walls. He tossed the bones of his supper into the fire and wiped his greasy fingers on the dry dirt beside him. Sir Claire stopped on the other side of the fire. He was carrying his shield from his saddle to the tent the squires had erected.

"Jumpjilter, you show a troubled face. I know Prince Max and Derek are removed from us. Be assured they are kept in greater comfort this evening than we."

Jippit shot a glare at the elder knight. "Comfortable prisoners unless I miss my guess. They should never have agreed to such arrangements."

Claire considered this. "To refuse the king's hospitality would have been unchivalrous. Such a mission as ours requires risks. Yet, I would give a pretty penny to know more of that great castle's plan."

As Claire moved on, the elf whispered, "And soon, I shall." He rose quietly and before anyone was aware of his having gone, vanished from the camp.

The moon shone bright above the trees, lighting the shadowy earth in blues and grays. Jumpjilter moved with such silence that only the wariest of the wood creatures sensed his presence. The campfires of the knights burned low and few sentries were awake. The elf's passage did not intrude on the dreams of those who rested for the morrow. Jippit came to the edge of the small wood at the bank of the moat and stood gazing up at the wall of the great castle on the farther shore. As he contemplated the silent fortress he tensed. Somewhere in the orchard behind him, someone followed. But not just anyone. Here was the soft grass step, the elf step that only elves hear. Mindful that he could be heard as well, if another elf were near, Jippit slipped into the black shadow of the nearest tree. He turned his eyes to pierce the dark of the orchard lane.

Whatever it was, it was no elf. Too tall and cautious of the dark. The step had been learned, Jippit knew. The shape revealed itself as a peasant — a beggarman perhaps. It carried a staff but here in the orchard, it was not used as a crutch. The peasant showed no bend of age or illness. Jippit smiled. A disguise then, but for what purpose? He had expected layers of lies and deceit upon arriving in Leorna, and now he seemed to be discovering them.

The figure checked its step and looked around. Jippit was no more than ten paces away but knew this stranger could not sense his presence. He smiled to see the *beggar* bend down and work at uncovering something in the rushes at the edge of the moat. Soon a narrow boat was pulled from concealment. In a moment, the mysterious figure had eased the craft into the water. Without a sound, the stranger had sunk his staff into the moat and pulled away. Jippit saw the hood tilt back, allowing the stranger to view the towers above.

The elf noted that the moon shadow of the wall cloaked

most of the moat on this side of the castle. The path of the boat was almost hidden from human eyes. His own eyes were not so guarded.

The puzzle that remained was how this strange one would enter the castle, for Jippit was certain that this was its intention. He decided he must follow and looked about for a means to cross the moat. A small log lay near the bank, the remnant of a recent storm. With some effort, the elf managed to bring this makeshift float into the water and cut a branch to use as a barge pole. Straddling the low riding log, Jippit followed the stranger's path across the shadowed waters of the moat.

As he neared the other bank Jippit knew his quarry had been well landed. He hoped that with good fortune his elfin skills might show him where the track resumed on this other shore. With a smile of discovery, he concluded that fortune did indeed favor the bold for as he gazed ahead at the nearing bank and the towering castle, he caught a brief flicker of light at the base of the great stones. It was gone in an instant. Had he been looking elsewhere he should never have seen it. Jippit steered for the remembered beacon. Soon, he felt his dangling feet touch against the shallow bottom along the bank. Sliding off the log he sank almost to his waist and fought to keep from cursing the cold water as he crawled ashore. Any noise here could bring a sentry's arrow.

Jippit considered the mysterious stranger he followed. If he were the king's spy, why choose this difficult entrance? Still, if he were not of the royal court, how should he know of a secret way into the castle?

Jippit needed all his senses to detect the recent passage of the stranger. When he reached the base of the wall, he saw that leaves from a bush had been disturbed and felt wet to his touch. He knelt to feel his way behind the branches and against the hard stones. There were vines growing up along the heavy blocks. The elf ran his hand along them, though he could not imagine that they were stout enough to climb. Then among these soft leafy runners he felt a hard branch near the bottom. It was not a plant at all, though it mimicked the twisting vines. It was metal. Jippit smiled with appreciation at the lever disguised with such cunning. The wiles of the 'Tall Ones' were worthy, but an elf's senses opened doors not seen.

Gripping the lever, Jippit strained to move it. In a moment he detected the faint sliding of weights in balance. The sound was muffled but Jippit waited, watching for any sign that he had been discovered. A moment passed before he grew aware of a deeper darkness opening in the shadow. A moist breeze worked past him from the secret door. The rank stuffy smell of dungeons warned him of what to expect beyond the entrance. Had not Max been inside the castle, Jippit would have turned back, for going on meant great risk. And, though he often chided Max about his curiosity, he also felt drawn to any mystery. He crawled into the darkness.

Pausing inside the tunnel, he felt the flat stone beneath him sink. The shifting weights, louder inside, closed the entrance behind. In this new darkness, Jippit crept forward; his fingers, ears, and nose taking the lead. He found he could stand but the narrow corridor turned and twisted tightly, sinking, and rising. The skittering of rats, and echoing drips of water, confused his senses as he moved along. He strained for any warning of his quarry, or other dangers lying in wait.

With relief, Jippit inhaled the odor of a burning torch. Someone had passed here recently. Here was a true guide to the labyrinth. In the stale brick tunnels, the spent torch smoke would leave an unfailing track. Jippit moved ahead with new confidence. He came upon stairs that rose in the tight spiral of a turret. It was quite late now, for he had heard no voices or treads within the walls. The castle slept. Turning a corner, he almost gasped. His hand, having grown accustomed to the cold stone of the tunnel wall, had plunged into soft fabric. Composed again, he reached ahead to explore the coarse cloth. Clothes. Robes, hanging on a peg. The stranger's disguise. Even a false beard. Jippit gloated to himself at his own prowess in tracking this clever one's path. He stopped to consider what he should make of what he had uncovered.

If this were indeed the disguise, he reasoned, then the spy must have left the tunnel. This meant that an exit from the secret passage was near. Jippit noticed something else as he held the cloak. At first, he doubted his senses or had perhaps a faint odor from a bordering room worked through a crack in the wall? He held the fabric to his nose. "So, your disguise hides more than even I had imagined. A clever spy indeed," he whispered.

Jippit resumed his pursuit with more appreciation for his prey. A moment later he saw a sliver of light ahead that could only mean a doorway. He leaned a cautious eye to the thin crack. It was a familiar hallway from his days in Leorna's court. A long plush carpet ran past arrow slit windows along the outward wall. Jippit frowned. The trail would grow fainter here, he knew. Listening to make sure he would not be detected, the elf opened the door and stepped into the hall. Closing his secret entrance, he found it was disguised as part of a wide support beam in the wall. A clever device to have remained hidden so long. He wondered whose secret he shared.

In the hallway, Jippit paused to listen at every door. He heard nothing more than snores. Then, at the last door before a corner in the hallway, he saw a faint light along its bottom. He moved to press his ear to the keyhole. As he listened, the hairs of his neck rose. He recognized both the voices. One was the voice of King Lull. The other was a voice he had not heard in long months. He scarce could believe he heard it now. Jippit covered his other ear to block out the distracting echoes and creaks of the castle corridor. His heart raced as he strained to follow the conversation.

". . . And you are certain the lance point will shatter the rounded tip? If it does not give way, then all your scheming is for nothing, Darkcloak."

"My king, do not let your impatience make you afraid. As I said, I have supervised its design and have tested it carefully. And the shield of Galen has already been replaced. It will give way, and our purpose will be accomplished. I grow weary of repeating these assurances."

"Yes, yes, but should our scheme go wrong by any means, then we would face not only the knights of Gaspaar but also the knights of Averon and perhaps those of Wotterham as well."

The other voice sighed. "Be brave, King Lull. If — and there is no such possibility — some angel of fate should show our trick, even then, it would be only thirty knights against your army. What are thirty knights against three hundred? Not counting the two hundred barbarian mercenaries of Garm who swell the crowds? And when the deed is accomplished, we may place blame on the princes of Gaspaar. Why, we can even claim sorcery against them. Many have heard of the great wizard of Doonadim's affection for their young crown prince."

"Your clever plotting is long and deep, Darkcloak. Your snare is not easily fouled. I begin to believe you would prove a match for even the great wizard himself."

So intent was Jippit on listening to the conversation that he did not hear the guard slipping up behind him until it was too late. Taken unaware, the elf was not able to draw his blade before the large soldier had locked him in his grip. Scuffling in anger, Jippit saw the door open and the surprised faces of the king and his counsel. At the king's command, the guard forced Jippit into the room.

"Well, well, what is this? A familiar face indeed. It seems this 'squire' appears on closer view to be none other than my old jester, Jumpjilter!"

"Tell this oaf to unhand me, Lull, and I'll give you a jest you'll not soon forget."

The hooded counsel drew away from the candlelight. "Your ears have proved too large for you, little man."

Jippit stared at the dark figure. "You — you traitor! Don't think your treachery won't find you out."

Darkcloak stiffened. "Mind your tongue, elf! In a moment, it may cost you your life."

Jippit glared but held his anger in check. He knew that there was a secret here that the hooded one held from the king. He knew the secret, for he knew who Darkcloak was and also that there was more than one spy in this castle. "Very well, Dark One, I'll hold my tongue for the time, but truth will be louder when the time comes."

"Take the prisoner to the dungeon," the king commanded. "And make certain he cannot be heard. I'll deal with my jester in good time."

As the guard led Jippit away from the room at sword point, Lull turned again to his counsel. "It seems to me that our visitor has some separate quarrel with you. I think I'd like to know of it."

"The elf has heard all our plans . . . his devotion to Prince Max fuels his anger against me."

Lull scratched his chin. "Hmm . . . I wonder."

"And I wonder how the elf came to be inside the castle," Darkcloak replied. "Is it so easy to slip past your guards? Secrecy is everything to us. Perhaps I'll question Jumpjilter more pointedly and find out the way of his entry."

"So, this does not alter our plans?" the king asked.

The hooded counsel shook his head. "They will wonder where the squire has gone, but he's such a fiery fellow, his absence will be unremarkable. The time for fear is past. We must proceed with caution, but we must proceed."

***

Max

Max turned over in his bed. The fine feather mattress was too soft, he decided. Dreams were stirring his mind. He had imagined that he heard a familiar voice cry out. Jippit's voice? But Jippit was at the camp. He sat up and listened long but there were no sounds now but only stillness in the dark. Had it been only his nerves? For all his worrying and doubts, surely King Lull had shown them nothing but courtly courtesy. Max wished he could think of Rhena's father as a friend, yet the outlaw's note had stuck in his mind as firmly as it had stuck into the tree on the path. He lay back down and closed his eyes. New sleep was slow in coming.

CHAPTER 7

PRESENTS AND SURPRISES

Morning was announced with trumpets. The fair was to begin. Max rose with tired eyes after a restless night of odd dreams. As he washed his face from the basin at the window, he heard a knock and Rhena's voice. Toweling off, he rushed to the door, pausing to comb his hair with his fingers before opening it.

The princess was leaning against the wall of the corridor. Her fingers tapped impatiently on the side of a package she held in her arms. "I did not remember that the nobles of Gaspaar slept so late in the day. Was the mattress soft enough for the *prince's* royal rest? Perhaps you felt a pea somewhere underneath?"

Max laughed. "It was a *princess* that was worried at a pea, if you remember the story, Rhena. You try spending three days in the saddle and nights with bare blankets on the ground, and see how well you leap from the covers at the crack of dawn."

"Well, it's more like the crack of noon than dawn. Still, we might be able to find you a breakfast. But first, I have a present for you, if you give me one in return."

Max took the cloth covered box from Rhena and ushered her into his room. "Let me see my present before you ask me for yours," he said with a teasing frown. His eyes widened as he opened the box and held up the beautifully sewn jerkin. "Rhena, it's fantastic! Its style and colors will make me the envy of all."

"I thought the prince who saved the princess of Leorna should shine a bit more than a common page. Those who've heard the tale would think less of me if they saw a dull covering on my rescuer. Appearance is everything to many in the court."

"Ah! So, it is a gift to me *and* a gift to you," he grinned. "Well, what is the other present; the one I'm to give you in return?"

The princess sat down on the window seat. "There is a braggart boy here, one Malvern by name, who tells it everywhere that I am to be his lady one day. He seems to think himself worthy of my worship by his eminence over the other lads here. In truth, I despise him! He is so arrogant and full of himself. His boasts tire my ears beyond endurance. What would best bring his flag down would be to fall before you in the archery contest. When he hears tales of you, his anger boils. He grumbles that you are only a strutting boy and a story I stretch to fit the occasion."

"So now you have made me an enemy I never met! I suppose it is too much to hope that he is a poor archer?"

"Malvern is a great shot and that is why you must beat him," Rhena pleaded.

"So, you're more *against* Malvern than *for* me?"

Rhena held her hands up and smiled her guilt.

"Derek has tried to council me on the ways of females, but your trails and traps are too much for me. It would serve this Malvern right if he did indeed marry you."

"I won't need any *boy* to help me rule! A good queen is worth twenty kings."

"It might take twenty kings to straighten out the mess you would make of Leorna," Max laughed.

Rhena was about to reply but checked herself and spoke in a calm consoling voice. "If you fear to face this challenge, Max, just say so — I couldn't really blame you — he is quite a formidable opponent."

Max started to answer with an angry response, but stopped and chuckled instead. "I'll do what I can, but someone should warn this fellow about the princess he wants to win."

***

Gerald

Jippit Jumpjilter sat staring at the hooded figure who entered the dungeon. Darkcloak waited as the guard closed the outer door behind him with a clunk. At the sound of the lock turning, he moved to the single stool across the small enclosure from the bars of the prisoner's cell. The silence continued until the figure threw back its hood and eyed the elf openly.

"Yes, Jumpjilter, it is me. Gerald. The 'traitor' as you must have it."

Jippit narrowed his eyes. "I knew you by your voice. One never forgets a snake's hiss no matter how he cloaks it. But now you surpass even the most wicked thoughts I ever suspected of you. You plot the death of your brothers."

"No!" Gerald's eyes blazed. "Only their imprisonment. I plot to correct a wrong. I waited on Father to see the folly of his choice in Max, but old age and illness have dimmed his mind. He would make that witless boy the king."

"Deeds done in darkness speak more of dim thinking, deceitful one. If there has been a mistake made, it is that Randrew did not see the evil in your heart before and make you prisoner."

Gerald laughed. "I *was* a prisoner in Gaspaar. To know

55

I would make a better king than Max or Derek, but always to be put last, to be snubbed again and again. Jumpjilter — I could make an empire of Gaspaar. And I will yet, but first I must have Leorna."

The elf crossed his arms. "I call playing toady to King Lull a distant cry from ruling this unfortunate land."

Gerald nodded. "King Lull is like a large boat without a rudder. I determine his course, and soon . . ." He paused. "You are not as foolish as you seem, elf. You have drawn far more from me than I from you. Such cunning as yours would fit well in my court. You might even prove wise enough to guide Max. He is young and his naive sense of right and wrong could still be turned to serve the greater truth."

Jippit grunted. "I would be interested to hear what you imagine that truth to be."

The prince looked evenly into the elf's eyes. "The truth is this. Good intentions do no one good. Honor is a pretty game played by pretty fools. All the fine words of virtue are just that . . . *words*. Power makes things happen in this world. Give me power and I can make it a better world. My mind is uncluttered with superstition and myth. What *works* is truth. The rest is folly." Gerald narrowed his eyes. "And you know this is so."

Jippit blinked. He was surprised at the cold discomfort in his spirit. Where Gerald had been boasting moments ago, now he seemed almost pleading. The elf hesitated. "I won't say that I hold with every fine whim Max calls good, or deny I hold little trust in the words of men — any men. When I lived here before, as a servant to King Lull, I might have agreed with you. I might have listened with an open balance, but things have happened to me. I've seen some of these *words* more than talked. I've seen some of those petty fools of yours, who don't seem so foolish. And fools or not — and maybe they are — I've joined them. So long as you war with Max, I am your enemy, be certain of that. Alive or dead — if there's more beyond — I am your enemy."

Gerald's face hardened. "I use no force on you to learn of Father's thoughts in regard to Leorna or of any knowledge of Catterline you might have heard — an elf hearing so much more than others — for Lull will do it for me. But remember, I care for Max's safety, and Lull does not."

Jippit was about to reply when he sensed a slight movement outside the outer door. Someone was listening. Who would listen so quietly to the words of the king's advisor or the prisoner elf? This was not Lull's spy, for Lull had gone to the fair and Gerald had come in secret. Whoever listened must be an enemy to Gerald. This might not make him a friend to Max, but at least there was a chance. Jippit spoke again, slightly louder for the sake of their eavesdropper.

"Well, be that as it may — If I could get one word beyond these bars, I would warn Max and Derek of your treacherous plan for the tournament! To kill a prince of Averon and blame it on Prince Derek of Gaspaar, is a heinous crime! If there is a heaven, you will be punished!"

As he spoke, Jippit heard another slight shift, perhaps of surprise, and saw that Gerald turned at the sound. The prince stood up.

"What is this? You raise your voice and something moves beyond the door? Is there *another* spy among us?" Gerald sprang to the entrance and looked through the barred window slot. He called for the guard and Jippit heard the quick tread of the sentry.

"Has anyone come past your post?" Gerald demanded. "I told you I must be alone with the prisoner."

"No one, my lord! I swear it!"

Gerald glared at the man then laughed. "Open the door," he commanded. He turned back to face the elf. "No, Jippit, no spy . . . no help for you, I'm afraid. Unless perhaps one of Max's fairy friends has sneaked through a crack in the walls. I leave you for now. If you change your mind before King Lull comes to visit, let my man here know."

Jippit scowled in reply as Darkcloak left the dungeon. Inside he smiled, for when the door was opened, he had smelled the same faint odor from the cloak disguise hidden in the tunnel. Someone knew how things stood, he thought, and that someone might make the difference. One thing Jippit was sure of — this was no fairy spirit.

CHAPTER 8

THE ARCHERS

Derek and Max had lingered at their breakfast in the great hall. Rhena and her maid had departed to see to some adjustments for the gown she was to wear at the final celebration. Moments later a page stepped into the hall to announce the arrival of Gaspaar's knights from their encampment outside the castle.

Sir Claire waited until the page had left the hall then stepped nearer Derek's chair and spoke in a worried voice to the brothers. "It grieves me to report it, sires, but your squire, the elf, is not to be found this morning. We assumed he had gone to hunt last evening, but as morning neared, he had not appeared. I know not what to make of it."

Sir Brian stepped beside Claire and spoke with more urgency. "I think this 'Catterline' has come upon him. The nobles of Leorna think this outlaw bold enough to threaten the very palace."

"Jippit — gone?" Max turned to his brother. "Do you think this is Catterline's doing, Derek?"

Derek frowned. "I hardly know what to think. I am not so fast to judge the outlaw, but something does feel wrong here. Let us remember to be on our watch." The knights all agreed to this.

A few moments later they were summoned to join the other nobles for the grand parade to open the festival. The colorful array of mounted knights was to ride slowly through the town to the peasant fair set in the open grounds just beyond the streets where the grandstands and hedged lanes of the lists awaited tomorrow's tournament. As they rode through the town, trumpets announced their arrival and growing crowds followed them to the waiting pavilions.

All was festooned with bright flags and bunting, and music jangled from traveling musicians. Everything looked so grand and exciting that Max was tempted to forget his worries as again trumpets sounded to proclaim King Lull's ascent to a raised dais before the assembly. Many lords and ladies had come from nearby lands to observe the festival of Peace and Trust as Lull declared it and cheered the king's welcoming to all the friends of Leorna. There were dancing troupes and magicians, jesters, and all manner of vendors vying loudly to sell their goods in booths forming the squared boundaries of the fair.

Yet while Max enjoyed the sights and sounds of the entertainers, another part of his mind remained worried at Jippit's absence and the strange mystery surrounding the mention of the outlaw. And in this tense state Max noted Sir Claire looking beyond the dancing, singing troupe before them and followed his gaze to the crowd beyond the roped stage. He became slowly aware of a vast difference in the appearance of the peasants beyond the nearest row and the nobles of the court. It was not that they were poor, for most peasants were poor, but here in the midst of a great fair there seemed little mirth among them. The thin, wane look on their faces, slowly made the prince realize with growing certainty that the festival was a show, not for the peasants, but for the visiting nobles. And everywhere were soldiers, well-fed, laughing, cheering the entertainments. It was their laughter and applause that served to cover the silent gaze of the serfs. Soon Max was no longer able to see it in any other way. The festival for him became a mockery of happiness. There was an evil here hidden behind the laughter and applause, and Max's heart felt heavy at the empty cheers.

As they applauded a jester's juggling show, Derek turned to Max and noted his brother's gaze. "What is it, Max? Do you think Jippit's captor might be in this great crowd somewhere?"

Max shook his head. "It is this fair itself . . . Do you see it?"

"What?" Derek was confused but Sir Claire had heard Max's comment and stepped close to the two princes to speak.

"Aye, young prince, I see it as well. This is all stage acting. There is no serf here who would smile without the soldiers at his back. It is the laughter of the keeper, not the captive, that we hear."

Max watched his brother look slowly about them. His face grew grim as he gazed longer on the sullen faces of the serfs behind the guards. Even the children were quiet, not chasing or tumbling as a sign of a true holiday. Derek nodded and whispered, "Yes. You are right. There is poison here. Heaven guard us from it."

The trumpets blared and the herald called for archers in the open tournament. Max knew he must take his mind off his worries to concentrate on the challenge at hand. He felt some of his confidence returning as he slid his bow over his shoulder and fingered the white goose feather shafts that Jippit had taught him to make. It had been important to Jumpjilter to train Max well at archery over the long winter and spring. "An arrow makes a point in an argument with any enemy, no matter how tall or tough," the elf had said. "When I leave this tangle of fiefs and feuds behind, I shall not have done badly if I leave you with a whisper of the elfin art." And Max had worked hard to pick up what he could from his determined and impatient friend. Jippit had shown him that accuracy and distance could be achieved with less muscle than he had dared to hope. Even more, the elf had preached the way of centering the mind and heart. With this he learned to align even his body with his will to extend the limits of his abilities. Archery was a part of the elfin way. Jippit, though he claimed to be no master, astonished Max with tales of skillful feats. The prince had to work at not questioning his fiery friend. He knew if such a level of mastery truly existed, no man in his father's army could approach it.

Max stepped forward to join the que forming on the open square. Target bales were positioned at a distance to test the accuracy of the merely interested against the more serious entrants. He dared not think he could best the true archers among the line but hoped to match himself with the younger ones. Gauging his skill against the best was always a good thing to do. As the herald pointed him to a rope-bounded portion of the line, Max looked to the royal box. Princess Rhena sat at King Lull's right hand where she waved to him with a wide smile. This would once have cheered him. Yet realizing the unhappy state of the peasants, he was distressed by the obvious difference in their faces. He was amazed Rhena did not see it also. Were all nobles so blind to the world around them? It was so easy to see only what one wished to see, to be blind to painful truth. This was a lesson he had learned from his friends, the speaking beasts of Gaspaar, and among the clouds of Izmah.

Max raised a hand to Rhena and saw her pointing just to his left. He turned and saw that the youth standing next to him must be Malvern. The taller boy was glowering, staring at him with cold contempt. Here was another noble with little on his mind besides his own pride.

"I guess you're the famous Prince Max, that Princess Rhena speaks of so highly?"

Max met his gaze and tried not to laugh. "I suppose you are the famous Malvern, that Princess Rhena speaks of so lowly?"

The startled boy made to reply but was interrupted by the herald's shouts again.

"Here ye, archers all. The challenge shall begin with the first trumpet. All arrows reaching the inner ring shall stay the field and remain as the targets are moved back. The groups of four to a target have been tapped. Should your arrow hit another target, even in the center, ye shall not argue but leave in silence. With each round the targets shall be moved back until none but four remain. These last four shall shoot until one is clearly master. To this one, the silver arrow of Leorna shall be given. The first trumpet will blow in moments. Archers, ready your bows!"

Max put his worries aside and stood into his bow, slipping the bowstring over the tip. He drew back the hard pull as he slid the notch of his arrow over the tensing line in a single motion as Jippit had taught him. *A single motion to settle many things*, he remembered. *Let your body learn the motions the way your voice learns a song . . . smooth, flowing, even. Don't think the song, sing it.*

Max measured the distance, traveling the rising curve in his mind's eye. He waited, lifted the bow, and pulled his arm back in a single rotation settling back into position, the angle of his arms and arrow forming a narrow horizontal triangle. He felt the assurance of his back muscles taking the load that would feed only the energy the flight demanded. "Not more . . . just enough," Jippit had said. "Waste nothing . . . not a breath."

The trumpet blew and the air whirred with bowstrings and whistling shafts like a wave of startled birds breaking cover on the heath. Max saw his white feathers stop inside the center target ring, along with another from his foursome though further to the edge. The field was down by more than half as the pages plucked the targets clean and waved the shafts at the judges who motioned the short entrants away.

Malvern grumbled. "You shoot well enough, anyway."

"And we both stay," Max said and nodded to Rhena.

"Not for long," Malvern replied. "I'm thinking your arms have reached their distance, and they are placing the targets back another fifty paces."

Max grinned. "Well, this should prove no difficulty for you I suppose."

Malvern grunted. "It will be a worthy test."

The herald held up his baton and everyone prepared for the next round. Max began to pull for more strength in his bow. He counted silently to steady his shaft and concentrated on his breathing. *A steady, even breath, is worth much muscle*, were Jippit's words. The elf had tapped his head. *Power you will gain as you grow, but nerve is in the mind now to master.*

The trumpet sounded and the arrows flew again. Max strained to watch his shot slide down to hit the line of the inner circle. He saw that Malvern's arrow had just hit inside the outer circle, at the bottom of the target, a finger's width from a miss. The cheers were high as many more archers walked away and Max felt that even the serfs were drawing into the cheers as among the archers were several woodsmen of no title. There were only a dozen men left and the two boys. Max knew the cheers were not for the two well-dressed youths of the court.

Max turned to meet Malvern's curious stare. The taller boy looked worried and Max thought he appeared much less offensive without his smirk. He saw his rival was gazing past him and turned to look back over his shoulder. Rhena was smiling and waving at him again.

"It seems you have a great admirer in Princess Rhena," Malvern said. "I must admit you are a good marksman. I had not thought you could even reach the target at such a distance."

"You shoot well also. Good rivals make better archers, don't they?"

The pages were carrying the targets back another fifty paces and Malvern groaned. "I can never hit the target at this range." He bowed his head. "I should quit the field and leave honor to a better."

Max frowned and reached to grip Malvern's elbow. "Let us shoot this last flight together. I do not know if I can reach it at this distance — but you have longer arms and I can tell you how, if you can take a lesson."

Malvern stared at the prince. "I have learned one already . . . that I am not the better archer. And I would learn another if you will give it."

Max nodded. "Good. We can't go beyond this target, and I never hit well at such a distance, but with your arm and muscle, you should have a chance. You are trying too hard to drive your arrow with all your strength — that is only part of the shot. The arrow must go with sureness you feel. Relax. Calm your mind. Release with a natural motion, not a sharp burst. See only the target in your mind . . . nothing else . . .let your eye become the arrow . . . let your body become the bow."

"That is strange talk," Malvern said as they drew their arrows. "It sounds almost like a poem or a magic chant."

Max smiled. "I was taught it by an elf."

"Ha! Then talk more as we shoot."

Drawing back the string Max continued, as much for himself as for Malvern. "Breathe evenly, draw your strength from your back. Grow stronger with each moment until you are ready." His hand gripping the bow trembled with the pull then stilled. "Trust yourself. Let go like a tree lets go a leaf. See your shot already done." His eye was on the dull red circle at the far end of the field. Beneath it, the grass shifted in a light breeze and he knew without looking, that Malvern was settling alongside him. "Wait only for the signal to set free."

And then the trumpet sounded, and the arrows were away, and Max was almost surprised he had released the bowstring as he followed the arrow's journey to the distant target as sure as an apple falls to the earth.

A hand slapped his back.

"Max! We did it! We did it!" Malvern was thrusting his bow into the air. "We both hit the target! It's at least a dozen paces beyond my best shot ever!"

Both Max's and Malvern's arrows were at the bottom of the target. Malvern's was just outside the last ring, Max's shaft a finger width inside it. They would not advance with the final round of archers, but the two boys shook hands. As they walked to join Rhena at the royal box, Max heard the serfs cheering the champions from their ranks who still shot alongside the king's best guards.

Rhena stood with her hands tucked under her elbows, frowning. "Well, I suppose either Max has lost his touch, or Malvern will gloat forever at his tie."

Malvern bowed. "Neither, Princess. I would have quit before the last round, but Prince Max taught me to shoot beyond myself. It is no failing of his. I would see him shoot further still, for little he does would surprise me now. He is as you have said."

Rhena blushed at this praise and grunted. "Defeat becomes you both. The true archers are still at it. Don't take too much pride in failing only a few paces beyond the beginners!"

Malvern glared, but Max laughed. "You best learn to hear only the compliments from Princess Rhena, Malvern. Else your head will have no room from her complaints."

"I will mind my boasts, my lady, if you will spare me your taunts."

Rhena sighed. "I had hoped the two of you would knock each other down to size. I find I have created a friendship instead."

The three youths watched the narrowing field of archers. After another round it had fallen to two. Then one. Amid cheers the champion prepared to shoot a final arrow at the farthest target yet. The arrow fell amid the hushed silence of the crowd to strike low on the target face. And then, just before anyone could shout, a strange thing happened in that quiet moment that changed the course of the day in a single instant. A sudden whirring split the silence as another arrow shaft whistled in from the crowd itself, striking the target loudly twanging in the hard wood center. There were shouts and gasps of surprise as everyone turned to look for the unknown archer. A guard ran to pluck the arrow with black feathers free. He rushed with the shaft to the royal box as the crowd stirred and soldiers turned to face the crowds behind them with their shields and swords ready.

Max edged closer to the king's chair as the soldier bowed, out of breath.

"Your Majesty!" the man panted, "There is a note attached to the shaft." The guard pulled the paper off the arrow and handed it up to the outstretched hand of the king.

Max was near enough to glance over the shoulder of the monarch from his place beside Rhena. He was able to read only a bit of the message.

Guests of Leorna, the king plots against you!
Be warned this tournament is a trap...

The king turned to look around him. Max leaned back, hoping he had not appeared too close. He raised his eyes as if in question and waited with the other nobles in cautious concern and curiosity. "Sire?" he asked, along with Rhena. "What of this?"

The king's face had gone cold, his eyes narrowed, and he crushed the letter into a crumpled ball. "Guards!" he called. "Search the crowd. The outlaw is among us. He must not escape. A fortune for the man who finds him!"

There was a loud commotion and Max was surprised to hear a sound he hadn't heard before, excited peasant voices. "Catterline!" they shouted. "Catterline!" Everywhere soldiers rushed, brushing peasants out of the way, running and searching, looking everywhere for the outlaw who had disappeared in their midst.

Soldiers moved in platoons through the streets, chasing strangers and echoes, pointing and shouting commands as they moved through the crowd, blocking off streets and alleys.

Rhena turned to Max and Malvern. "This Catterline is like some ghost that haunts our kingdom. I would like to see him bound, for he must be a desperate villain!"

Malvern nodded. "He might have killed your father with that arrow! And look how the rabble hide his escape. They think it a game if some fellow defy the king. It's treason!"

Max said nothing. Catterline might have attempted to kill the king but had not. Just as the warning arrow on the trail had hit cleanly beside his brother's mount, murder had not been its aim. This fellow might be a villain, or perhaps something else again.

As the crowds parted, Rhena saw the chief of the guard passing down a near street. "I'm going to speak to Sir Vernon to see if the outlaw has escaped completely," she said, and started down from the royal box into the commotion.

"No, Rhena, it is not safe!" Malvern called after her.

Max agreed. "Then we must follow." He lifted the rope of banners and slipped off the wooden platform into the crowd.

Princess Rhena was moving anxiously through the passing crowds when she saw something that brought her to a sudden halt twenty paces from the chief of the guard. A yellow movement shifted at the corner of her eye. She turned to see someone slipping something under the folds of a lady's cape. That something was nothing other than an archer's bow. Her mind raced as she prepared to shout the alarm but froze as the fugitive turned round to stare into her face. It was the lady from the grove, the Queen of Lost Friends and Last Hopes. The princess' voice was stolen as the lady placed a finger to her lips.

"What is it, Rhena?" Max asked as he and Malvern caught up to her.

She turned to look at them and when she turned back. The lady was gone. Rhena looked in all directions but could find no trace of the yellow dress and long green cloak.

"Nothing," Rhena answered. "I — I just thought I saw someone. It's nothing." But Rhena knew one thing. This evening she intended to visit the grove beyond the moat, and she wondered if the Queen of Lost Friends and Last Hopes were indeed a lady of her word.

CHAPTER 9

I ALMOST REMEMBER YOU

Princess Rhena sat uneasy at the evening banquet. She had long looked forward to Max's visit in the days leading to the tournament. Now, though they sat together at the table, she felt she could not speak to him with the ease of friendship that they had shared. She longed to tell him of her discovery of the lady in the crowd that morning. All day they had followed the procession from one event to another viewing the parade of performers who had come to Leorna to entertain. Yet she could see only the face of the woman in the crowd and think of their meeting in the quiet grove. Despite this fantastic secret, she knew that she had given her word. She must not tell, at least until she had heard the lady speak. Rhena knew the word of a princess was not a thing to be broken lightly.

She vowed to be careful of giving it in the future. Yet it was not her secret from Max that troubled her most. Why did she not wish to tell her father? She had not even considered speaking of such a thing with him. Yet were not the bonds of family stronger than the threads of even friendship? Rhena was afraid she knew the answer to these questions but did not wish to face it. These thoughts were at war in her mind as she sat unable to taste the food before her. The hall was ablaze with the merriment of the gay ladies and lords of the court. She knew her silence was marked by Max but was also aware that all of Gaspaar's company, seemed much reserved since the events of the day's festival. And where was Jippit? Had the elf left of his own accord, or had some evil misfortune happened to him? At this thought she shuddered, and Max, seated beside her at the table, spoke to her with concern but also in an almost secretive tone.

"What troubles you, Rhena? You seem sad to me since this morning."

"I, I have only wondered at Jippit's absence. I so wish he were here with us."

Max nodded. "I also," he answered.

Rhena tried to appear calm. "Perhaps you have some idea of his whereabouts, or of what might have become of him?"

Max glanced over his shoulder before he answered. "Your soldiers say he may have been captured by this outlaw, Catterline."

"Do you think this is so?"

The prince considered his answer. He did not like holding back his thoughts from his friend. He knew much of what he thought would upset her, and he might be wrong. "No. I do not think so."

"Are you not afraid of this outlaw?"

"I am not. I am told to be by everyone here — but I am not."

The lord sitting next to Max turned from his conversation with the lady beside him. "What's that, young prince? You do not fear this terrible Catterline? You must be another David not to fear meeting this Goliath of evil!"

Max colored as the lady snickered and the noble laughed at his joke, but he said nothing. When the man turned back to his lady, Max whispered to Rhena, "I can't speak here — but I think things may not be as they seem." He stopped as King Lull stood and called for quiet.

"Lords and ladies, knights and nobles . . . I, King of Leorna, as protector of all her peoples, give you cheer and fortune. We salute the princes of Averon, Wotterham, and Gaspaar, who have accepted our hand of friendship to bravely lead their knights in the morrow's lists. Leorna is honored by their presence. We pray, with all our good will, the blessing of peace on all their houses and lands."

Everyone cheered this and drank deeply to the toast. When Max turned back to speak with Rhena, he saw that she was gone. Had he disturbed her with his remarks about Catterline? He felt a pang of conscience at taking the praise of the king while whispering hints of treason to his very daughter. Max had no more appetite and wondered if he might not best search out the princess wherever she had gone as soon as courtly manners would allow him to leave the table.

***

Rhena

Knowing her dress drew great attention, Rhena had made fast for her chamber and changed into her leather britches and soft boots along with a dark hunting jerkin. Making sure no servants saw her on the stairs, she hurried to the courtyard where the day's laborers were leaving for the night. The guards seemed far more occupied with watching for those attempting to enter than with anyone leaving as twilight settled. She used the cover of a departing wagon, slipping along, on the opposite side from the sentries to cross the drawbridge. Remembering Jippit's lessons from years ago, she moved from shadow to shadow until she was free of the busy village beyond the gates. Finally, she was alone on the bank of the castle moat at the edge of the small orchard.

71

Now, entering the grove, Rhena began to think of the object of her visit. Fear began to tempt her. If this lady in yellow and green were in league with Catterline, then might she be a fiend indeed? Still, the princess could not imagine evil in the eyes of the lady in green. Yet, had not Sister Angelique, her favorite of the nuns, warned that evil often speaks in soothing tones with a pleasant face? To be ruled by one's feelings was a dangerous business, the heart must not travel far without the head. Half her mind told her to return to the castle, even to alert the guards. The capture of one of Catterline's band would mean much to her father, she knew. What would he think of her purpose here?

Sitting thinking, she was shocked to realize a figure now stood before her. How long it had been there she had no idea. With a gasp she realized that it was Catterline *himself*. It was the subject of the crudely drawn posters of the sheriff. The outlaw stood before her, his broad-brimmed hat hooding his face in the twilight. When he raised his head, the dark eye-patch, stood out black against the thin face. It seemed to accent the single iris that glistened like a tiny lance of light, piercing her heart. The mouth below the bushy mustache was a straight firm line. Rhena stood, bracing to run. She would be no easy hostage.

"What do you fear, Princess?" the outlaw asked in a surprising strained, high-pitched voice. "You did not expect to meet me here?"

"I feared no less, but I trusted the word of another to meet me. A princess is bound by her word." She felt her heart beating as she watched the outlaw fold his arms and smile.

"The one you seek has kept her word, as you kept yours today at the fair. She thanks you."

Rhena grew more tense with each word the outlaw spoke. "Where is she then?"

Catterline reached up to grasp his hat before answering. As the brim came away, Rhena saw long folds of auburn hair fall to the outlaw's shoulders. "Here," Catterline replied in a softer, smoother voice, and with a gloved hand peeled away the mustache and beard. As Rhena stared speechless, the outlaw undid the eye-patch. To Rhena's astonishment, the moonlight revealed the face of the lady in yellow and green, the Queen of Lost Friends and Last Hopes.

"You — you are Catterline!" Rhena stammered.

The lady laughed. "You might as well say that Catterline is me."

Rhena was still unable to believe the transformation she had witnessed. "But why? Why?"

The lady sighed. "Because men, by their natures, will not readily follow a lady into rebellion. There was no man to lead them. It is not a disguise I wear happily."

Rhena could only stare. "Who *are* you?"

The lady gazed at her, measuring her words before answering. "My name is not important. And remember we are in your grove where names and titles are still the ones, we choose."

"Why are you against my father?"

The mysterious lady sat down on the log next to Rhena. "Princess, you are old beyond your years — that I saw today at the fair. That I saw in your eyes in this grove, and even long before . . ." Her voice trailed off before she spoke again. "It is because of this that I will speak to you freely. I have already trusted you with my disguise, which no one else guesses, even among my men."

"But why?"

"Your father has grown hard and unfair in his rule of Leorna, Rhena. His lords twist the laws tight around the serfs, squeezing them harder and harder to increase his wealth. This wealth he spends on soldiers and armor, and always with an eye on the kingdoms of his neighbors."

Rhena started to speak, but the lady continued. "This was not always so. Your father was once an honorable man . . . always proud, but his greatest pride was his queen. Even this prideful love of someone outside himself worked to correct many faults. But when your mother died, no longer did the king's love move toward another but fell away and back, at last, on himself. He seeks to replace the treasure he lost with a treasure he can own forever which will not die. It is the dream of many before him — the madness of empire. Princess Rhena, the king is ill. His mind is lost to this false dream of building something he can love as much as his lost queen. This growing evil is reaching a bitter harvest. The king has found a counselor of darkness and makes a plan to divide the kingdoms and throw them into blind war against each other."

Rhena jumped up from the log. "No! It is not so! How can you know of such a thing? How can you know of the king's mind and heart?"

The lady waited for Rhena to be silent and spoke again.

"I am sorry, my princess, but do not my words ring true? You have told me yourself of your father's nature. Have I said ought that you think false?"

Rhena trembled. "No . . . though I hate them . . . your words are true. But what of this plan? How do you know of this?"

"In another disguise I entered the castle. It was the first time in many years I have done so in this manner, though it is still familiar to me. I visited the dungeon this very morning in secret, hoping to find others who had resisted the king's rule. They might know better the state of the inner court than I in these days. I found a bold elf who once served as a jester here for a time . . ."

"Jippit!" Rhena exclaimed. "A prisoner in our castle?"

"And being visited by Darkcloak, your father's favored counselor. I heard just enough of their plan before I had to hide. Now you know what I have attempted to tell the princes of the tournament. It was a wild chance. I was near caught as you know, but the plan must be stopped.

"Are . . . are you certain of what you heard?" Rhena's words caught in her throat.

"The elf sensed my presence. He spoke more loudly so that I would overhear. But I must know more. Tonight, I must try to speak directly with him, but this shall not be easy. I am certain that the guard will be heavy. Darkcloak knew something was amiss as Jippit spoke loudly."

"I . . . I could speak to Father . . . I could try to change his mind . . ."

"Princess, you know that is a lost hope. When has your father truly heard you last? When you were rescued from the tower of the witch last summer, did this open his heart to Gaspaar? The young prince who saved you was none other than one he plans to enslave. He grants you any gift you wish, but has he sought to know your thoughts or the dreams of your heart? Has there been an hour when he has spoken with you as we spoke in this grove last twilight?"

Rhena felt her heart breaking. Tears rolled hot down her cheeks and sobs shook her. "What . . . what can I do? He is my father."

The lady held out her hands and Rhena clasped them and sat down again beside her. "It is a terrible tale I tell you, princess. Stronger hearts than mine have been broken by it. But we who were born in the high houses must act for all who suffer. We have been given much, and much is expected from us."

Rhena nodded. "Sister Angelique says that."

"It was said long before your Angelique," the lady nodded. "If only the king's brother would come home again, he would make a just ruler, a restorer of much that is broken. He could be a prince for all the peoples, high and low. But his mind was so clouded by a broken promise and a lost hope."

"I — I know something of that story," Rhena whispered. "I can't remember where . . . or how I know."

The lady shook her head. "That is a time past. Still, Leorna would better follow a true king than a secret outlaw."

Rhena swallowed her pain. "How will you save Leorna from all that comes?"

"I must know the king's plan fully before I answer that. I know tomorrow will be a great day in that plan. We must be ready. I need someone to alert the princes. I would not be trusted . . ."

"But I might be," Rhena finished her words. "I can go to the princes of Gaspaar. They do trust me. Perhaps with Max and Derek's help, something may be done."

The lady stood. "Then we must both be about our

business. We will both have a long night I suspect."

Rhena stood and looked into the lady's face before she spoke. "I almost remember you."

The lady took her hands again and turned toward the castle. "I will take you with me into the castle by a way you have never known. It is a secret that is lost now, even to the king himself." Saying this, she led Rhena to a large overlapping of undergrowth. Pulling branches back, she revealed a small punt. "We must be quiet above all else when we are on the water," she cautioned, "and stay in the moon-shadow always."

CHAPTER 10

DARK PASSAGES

Max opened his door with caution and peered up and down the hallway. There were no guards here. He took a deep breath and stepped into the hall. He needed to speak again with Rhena before he told his full mind to Derek. The princess' room was on the next floor above his and the only way up was through the winding stairways in corner towers of the inner keep. The guests had all retired to their quarters for the night. If things were as Max suspected, then all rested under the careful eye of the king's guard. He risked perhaps more than embarrassment if he were discovered stalking about in the night, yet he had to do something. First Jippit had disappeared, and now Rhena herself seemed to have vanished. He had to have some answers and he would not get them by waiting in his room.

At the end of his hallway, he stopped to listen before approaching the staircase where another hall met his to form a corner. Starting forward again, he recoiled, pausing in mid-step. A guard's foot stood out from the other hallway. With relief he realized the man was asleep on duty. Taking a deep breath, Max moved past the sentry and entered the tower stairs at the outside point of the corner. As he carefully climbed, his eyes came even with the floor of the next level and he heard the even tread of a sentry on the carpeted hallway. By the low flickering torches spaced at the corners of the keep, he watched a single sentry march past the entrance. Crouching, he waited for the sentry's return and counted the route in silence. Patiently he waited for the sentry to make three rounds and he reckoned the guard arrived every time he counted to ninety. This was enough time to get to the princess' door, but he did not know how long it would take the guard to round the corner onto Rhena's hallway. In that instant he would be visible if he could not get inside.

Max could think of no way to lessen his risk. He crouched waiting for the instant that the guard passed the entrance. He bounded up the last stairs and scurried to the princess' door. It was locked. He tapped urgently and called to her in a whisper. There was no answer. He dared to call louder. Still there was no answer. The sentry would come around the far corner soon. Near frantic, Max looked for a hiding place. There was a tapestry hung against the wall and he slipped behind it. Waiting for the guard, he knew the toes of his boots were visible below the bottom fringes. He could only hope that the guard would not notice them in the dim passage.

The sentry's tread approached, rounding the corner at the head of the hallway. Max counted to himself, wondering how vigilant the night watch was. He hoped that the repeated rounds had the effect of dulling the soldier's senses. Max had counted twenty seconds before he knew the guard had turned another corner in the hall. He slipped from behind the tapestry.

He had remembered an old trick he had learned from Jippit, to whom locks were a form of entertainment. He drew his dagger from its scabbard and inserted the thin blade tip into the keyhole. This knife was a birthday present from Derek that he had had made for Max. It was forged from good steel, just as Derek's sword had been, yet its blade was small and not so wide. He was happy to see that it could penetrate the keyhole far enough to make contact with the metal lifters. Twisting the blade in his hand, he could feel the shifting of parts inside the lock. Then the footsteps were approaching far too soon. Had the guard quickened his pace? He would not have time to hide. Concentrating, Max knew his only hope was in opening the lock. Just as he knew he must be seen — knew the sentry was turning the corner — he felt the lock give. The doorknob moved in his hand. To open the door and close it behind him was the work of a single instant. Max stood frozen against the inside of the door as the guard's footsteps moved past again without stopping.

He let out his breath and turned around to face the princess' chamber. The room was dark. Only the light from the windows showed him the outline of the room's features and furniture. Rhena was not here and the bed was still made from the morning. Where had she gone? And had she gone by her own leave or been taken? Did her father know of this, or was he perhaps the reason? Max heard the doorknob beginning to turn behind him. He rushed to crouch behind a large trunk almost without thinking. Kneeling low behind the barrier, he sensed that the door had opened. Someone was standing in the entrance, surveying the interior. Then he heard the voice. It was a question. A single word.

"Princess?"

The question was answered by silence, yet the voice had turned Max's heart to ice. He knew the voice.

The door closed. Max knelt still for a time, trying to piece together the mystery he had uncovered. Finally, he began the precarious journey back to his own room. He timed his exit to follow the next round of the sentry. He followed just enough paces back to remain out of sight and earshot and listened for echoes from the staircase before descending to the lower level.

Reaching his own door, he thought he heard something behind him and turned. There was nothing there. No one stood where his imagination had painted an ambush. Had the sleeping guard stirred at his passing? He stepped inside his room and closed the door behind him to ponder what he had learned. But he did not want to believe.

***

Rhena

Rhena traveled the hidden passages of the palace. She marveled, amazed, as she trailed her mysterious acquaintance. They moved in silence through narrow secret tunnels that led alongside the rooms and halls she had walked since childhood. The princess was stunned to think that always there had been an unknown world just out of sight. Her guide motioned her to stop.

"Here is a good place for you to enter the palace, Princess Rhena. You must be careful. Look and listen as you enter so not to draw notice. I shall travel further on. Should the day come when you must flee this place unknown, remember this way. Be careful not to use it unless the need is great. And watch always for eyes that follow."

"When will I see you again?"

The lady paused before answering. "I shall be in the crowd tomorrow as a lady. If you must speak to me, it will be easier to approach one dressed as a noble than a beggar."

The lady opened a narrow doorway in the wall and Rhena turned to slip through. When she turned back, the door closed again to reveal only a wooden beam. A round peg head revolved to seal the way. She would not have believed this to be an entrance if she had not just stepped through it.

Facing her new surroundings, the princess determined to go to Max's quarters. He was the one person she could trust. Walking freely to attract no attention of sentries or servants at this time of night, Rhena sought the North-most

80

rooms. She wondered what Max would say to her news. What would he, or Derek for that matter, do? What *could* they do?

Her mind turned from her father's treachery to "Catterline's" story, then to her betrayal of her father. This was the most miserable night of her life, far worse than her imprisonment by the Witch. No witch could ever have hurt her more than her father . . . more than someone she loved.

Nearing Max's hallway, she noticed a watch had been set but that the guard was asleep. Sensing movement at the stairs, she drew back from the corner of the hallway. Peering around the corner again, she was surprised to see Max himself! He was striding on tip-toe toward his room. She started to call to him with a whisper, but a hand clasped her mouth from behind, smothering her words and drawing her back.

*** .

Jippit

The guard had set a fresh torch in the wall holder. This much increased the light of the dungeon from the flickering dimness Jippit had so far endured. Jippit Jumpjilter stared at the new prisoner who was brought to the cell beside his own. When the jailer had again closed and relocked the door to the dungeon, the elf addressed the princess from the rude cot that was his only furniture.

"So, the king has even thrown his own daughter into prison."

Rhena twisted around at his voice. "Jippit! Thank goodness, I've found you!"

"I'm sorry to have found you here, Princess Rhena," Jippit replied. "And surprised that even your father has chosen to send you to greet me."

Rhena shook her head. "Not Father, but Darkcloak — and I know who he is now."

"I know also," Jippit nodded, "but Gerald's power extends only as far as Lull permits. You must know that."

Rhena raised her hands to the bars and bowed her

head against them. "Yes . . . I know it now to be true, though I would believe anything else if I might. It is as Catterline said."

"Catterline?" Jippit was surprised. "You know the outlaw?"

"We . . . are acquainted. *Catterline* at least can be trusted."

"I thought as much! Then his spy caught my message. What is the outlaw planning to do to prevent the king's design?"

Rhena strolled to stand below the barred outer window of the cell which was a narrow slot in the stones near the ceiling. "The spy only heard that something would happen tomorrow, was there more?"

Jippit jumped from his bed. "What? He does not know of the steel point and the soft shield? Tomorrow will be murder!"

Rhena moved to the bars to face the elf closely. "Tell me everything, Jippit."

***

Lull

". . . but my own daughter, Darkcloak! I can't believe it!" King Lull huffed at the counselor who stood facing him in his chamber.

"Your own daughter would have warned the young prince as surely as we speak."

"Of what?" Lull sulked. "She knows nothing of our plan. She's only a child! This is a child's prank. She was sneaking to visit her friend. They have had little time to visit in all these festivities, she said as much to me earlier this morning — or yesterday morning. Great Uthur's ghost! Do you realize how late this is? I need my sleep to face all that comes tomorrow."

Darkcloak crossed his arms. "I do not sleep easily when this castle is a burrow of spies. First the elf, then whoever I heard outside the dungeon cell, then Max's visit to the princess' room, and now her stroll at midnight. I warned you that without secrecy we cannot win."

82

The King tucked his chin down. "Well, it is certain that Rhena will be safer in the castle than at the tournament tomorrow. There may well be violence — and whatever Rhena knows or doesn't know — it could prove dangerous to her. But how am I to explain her absence?"

The counselor nodded. "You shall simply say that the princess is ill. You'll convey her regrets to the princes, perhaps bestow her handkerchief on Derek for the tournament. Yes, a nice touch that would be. There should be no hint of your true intentions in the treacheries to be witnessed by the princes of Wotterham and Averon."

Lull scratched his head. His voice was weary. "What next? I don't like making such changes so suddenly. Sudden steps are often missteps."

Darkcloak bowed. "We seize the moment and master it, my king. No emperor rises to the throne through caution."

CHAPTER 11

THE TOURNAMENT BEGINS

Max was helping Derek strap on his mail leggings overlapping his soft undergarments. The morning trumpet had blown, announcing the first call to the tournament grounds. "You are *certain* it was Gerald?"

Max swallowed. "I could not see him. It was just the one word. But, I . . . I *felt* it. I . . . cannot be sure."

Derek stared at his younger brother. "Gerald has been on all our minds for many months." He took a deep breath. "And *of course*, you crept around the castle after dark spying? Max, you could have gotten yourself in terrible trouble. What if the guards had caught you last night? If Lull has really planned something against us, he would have a good excuse to declare us treacherous enemies. It's just the sort of thing that he might be looking for."

Max moved to tighten the laces at the back of Derek's waist. "I know, I know, and I also knew that you wouldn't have let me sneak out like that. *That's* why I didn't tell you."

Derek bit his lip. "You always assume everyone else is too thick-headed to listen to your plans. Did it occur to you that I might have *helped*?"

Max flushed. He knew that he often gave little credit to Derek to share his own plans. "It's just that . . . well, I know I'm young, and I know you feel responsible for my safety. Father even charged you with it. I knew it would seem dangerous to you and you would not want me to go."

Derek turned around to face his brother. "You are the crown prince. I am your older brother, but *you* are the crown prince." He placed his hands on Max's shoulders. "I will advise you, and try to protect you, but I am not your master. I learned on the quest for the wizard that I was your *brother* not your *keeper*. Jumpjilter and the great fox taught me that without saying it. Whatever you choose, Max, I am your servant. Remember that when you are king."

"I am sorry, Derek. I will remember."

Derek handed his helmet to Max. "Well, squire, whatever awaits us in this day, we will be late for the breakfast table if we don't hurry. Perhaps you can question Rhena about her whereabouts last night, without being too obvious. The walls have ears in this place."

Max slid the helmet into a cloth bag. "I'll be glad when we're out of here again."

His brother shrugged, "If the fates allow it, we should leave tomorrow. *Hopefully* with a pledge of peace from all four kingdoms."

Max cinched the helmet bag cord and drew it over his shoulder. "It's a strange thing, but every time King Lull smiles at us, I feel less certain of his trust."

"Don't let any of the others hear you speak that way. We don't want anyone to blame Gaspaar for balking at offered friendship, if that is truly what is offered. So far we have nothing solid to show us it is not so."

"Catterline's warnings."

"It is taking much on faith to trust shadows that disappear when you approach them. I will listen to this outlaw when he steps forward to meet me face to face."

"But you've seen the people — the serfs, yesterday when the crowd hid his escape."

"Excited crowds are useful to thieves too, though I must say that I have never been to a tournament with more forced merriment and less true cheer. This is not a happy kingdom, but that is not our affair, Max. When you become king, you must remember where your duties begin and end. Perhaps this festival is a mark of turning, a sign Lull has decided on a new course for Leorna. It may be his people wait to see his true intent as much as his neighbor kings."

"I am glad not to be king yet. It seems a harder job than I ever thought."

Derek grinned. "Now you see why I am glad only to be a knight."

"Well, when I am king, you may regret it."

In the hallway the brothers greeted the other princes from Averon and Wotterham. The nobles wore their mail beneath their robes as did Derek. Only the princes and their squires were quartered in the palace. Their larger parties were still camped outside the walls of the town.

"Ah, Prince Galen," Derek nodded. "Are we to ride against each other again?"

The black-haired heir of Averon smiled. "We have many riders in the field today, my lord. Still, if the fates play as they seem, I expect we may well end lance to lance."

Galen's squire grinned. "And with the same result, if form runs true, sire."

Max glared. "Don't count on Derek's horse stumbling twice."

Derek laughed. "Don't mind Max's manner, gentlemen! He has the loyalty of a brother."

Galen looked down at Max and put a hand on his shoulder. "No one wishes for a truer field than I, Prince Max. No knight likes a faulted victory. I took no glory in your brother's fall in our last match. Perhaps one day you shall join him in the lists. I was much impressed by your skill as an archer yesterday."

Max nodded. "I thank you, sire. I apologize for my remark. It is my hope that both you and Derek make the last runs. That way this tournament must produce a true champion."

Galen turned to his squire. "Well, Thomas, you can't ask for a more gracious foe than that. If we tumble today, learn that lesson."

As they entered the great hall for the breakfast, Lull greeted the nobles.

"I trust each of you has enjoyed a good night's rest in preparation for today's lists. We look forward to observing the prowess of all the champions of Averon, Wotterham, and Gaspaar. However, I regret to inform you that Princess Rhena will not join us. Though she would desire nothing more than to accompany you on this grand occasion, she cannot. Last night found her ill, and she has broken out in splotches. While my physician promises there is little danger, we must insist she remain apart from the court. The princess must stay in her chambers and may only observe the tournament from her high window. Perhaps she may hear the cheers that accompany your brave deeds."

Max glanced to Derek, then spoke to the king. "Sire, are you certain that no one can visit the princess, even from outside her door? I would very much like to encourage her."

Lull shook his head. "No, no, young prince. We cannot run the risk of starting a 'rash' of such rashes among us!" The king laughed. "Oh, there is one other thing; she did wish to send this token to you for Prince Derek to wear in the lists." He held up a long green and gold silk scarf. "May you other lords not think unkindly of Rhena's partiality. Remember, it was a prince of Gaspaar who gallantly rescued her from the Witch of the Runruggle Mountains!"

Max took the scarf from the king among murmured assents from the others at the table.

"We shall do our best to honor the princess in the manner we ride the field today," Derek said. There was light applause from the court.

Prince Linus of Wotterham grinned. "That would look nice on my saddle, Derek. Perhaps the princess shall be better educated in the chivalrous arts after today's tilting."

Amid the laughter, Derek patted Max's arm as he smiled at his antagonist. He whispered to his squire, "Replies are served best on the field, Max."

***

Jippit

Jippit Jumpjilter stopped his pacing and looked from his cell into the one next to his own. "Every plan boils down to a risk. Risking my own life is not so hard as taking chances with yours, princess. Yet we need a key, and the one we possess is your being the king's daughter. Using that key could get you into very deep trouble. Even now you could persuade him that he is mistaken in thinking you side with Catterline. After this gamble, he would no longer be in doubt."

The fearful night had been long and sleepless, and Rhena yawned as she replied. "I am already in the dungeon, Jippit. And I *have* sided with Catterline. I won't lie to Father. We will do what we must do to warn Derek and Max. To do nothing would be more dangerous. Dangerous for us and all those gathered here. If war should come . . ." she did not finish.

The elf bowed before speaking again. "You are indeed a true princess, my lady, and one day you shall make a great queen. Let us pray you prove as good an *actress* next."

The jailer heard the muffled shouts through the outer door of the dungeon and slid the viewing panel open. He could not see fully what passed inside. The elf gestured in excitement from his cell, pointing across the floor to the further stalls of the chamber. The guard could not see the princess through the narrow slot and unbolted the heavy outer door. Rushing inside to unlock the first bared door, he heard the angry cries of Jumpjilter.

89

"Guard! jailer! The princess is ill! Hurry, fool! Come quick!"

The guard stopped at the door of the cell and drew the long keys from the ring at his belt. He paused to peer with anxious caution at the girl lying on her side on the floor against the bars. "Why is she not on her bed?"

"Hurry, you oaf! Do you want the king's daughter to *die* in your filthy prison?" The jailer jumbled the long key into the lock and pulled the frame wide. He was always cautious of treachery and faked illness was a common ruse — but he made one mistake. He failed to pay notice of the princess' cloak spread on the floor as he stepped forward. Looking only at the stricken girl, he did not see the elf grip hold of the cloak. In that instant Jippit tugged with all his might, upending the man's footing. As the jailer crashed down, Rhena sprung up and gripped his key ring, attempting to tug it free.

Though stunned, the guard fought back. Rolling on his back, he grabbed hold of the ring Rhena held now. However, just as he broke her grip, he felt a firm hand clutch his neck. His head was pulled back against the bars and his own dagger pressed his neck from the elf's other hand.

"That's enough bravery, lad," the elf said. "Rhena, take the keys and open my cell. We'll have to tie up our friend here, unless he insists on dying."

The jailer swallowed. "You'll not escape this dungeon. No one ever has."

"Then you'll get to watch something special, won't you?" Jippit said as Rhena stepped out of her cell and began trying keys on Jippit's lock. "Now, be a wise fellow and pass your arms back through the bars. That's right. Princess take my belt and tie his hands together. I shall make certain of the knots. Elf knots are wicked spells that do not like much tugging. They tighten spitefully. Don't count on shouting once we're gone, you'll have a mouthful of handkerchief. I should hate to choke to death when a little patience will grant a tale to tell your grandchildren."

Leaving the jailer tied and gagged, Jippit and Rhena made their way up the stairs. They stopped at the dungeon door. Jippit frowned, "I hear steps coming, they'll be on us in a minute."

"We'll be trapped!" Rhena hissed.

"I'll delay them," Jippit said. "You must get to Max and Derek, it's their only hope."

"But you're stronger and faster than me. You should go!"

Jippit pulled the princess into the hallway with him. "They'll not send an arrow after the king's daughter. Even an elf can't outrun that in these narrow halls. Now hurry, or our escape is for nothing!"

Rhena started to reply but saw the feet of the guards coming down the stairway. She turned to run in the opposite direction. She did not look back as she heard the guards shouting. "Look! The elf! He has a sword! Shields up, men!"

CHAPTER 12

PAINFUL ESCAPE

All the knights and squires were saddled and waiting in rows in the clearing before the castle. Even this far from the lists, the fields were bordered by larger crowds than had yet been seen. Derek and Max saw that their mounted party waited beneath the flapping banner of Gaspaar, a scarlet lion rampant on a gold field. Sir Quinn and Sir Claire were foremost. Quinn's charger was snorting with impatience as if it sensed a coming battle. In contrast, Sir Claire's mount munched the grass at its hooves. With a flourish of trumpets, the knights saluted their lords and wheeled in place to follow them through the streets of the town. Sir Quinn brought his mount up to tread alongside Derek's horse.

"Highnesses," Quinn began, though he looked ahead as he rode. "Last night many men entered the town. They look to be mercenary bands, soldiers with no king but money. As to their purpose here, I can only guess, but I do not like it."

Max looked over the crowd, noting clusters of rough-looking men in various colored cloaks and tunics. Swords and daggers hung at their sides. These were not peasants.

"Could this be *Catterline's* band?" Derek wondered.

"I think not," Quinn answered as he continued nodding to lords and ladies along the path. "I know some of these scoundrels from troubles in other days. They come from well beyond these borders. You will notice they are avoided by the peasants. Hardly the way they hid the outlaw's appearance and covered his escape, yesterday."

Derek waved to a lady on a balcony as they rode but spoke to Quinn as he did so. "Agreed. I'm afraid these rough fellows must be the paid allies of our host." He waved cheerfully to a cluster of children. "It may be that we have to fight our way out of this, Quinn. Can we count on Wotterham and Averon's knights to join us if it comes to battle?"

Max tensed at this thought. Fighting for a prize and fighting for survival put very different feelings into his heart. He knew the skills he was learning were useful in both cases. Keeping calm was just as important as the courage he might need to survive. He did not feel it.

They were passing through the gates of the town when Quinn replied to Derek's question.

"Prince Linus of Wotterham, suspects all of us equally, I think. That court has no love for Leorna. There are old wounds between our lands that must heal for generations. This I gather from the campfires we have shared outside the gates. Men without their lords often talk more boldly than they have been bid. It is a good time to drink little and listen much."

Max licked his lips, which were dry. His palms had grown moist with sweat. He felt his body readying itself for danger even without certain knowledge of its nature. "What of Averon, Sir Quinn? Did you listen at their fires as well?"

"Indeed," Quinn replied, again without turning to the princes. "It seems they wish first to avoid conflict with any foe. Their courtesy seems as rigid as a command they must have been given. It is hard to know how deep goes their regard for more than our lances. Perhaps they study us as much as we study them. Still, if even the three parties all stood together, we are but thirty lances and thirty squires against at least five hundred of Lull's men. Add to that, half again as many of these bloody mercenaries. Not good odds I fear."

Max closed his eyes to steady his nerves. If only Jippit and Rhena were here. He looked back at the castle and wondered if he shouldn't be trying to find the princess even now. He knew it was not sickness that kept her from this day's parade. His gaze fell upon the king. Lull was nodding to the crowd amid the forced cheers that the presence of his guard demanded. The applause lasted only as long as the soldiers passed. At that moment Max noted a mounted guard gallop to a sudden halt as he reached the royal party. Max watched the king lean forward in his saddle to hear the rider's message. Lull's face changed from a kindly smile to a hard mask of controlled anger. The monarch turned in his saddle to look back at the castle. Lull grasped the rider and pulled him close to speak in his ear. The rider turned his horse and galloped off.

Derek tapped Max. "Mind yourself, it's never wise to stare at a king."

"Perhaps it's wiser here than looking away, Prince Derek," Quinn added. "I'd give a pretty coin to know what that message was about. It certainly upset the king."

"It may bode well for us, Quinn, if it grieves Lull. I'd like to know as well," Derek replied.

"Then we shall," Max said, and pulled his reins, turning Blueberry back along the procession. He heard Derek call out a warning to him but continued. As he neared Lull, he heard the unmistakable sound of Moonstone's hooves drawing up to match Blueberry's. He saw that Derek was not going to leave him to any more adventures — alone at least.

The soldiers that rode before the king looked to each other at the approach of the two princes. They raised their shields to block the way as was the custom, but at Lull's command they lowered their guard, stepping their mounts to the side.

"Your Majesty," Max gave the courtly nod that served

when approaching a monarch on horseback and awaited the king's response.

"What is it, my young friends, that turns you back from our parade?"

"Sire, forgive me, but I noted that your messenger seemed in a great hurry! I hope there is no misfortune?"

For only an instant Lull stared at Max with a hard gaze. A quick smile spread across his face. "Ahh, young prince, I do appreciate your concern, but no, there is no calamity."

Derek reined up beside his brother. "Highness," he greeted the king also with a waist bow. "I hope this message brought no bad news of your daughter's condition?"

King Lull was in control of himself now. "Let me assure both you noble princes that the messenger was only informing me that the . . . outlaw — Catterline — had been spotted by my men. My captain hopes to have him soon in custody. Perhaps you have noted many of my soldiers among the crowd? You see, I have taken every precaution for your safety."

Derek and Max bowed their assent and turned their mounts apart from the king's company. They urged their horses ahead to rejoin Quinn and the double file of Gaspaar's knights.

Quinn frowned. "Prince Max, forgive my tongue, but if you insist on acting without council in such matters as this, I fear you will not live to see the crown on your head."

"I beg your pardon, Sir Quinn, but some things must be done in the moment or they can't be done at all."

Derek grinned. "Max is right, Quinn. To have waited to question the king would have made his inquiring all the more suspicious."

"And what do you suspect, sires?" Quinn asked, looking away again.

"I suspect we shall be in for a hard time today," Derek said. He turned to his brother. "It may be that we should make a dash for safety, yet with so many soldiers, there would be little chance. I think we must follow along and look for our best opportunity — but not you, Max. We must be certain of your escape. You can find a reason to go back. Perhaps you've forgotten my gauntlets. You can drop out of sight and go for help. Turn your horse for Gaspaar as soon as you clear the town and keep riding. The king must be warned."

Max was astonished at the look on Derek's face as he spoke. It was the face a knight wears into battle. He wanted to speak but Derek stopped him with an insistent, "Go!"

Max looked across at the sober-faced Quinn, who only nodded. The prince swallowed his protest and turned Blueberry back again. As he rode away from the party he wondered if he had seen his brother and the brave knights of Gaspaar for the last time. As he rode past the other knights he saw one of Lull's mounted soldiers move to block his path. The rider held up a hand to halt him.

"Your Highness? Where do you go? All parties are to proceed to the tournament field. It is the king's request."

"And I shall," Max replied and laughed. "Only I am acting as my brother's squire on this day, and I have let him down! I have forgotten his gauntlets for the lists. He will be furious with me if I do not bring them from the castle this moment."

The soldier seemed doubtful but looked over his shoulder at the castle. "And Your Highness promises to return as soon as possible?"

"That, you may most certainly count on, faithful guard. I shall indeed return." The prince imagined himself leading a long line of soldiers on the road from Gaspaar.

The guard was cautious, mindful of his king's orders. He also knew that interfering with any noble might as easily result in punishment. The man dropped his hand and bowed. "By all means, young sire. Hurry and do not disappoint your brother."

Max spurred his horse forward, thankful the man had not read his nervous manner. Passing the procession, he saw that others watched him with curiosity. He knew his safety lay in looking of a purpose. He must not appear fleeing to escape. As he neared the edge of the town, he began to consider his best path out of Leorna, yet he noted an activity that puzzled him so that, in spite of his hurry, he pulled Blueberry to a halt and stood in his stirrups for a better view.

Ahead, beyond the town, he saw guards rushing across the castle battlements. The great drawbridge was being drawn upwards, cutting the fortress off from the surrounding land.

***

Rhena

Princess Rhena caught her breath as best she could. She had just outrun the guards on the stairs and made her way into the kitchen. Hiding herself behind a stack of baskets, she heard a guard shouting orders just outside the entrance.

"The king orders the drawbridge to be raised! No one is to be let out of the castle — man, woman, or child! He'll have the head of any sentry who allows so much as a housefly to escape!"

Rhena knew this was no time for panic. She bit her lip. She wondered if Jippit had been captured or killed. Whatever had happened, he had fought to give her the time to escape. She must find a way to warn Max of the terrible plan, or all was for naught. Now there was another voice, this one irritating and familiar, arguing with the guard who had just passed the kitchen doorway.

"What do you mean, no one's to go outside the castle? Do you know what day this is? I shall miss the tournament. I came back for my father's pipe. He's the king's best friend, you know. I would dare not be in your shoes when he learns you pester nobles with such ridiculous commands!" It was Malvern. Rhena almost shouted from her hiding place. She knew Malvern would do anything she asked, though she would certainly regret having given him claim to favor in return.

"The commands are the king's, not mine!" the guard barked. "The drawbridge is rising. Unless you choose to test yourself against the king's guard, I suggest you go sulk in some fine chamber. We have orders to slay those who will not

98

be stopped by other means."

"How dare you!" Malvern shouted back.

Malvern would be no help if he were locked up. Rhena took a potato from a basket and hurried to the entrance. Leaning around a corner she saw the back of the belligerent youth. Taking careful aim, Rhena threw the spud with enough force that Malvern uttered a sharp shout.

"What was that?" Rhena heard the guard turn at Malvern's cry. "You'd best keep your tongue to yourself. Noble or not, you'll feel the flat of my sword on your backside!"

Malvern was too confused to speak as he stood rubbing his back. This was well, for the soldier took this for submission and went on his way. Rhena stepped into the hall and put a finger to her lips as Malvern started to speak. She motioned him to follow her into the kitchen.

Once inside, Malvern glared at the princess. "What trick is this, Rhena? First, I am shut up in this castle to miss the tournament and now you hit me in the back with —"

"A potato — and you're lucky it wasn't a pot! Now keep quiet and listen to me, Malvern. What I must tell you now is the most dangerous thing you'll ever hear. Say nothing and listen!"

Rhena told Malvern of the terrible plan to set the princes of the other kingdoms against Gaspaar. She told of her imprisonment in the dungeon and of her escape. When she had finished, Malvern stared at the princess, open-mouthed in amazement.

"It . . . it is the most incredible thing I have ever — that *anyone* has ever heard! Can it possibly be true? Are you certain? I heard you had been ill — perhaps a fever?"

"Malvern!" Rhena's eyes were hard and dark, and not at all feverish.

"Uh, well, certainly. I — I am your servant, princess, whatever you command."

"Thank you, Malvern . . . I can't blame you for your doubts. I only wish they were true, but there is no mistake. The problem now is what to do. We must find a way to warn Max and Derek at all costs. If Derek rides against Galen, there will be murder and war."

Malvern chewed his lip. "If only there were some other way out of the castle."

Rhena looked down the hall. "Well, there is, but it requires rowing all the way across the moat in full sight of the walls and would be impossible in daylight with every sentry watching."

Malvern plopped down on a stool. "Then what good am I to you? I can't fight through the guards. I'm already in trouble with them for just complaining."

Rhena took a breath. "There is one very thin chance of getting word to Max out of this castle. You are perhaps the best one to try it."

Malvern looked up, confused. "I . . . uh, I can't swim, Princess," he confessed, blushing.

"No, no . . . that would be no use. Now I must get a quill and parchment, and you, brave comrade, must get your bow and arrows."

The light came at last to Malvern's eyes. "I believe I understand your plan, Rhena, but it is still an exceedingly small hope. The moat is wide and who outside might find our *letter*?"

Rhena pulled the boy out of the chair and pushed him ahead of her. "When you've only one hope, you leave the rest to heaven."

***

Max

Max saw that the castle seemed to be coming into battle order. As the drawbridge clanked upwards to seal off the fortress, he could see several of the guards rushing across the ramparts, shouting and pointing. This seemed more than a common drill as his father's men of arms would practice back in Gaspaar. The message from the king had been to give this order to close the castle. Why? No army threatened Leorna. No one was attempting to force their way inside. Then it struck him. Was someone perhaps attempting to escape?

100

To Max's mind there sprang the image of Jippit Jumpjilter. Was he held prisoner inside those walls? Before riding for Gaspaar, Max knew he must learn if this were true. The dungeon might be below ground or in a high tower. He must study the castle walls for some clue to the prison.

Max slipped off his horse and led Blueberry near the bank of the moat. Carefully using the trees and brush for cover, he moved closer for a better view. He saw that none of the sentries on the battlements were even looking in his direction. They were not searching outside for any danger but were focused on searching within the walls.

There was a sharp cry and Max thought for an instant that he had been spotted. Then he saw movement along the top of a castle turret. Freezing in his tracks, he felt Blueberry stumble against him. This sent him tumbling forward through the brush, rolling out onto the bank of the moat in the clear. A moment later, he heard a whizzing sound and a firm knock as an arrow stuck in the mud some dozen paces away. Scrambling to his feet, Max struggled back up the bank, bracing for the arrows that were sure to follow the first. Yet as he grappled for a handhold of the brush above him, he realized that no more shafts had come. Over the loud pulse of his beating heart, he heard a faint call from behind him and far above. Despite his fear of the guards' arrows, he saw the distant figures of Rhena and Malvern struggling with soldiers at the top of the tower.

Watching the plight of his friends, Max felt helpless and angry. He saw something falling from Malvern's hand. dropping down the face of the wall. It was a bow. The prince looked back to the arrow that had struck the mud. It was one of Malvern's yellow feathered shafts. The shocking idea of Malvern using the skill he had tried to teach him to try and shoot him rushed across Max's mind. Then he saw the scroll of paper wrapped tightly behind the arrowhead. A message! Rushing back down the bank now, Max grasped the arrow and heard shouts of discovery from the wall. He began to hurry back up the bank toward his horse, determined to make his escape. The red feathered shafts of the guards were flickering after him.

In the very moment he mounted Blueberry's saddle, he felt an arrow point slice into his thigh. He screamed in pain and fear. Blueberry bolted away with him as he gripped her neck, his hands tightening on the reins with the agony of his wound.

CHAPTER 13

THE BLACK KNIGHT

Derek's face was grim as he watched King Lull open the tournament with a grand speech, cheered by the soldiers and the new "peasants" who had drifted into the town in the night. These visitors did not have the look of farmers or shepherds, and all seemed to have swords or bows which were not questioned by the guards along the way.

The knights of Leorna rode first against the knights of Gaspaar, five at a time over the five doubled lanes separated by narrow hedges. Each rider would salute his opponent from the far end of the field. Then, at a signal from the king, the combatants launched their chargers forward. Thundering at full speed toward the meeting at mid lane, the knights steadied their lances, striving to place the blunt tips so as to unhorse their opponents with a solid strike. Loud was the crash of point on shield or armor. Louder still were the cries of the crowd at each meeting.

Lances sometimes shattered, sending the riders down, or swaying in their saddles. Unhorsed riders were seen to by the stewards of the lists and their servants. Those who remained upright were attended by their squires who replaced lances and saw to any repairs needed for the coming round. Little else would excite Prince Derek more than such an event, but today was different. His thoughts were on Max's safety and his eyes were fastened on the king's party. Despite his anxiety, he was pleased to see that of Gaspaar's knights, Sir Brian alone had been unhorsed in this first series. Brian's only real dents were to his pride. Of Leorna, fully three of the host's champions had been knocked from their saddles. Another had dropped both lance and shield to hold himself upright, but Sir Tarand had beaten Brian in combat.

"Brian could use a knock anyway," thought Derek. He noted with satisfaction that Sir Quinn had already sent his page to request the honor of facing Tarand when that knight had rested.

***

Max

In his pain, Max's mind seemed to stumble in and out of a dream. He was in Izmah again, borne on a great cloud, floating on a soft wind. The face of the Queen of Izmah was before him, that timeless, beautiful face, not young or old but somehow both, staring into his eyes. She was speaking, yet her words did not sound like her voice. Then her face was no longer her face but a bearded man's, kneeling over him with treetops towering above. A searing pain shooting up his leg told Max he was awake now, and all that had happened was clear again in his mind.

"How did this happen, boy?" The man's grey eyes were searching Max's. He wore the rough cloak of a forest agent, but Max saw that beneath this was a shirt of mail. The prince pushed himself up from the ground to sit. He could see a shield and lance strapped to a charger not far from them. The shield was covered with black fabric and showed no device or sign.

"Who . . . are you?" Max asked and gasped with the flickering pain. "How did you find me?"

The man's eyebrows raised and he stood up, crossing his arms. "A question for a question? That is a wise answer in this place. Your clothes tell me you are a squire," the man said. "And mine tell you I am a knight. As to how I found you, that tale you might not believe if I told it. Had I not seen it, I should not believe it myself."

Max saw that his leg had been bandaged. "Try me," he said. "I have seen a thing or two that others doubt."

The man nodded. "Perhaps. Well, take it as you will. I was riding to reach Leorna before the tournament. But as I rode this morning, I saw a fox sitting in the road. It faced me bravely, not moving. Finally, as if waiting for me, this creature rose when I drew to a halt. It stepped off the road, pausing to turn back as if it made certain of my following. I am not a superstitious fellow — wild tales do little to move me — but the look and manner of this creature spoke clear as words, though not so much as a snarl or snap was uttered. Despite my journey, I dismounted and led Storm down this hillside. Here I found you with your mount, all bloody from that arrow. I know it to be of the guard of Leorna." He paused, "I have done what I may for your wound. By good fortune, it sliced little more than skin. Though painful, you have lost but little blood and need only rest to regain your strength. There is a farm a mile back I know and planned to take you there for proper treatment. Then you began to wake, talking wildly of *Izmah* and other things. I wished to hear you speak more fully before taking you anywhere."

Max was attempting to rise. "I believe you, for I know that fox well . . . and you know nothing of his true wonder. Where is he now?"

The knight helped Max stand. "You should be careful young sir, for I gather you are no common squire. Can you tell me of Gaspaar's knights? Can you tell me of their princes?"

Max swallowed as he steadied himself. "I can tell you more than that. One who I trust has already trusted you. I will tell you, sir, I am Prince Max of Gaspaar. I warn you that treachery awaits all on the field of the tournament. That secret has cost the Princess Rhena her freedom and my other friends as well. There must be a warning for my brother, Prince Derek . . . and a message sent to my father the king." Max held out the crumpled parchment he had taken from the arrow and stuffed in his tunic.

The knight took the note and stared at the boy prince who leaned against the side of his pony. "If heaven is on our side, I shall warn your brother. You must reach the farm I spoke of. I knew this farmer long ago, and he would be a friend of Catterline, of that I am certain. The outlaw should move — must move — now. You will make that case better than I. I will lead you to the road, my prince, but you must make for the farm yourself . . . I am needed at the tournament." He helped Max onto Blueberry's saddle. "I believe you know more than I have time to learn!"

***

Derek

The shock of his lance hitting true on his opponent's shield sent a clear message of victory to Derek. In the next instant he watched Sir Rondell rolling off the back of his horse. Rondell's lance swung high as the noble of Leorna bounced hard on the worn path. Applause erupted with each pass of the combatants. Derek noticed that when Leorna's knights fell there was an especially loud ring of cheers. Gaspaar's knights were acquitting themselves well enough to challenge for the tournament trophy. But Derek wondered where Max was. Far on the road to Gaspaar, he hoped. The longer his knights could keep fending off their opponents, the longer it should provide his brother time to escape without pursuit. At that moment the herald of the lists announced the finish of the round.

Derek looked to Sir Quinn and Sir Claire who had both

dismounted. Derek pulled off his helmet and took the gourd of water that Claire held up to him.

"Well ridden, Derek," Quinn said as the prince drank the water. "You must keep yourself fresh. I advise you to sit out this next round. You have already ridden against three knights this morning. Remember, we may need all our strength at any moment if Max's fears are true."

"True enough, Quinn, but if I hold back from any turn, it may warn Lull that we are suspicious. It may also remind him of Max's absence, which now is far past the time it takes to find gauntlets. My guess is that guards are searching for him at our camp by now. When they return, hopefully without him, anything might start."

Claire took the gourd back. "Something may be starting now. Here rides Sir Holbert. He is one of the few champions of Leorna to still ride at the front of the list. His squire follows him."

"Sir Holbert," Derek greeted the blond-haired noble as he approached on horseback.

"Prince Derek, my gentle lords, it has come to our attention that your party is running low on squires to aide you in the field. I have the honor of offering the services of my squire, Teller, to act as your servant in the tournament until your brother returns, or you have departed the lists. He is excellent in choosing the best lances from the racks and repairing broken bindings. He is good with bandages too if it should unhappily come to that."

The squire bowed. "It would be an honor for Leorna to serve Gaspaar's champion in any case, sire."

Derek looked to the other knights. "Then I should be a less than gracious guest to refuse such an offer. I trust you will be busy, squire Teller, only with the lances on this day."

***

Max

Max rode slowly up the hillside on Blueberry, clinging to the saddle. He saw the knight urging his horse back onto

107

the trail ahead. As he neared the roadway, Max watched his rescuer motion back down the path and call a farewell.

"Tell farmer Goosell that Leo calls his boon!"

Max only nodded in reply. He knew he must keep his strength. On the road, he gently urged Blueberry on. Then he heard a voice he had expected, once he was alone again.

"Try to rest as best you are able, Max." Fanzig stepped alongside the boy and horse as they plodded on. "I shall make certain that Blueberry reaches the farm the knight spoke of. By my nose, I think your wound is clean enough. The arrow point must have been a fresh one. The knight used a healer's dressing of herbs after he removed the arrow. It is amazing the ability of those hands' you humans possess and take so little notice of. My work with tooth and paw would never have removed such a fearsome thing without making the wound worse than before."

Max did not feel so fortunate as the fox seemed to consider him. "Fanzig . . . you know the treachery is real. Father's army must march as soon as it can — though I doubt if it left tomorrow it would reach us in time, even if Derek should manage some sort of . . . stand for the next few days. No horse could take Gaspaar this message in less than two days of this place. By then, Lull will have not only his men with him, but the army of Averon and perhaps Wotterham alongside him. With the armies of three lands, he would force Gaspaar to surrender or be crushed!"

The fox sniffed the air. "Sire, the logic of your words is true, but there are other ways than horses for messages to take wing. You'd best give me the message you spoke of, for I fear I smell trouble approaching. You must make for Goosell's farm and I to gain speed for Gaspaar."

Max pulled the note from his jacket and bent to let the fox nip hold of it. Pushing up from the saddle he saw three soldiers riding toward them. A patrol of Leorna sent to find him after his wild escape. He reined Blueberry in the other direction but saw another pair of guards pointing to him from the bend. There could be no escape. The pain of his wound denied any foolish attempt.

"Well, Fanzig, it looks as if I'll not ask that boon of Goosell, and no hope of aid from Catterline." There was no answer and Max saw that the fox was gone. His pain was too sharp to think of spurring Blueberry into the brush or of charging through the riders on the road, and dizziness moved over him. He was almost glad when the first guard steadied him in his saddle.

"There, there, highness, no sense in stressin' yourself so! You need tending to. We'd best see you back to Leorna. Master Darkcloak wants you safe and sound."

With those words, consciousness again faded from Max's mind and he fell into the arms of the soldier nearest his mount.

***

Rhena

Malvern sat on the straw-covered floor of the dungeon. His left ankle was clasped by a metal band, chained to an iron ring in the wall. "I refuse to believe what has happened today. Since this morning, I have not only been hunted like a common criminal in my king's own castle but thrown into a dungeon. And I find myself in rebellion to the king my family has served all my life. What will father say? What will everyone think? What is to become of me?"

"Don't ruin your life's one moment of worth with such drivel." Jippit Jumpjilter stood against the wall beside Malvern with both his hands raised in short chains above his head.

Rhena stared from her cot in the cell across the short aisle from both her fellow prisoners. "I shall plead your case, if it comes to that," she sighed. "The king will know that it was only your foolish devotion to me that brought you to resist the royal command. It's clearly no rebellion in your own mind, now that you have come to your senses."

"Quiet, down there!" a guard shouted from the landing above them. This inner guard was a new precaution brought on by the morning's escape. "I am not to allow you to talk! Much more chatter and I am to have the elf and the young lord

109

gagged!"

Jippit growled. "If I had known that Max would be shot by these dogs, they would have had to bury me before my surrender."

"Please, Jippit," Rhena whispered, "We may need your strength again, not a brave *memory* of you! Don't be too harsh with Malvern. He has had to turn his world around in an hour. I had years and still it hurts too much to say. We can only pray for Max and for our friends outside."

Malvern nodded. "Perhaps someone should pray for us."

***

Max

Max jerked awake. A fresh pain burned his thigh and he started to rise but felt a strong arm pinning his chest. His eyes flew open wide. He stared at the grizzled face above him. "Am I . . . in prison?"

The white bearded old man chuckled and shook his head. "Good — you are awake. No, lad, the guards have brought you to my farm to look at your wound. They were afraid you might not live to be taken to the castle just yet. The blood on your clothes frightens them far more than it warrants. Someone has done a good job of your bandage already. Cleaning your wound with salt water has brought you back as I thought it would. The soldiers have very direct orders about you I hear. The king's counselor has set a wide net for you."

Max whispered, "Where are they now?"

"Two wait outside, eating my stew. I have sent the third for more water from my well when I thought you were reviving. He shall be back in a moment. I wanted to hear what you have done to be hunted by the king's men while we were alone."

Max swallowed and attempted to rise up on an elbow. "You must get word . . . to Catterline that — "

"*Catterline*? Why might you think I should know of Catterline?"

"I ask . . . *Leo's boon*."

The farmer stared at Max then glanced behind him before answering. "Very well, say what you must, but hurry. They will take you soon after I have redressed your wound."

Max squinted with the throb in his thigh. "King Lull has planned for the prince of Gaspaar to kill the prince of Averon in the list."

"Is Gaspaar *in league* with Lull?"

"No! Prince Derek has no idea of the plan! It —" he grimaced, "is a trick lance and false shield!"

The old man ran a hand along his bearded chin. "You are certain of this?"

"On my heart's honor, I swear it." Max's head was spinning. He felt himself drifting away again.

"Who *are* you, lad?" the old man asked. "What is your name?"

 A guard was at the door. "Hey! Farmer! What've you done to the boy?"

The farmer looked over his shoulder. "Why are you so late with the water? He has fainted."

He'll get water when he comes to. It's time to go. Yarn! Come help me with the prisoner."

CHAPTER 14

THE FINAL LISTS

Derek watched his knights riding back to their stations. The victors climbed down to stretch and take their rest. Those whose rivals had withstood the run, tightened their cinches and took fresh lances from the squires if their own had broken.

Hours had passed with no word of Max. Derek could almost convince himself that all was normal but he knew it was not. The last of the champions were to ride against each other. He would lead his remaining knights, now five, against the champions of Averon. Vanquished knights, some bruised and battered, stood cheering on their friends and making wild boasts against their rivals. Prince Galen of Averon would finally meet him in the center lane. This was the first time they had crossed lances since Derek had fallen and broken his leg two years before.

Brian handed Derek's helmet to him. "Sire, fate has surely set proud Galen before you. However tired you are, pull up your last best strength to see him off. For the glory of Gaspaar!"

Though he worried of hidden plans, Derek felt a growing desire to meet the challenge of the lists. No victory could be counted true in his mind if he did not face a rider of equal skill. He raised his visor to breathe while the others readied at their stations. "Perhaps we *shall* teach Leorna what knights we have in Gaspaar." His heart was light with energy, and he felt Moonstone stirring eagerly beneath him.

"Sire, a new lance for a true strike." Squire Teller held up a sturdy striped lance with a large ball tip. "May you take him cleanly," the squire said as the prince gripped the weapon.

Derek could see Prince Galen taking up a fresh shield with his colors burnished bright.

Brian laughed. "Spear that bright gold eagle dead center, Sire, and Galen will truly fly without wings!"

***

Lull

King Lull felt a tense stirring as he watched the two princes preparing to lead their knights in this final round. In moments, the attempted murder of one prince by another would break the peace of decades. In the shock of what must follow, only Leorna would be ready to seize the day. Something twitched inside the king as he eyed the knights. His look was that of a cat watching a bird hopping near on the ground. Then, for a fleeting instant, the king felt a troubling twist in his heart. One of Derek's knights was holding up a familiar kerchief of green and gold.

***

"Here, Derek," Sir Claire called, walking his horse across from his station near the prince. "You have forgotten the scarf that Princess Rhena bid you wear today. My squire saw that Max had left it with your kit. It may bring good fortune to ride in honor of the noble young maid."

Derek took the scarf from Sir Claire and tucked it through his belt. "Certainly, Claire. I thank you for reminding me. I should not like to disappoint such a true-hearted one. Let us remember that we do have friends in Leorna that we *can* trust."

The trumpets sounded again, and Derek walked Moonstone forward. He gathered his reins and adjusted his grip on the shield and lance. Across the field he saw Galen prepared to make his run as well. The two princes nodded to each other and pulled down their visors almost as one. The crowd came alive, aware that the two famous princes would face each other. Pages, squires, peasants, soldiers, lords, and ladies, all pressed forward against the rails. The crowd strained to get the best look at the duel that all had hoped might come. The sons of the kings of two kingdoms who long ago had fought great wars against each other, rode in a challenge of honor.

Derek turned to see King Lull watching them from his dais. He glanced to another tent and saw the Prince of Wotterham watched a little apart from his men. Prince Linus stood alone as usual, arms folded across his chest. The sullen prince waited to observe the action upon the field. Derek realized that everything had been coming to this very point since the summons arrived in Gaspaar's court so many days ago. A fire burned inside him to give every ounce of his skill and strength in the next fateful minutes. He knew Galen's heart and that until one of them was unhorsed, this challenge would continue. No shock or wound would stop their combat so long as their minds and muscles moved.

King Lull raised his scepter and silence settled down like a hot mist over the crowd. Derek felt his senses widening

He was aware of every tremor in Moonstone's legs and heard his own breathing inside his helmet. He saw everything so clearly that even a tiny yellow butterfly tumbling across the field stood out like a signal. The heavy battle flags seemed to roll in the wind at the same pulse beat of his heart. It was this quiet, slowing-down feeling, that let Derek know his whole being was ready for what waited. The king's scepter swept down, and the warhorses launched forward.

Moonstone's hooves pawed for traction in the worn lane. Bits of grass and dirt flew upward around Derek. At a sudden cry to his right, his eyes cut to catch a flash of sunlight off the armor of another mounted knight leaping a rail onto the field, knocking aside the guards. The intruder was rushing directly into Derek's path. The unknown knight held his shield high, reigning his mount to a skidding halt, brushing against the border hedge between the lanes of Derek and Galen.

There was bedlam in the crowd as the jousting knights pulled their mounts to a stop. The horses pawed in uncertain anger as they strained back from their charges.

The soldiers and marshals of the lists were rushing onto the field, shouting and lifting their spears at the stranger with black shield and armor, who had dared to halt the joust.

Derek had never felt such confusion. He saw that Prince Galen was pacing his horse forward to call to him across the hedge. Galen's visor was up.

"By heaven, what goes here, Derek?"

"I dare not guess, but this bold fellow owes us all an answer, I think."

The knight, still on his stallion, was now surrounded by guards. "Escort me to Lull," he called, "and before these witnesses, I will give an answer, and demand one of the king."

"We shall hear you out," Galen replied, "but be advised it is Lull's judgment you face."

The black knight turned his horse toward the king's pavilion. "I shall answer to Leorna."

The soldiers moved with him, their spears held in readiness.

Derek paced Moonstone alongside the stranger's

mount. Galen trailed along on his side of the hedge before stepping his horse through a gap to join them as they neared the king's party.

Now the crowds had surged near the scene of this unusual confrontation. King Lull was looking about him both with anger and surprise as the black knight approached. There was something ominous in the dark rider's bearing that drew all eyes. This silent, armored figure, his shield with no sign, might be death himself visiting the tournament in the light of noon.

Lull quieted his court with a raised hand and called down to the waiting figure. "Who are you, sir, that you come unannounced and uninvited into our celebration? By what right do you disrupt our tournament? I will have your answer before passing judgment at your rash show but hold not your tongue if you wish to keep it."

The helmeted figure bowed in the saddle then spoke loudly to be heard by all. "I claim the right of all paladins to strive for mastery among their peers. I serve no king but the one whom all kings must serve yet am servant to all."

Lull hesitated in ordering his soldiers to seize the fellow. "You are over-bold, *Black One*. I would see if your skill is as great as your pride. Who would you challenge here?"

The black knight's reply astounded all who heard it. "One who used to ride well, and ruled well also, but has turned his sacred vows to mockeries. One who reigns no more with wisdom, but only the weight of might. I challenge *you*, Lull. I challenge you to prove your right on this field of honor . . . if *honor* you still hold!"

The silence was as great as a shout. All eyes were upon the king. Lull's face pulsed with anger. "Rebellious traitor! No man challenges a king in such a manner. The dungeon is too kind an answer for you."

There was a roar from the crowd as the guards stepped closer. The soldiers glanced over their shoulders. The mood of the throng was growing ugly. There were catcalls and shouts.

Quinn had ridden to join Derek and leaned near to

speak. "Should we not come to the aide of this fellow? His words are our own thoughts." Behind him, the party of Gaspaar had lumbered forward, their weapons lowered but ready. Galen's followers gathered behind their prince as well.

The black knight gripped the dark fabric cover of his shield and tore it away, revealing its true surface, a green field with a gold rampant lion. At the sight of this shield a cry rose.

"It is Leon! Leon de Leorna! Leo the Brave!" The crowd took up the cry. Faces of astonishment and joy spread along the course. Confusion and concern clearly showed on the faces of visitors to Leorna.

The knight raised his visor to address the king. "Yes, Brother, it is true. I am not dead as your agents would have me. I come to reclaim the kingdom, not for our family's fouled line, but for the people who suffer at our hands. Yours for your greed, and mine for my sorrow. We must right both wrongs. Do you yield your crown? Or do you answer my challenge as the warrior you once were?"

Again, Derek felt everything slowing down and knew his wise body was preparing for war. Against his prayers, he sensed a battle gathering strength around them like a coming storm. Soldiers stirred, lances lifted, banners flapped. Everything hung on the words King Lull would speak next.

CHAPTER 15

CATTERLINE ATTACKS!

"Max! Wake up! Can you hear me?"

Max opened his eyes to the words echoing around him as if he were in a deep well. As his eyes cleared, he saw that Princess Rhena peered down at him. Jippit Jumpjilter stood above her. Malvern was frowning just past Rhena's shoulder. He was surprised at how much better he felt.

"Yes . . . I hear you . . . I've been . . . wounded."

"And lucky not to be dead!" Jippit growled. "When I get out of this dungeon there will be payment made. Rest assured of that, Prince Max."

Malvern shrugged. "*If we get out of here, you mean! It*

looks pretty bleak if you ask me. If Max had got away, I would have a hope, but our letter has returned with no answer."

Max drew himself to a sitting position on the cot. "Is that — the sound of battle, I hear?"

Jippit nodded. "Yes, and it should be a short one if Lull's plan continues as it has. Don't strain yourself to look, sire. The window is too high. They have been at it now for no more than half the hour by the sunlight moving across the floor."

"How long have I been here?"

Malvern sighed. "Oh, you woke within the minute they dragged you in. At least they left your bandage alone, and you don't seem to be bleeding."

Max touched his bandage. "Yes. A strange knight dressed my wound and I shared what I knew with him. He sent me to a farm to be tended by an elder man, but I was captured. By now he may be on that field of battle . . . with Derek." He looked to the elf. "Jippit, I have to help Derek. We have to *do* something."

Jumpjilter slouched down, his chains drawing tight. "I've been no help on this journey. For this I offer my apologies, young sire."

Max gripped the edge of his cot. "There is still hope, Jippit." He whispered softly as the elf leaned close to listen. "*I...I saw Fanzig . . . if it was not a dream . . .*" He dropped back and shook his head. "And ... we are alive — all of us, yet."

"Yet?" Malvern grunted.

"It is all my fault," Rhena's lips trembled. "If I hadn't pleaded for you to come to the tournament we wouldn't be here now. Oh, what has my father *become*?"

Max placed his hand on Rhena's. "He is ill, like a spell. I have seen his eyes when he did not see mine. They burn wild, like a wolf."

"Max is right, my lady. I knew your father before when I was jester in this court, as you know. They said that after the death of your mother, Queen Lynette, he began to change. That was why I left finally." Jippit looked to the others. "But in this murderous plotting, he has help . . . Darkcloak, his new counselor."

"What is it, Jippit?" Max asked. "You are holding something back. What is it?"

Jumpjilter looked to Max. "Darkcloak is your brother, Gerald."

Max felt blood race in his head. "It can't be! Jippit, Gerald could never plan my death!"

Rhena put an arm around Max shoulders. "We have lost too much. It is too hard to bear."

Max could think of nothing to answer Rhena but they all turned to the window as a loud clattering of chains announced the lowering of the drawbridge.

***

Derek

Derek backed his warhorse into the frame of the pavilion at the edge of the field and sheathed his sword. Moonstone's battledress hung in rags, blood and sweat staining through. The field was strewn with bodies and wounded men calling for aid. Both sides had drawn apart at a trumpet call from Lull's dais above the field of battle.

The fighting had moved in a dream-like blur for Derek. Noise almost vanished though the shouts, cries, and ringing of sword on shield had not deafened him. His mind reeled back to the moment the battle had started. It had not been half an hour, but now seemed as distant as the start of an age. The words of King Lull echoed loud in his memory.

The king had stared at the figure in the black armor. His eyes burning with fearsome anger. He looked about him at the crowd before answering the accusation and challenge of the paladin. Then, in a voice so cold it seemed to chill the very air, he shouted. "You are no brother to me! *Traitors* have no lineage! Master of the guard, seize the black knight!"

As the king's men had started forward, Derek had moved his mount between them and Leon. He spoke — his bold words almost as surprising to himself as to the king and the crowd.

"Nay, Sire! Call back your soldiers and answer this knight's charge. If his words are *false,* then you have nothing to fear. Let him prove his slander. Sir Leon, what evidence do you claim against your sovereign? Such an unproved charge against a king is death in *any* kingdom." The crowd surged closer and the guards held their ground.

Leon pointed to Prince Galen. "Prince of Averon, where did you receive that shield?"

Galen lifted it up. "It is a fresh one given me for the damage to my old one in the last run. It was fetched from our camp just now."

"Throw it upon the ground," Leon ordered.

There was murmuring as the Prince of Averon did so.

Now Leon turned to Derek. "Prince of Gaspaar, is that a new lance?"

"Yes, just handed me up by the helper in the pits. He had found a flaw in the old shaft."

Galen nodded. I see it has the rounded guard upon the tip. Let me hold its balance."

"This is ridiculous!" Lull shouted. "We shall judge you at our leisure. Master at arms —"

Prince Galen held up his hand. "I pray you, Lord Lull. A knight's challenge is answered on the field in which it is charged. Stay your judgement a moment to hear his word."

Sir Leon held the lance above his head. "Lords, and people of Leorna, look well on this." Without another word he threw the lance at the shield on the ground. The lance sheered through its round tip and drove through the shield, pinning it to the ground below. There was stunned silence.

"Murder!" Sir Brian exclaimed from behind Derek. "It would have been death for Galen."

The king shouted over the cries. "Silence! This — this is a plot by you and Gaspaar. You try to lay a lie at my head, but it is yours that will fall!"

In this moment Derek saw a fierce chieftain near the king nod to a bowman. The man drew his string tight, raising his bow. The prince had only time to lunge across his saddle with his shield to take the force of the arrow that streaked toward Sir Leon.

That was how it had begun, Derek remembered. The princes of Gaspaar and Averon and their parties had drawn together as one to stand the attack of Lull's soldiers. The narrowness of the arena made horsemanship difficult, though the king's men could not first outflank the princes' bands. Yet the greater numbers of Lull's men pressing in had slain several of the horses and forced the princes back toward their tents at the far end of the field.

Derek saw that Sir Claire stood beside him now, his horse lost. His squire, Goodwin, was tying a bandage around the knight's knee. Gaspaar and Averon's men were ringed in a small circle at the edge of the rails, which were broken through in many places. The banners of both lands flapped behind them on splintered shafts that squires had driven in the ground. The prince turned to see that Leon was still on horseback and riding toward him. Galen rode at Leon's side. Derek pulled off his helmet. "What of Wotterham? Where are the knights of Prince Linus?"

Galen spat. "That coward has run. He will be happy to see us perish. A war between our lands and Leorna would suit his purpose fair enough. Wotterham has the largest army of the four kingdoms. They would have an easy time with the survivors, no matter who prevails."

Leon shook his head. "*That* was Lull's plan. Gaspaar and Averon fight each other and Lull would join the winning side. Then it would be easy to vanquish its weakened partner later."

"That much at least has come unstuck," Derek said.

"That does us little good, sire," Claire spoke from below. "We cannot stand another attack from such numbers. Some of Lull's soldiers changed to our side when they saw Lull's treachery, and perhaps two score of serfs have brought rakes and hoes, but they are not soldiers, and we have not enough to hold another fight. At least five of our knights have fallen, though three still live. Three of our squires are badly hurt, and Averon much the same."

Sir Brian limped up; his head wrapped in a loose

bandage. There was blood over his left ear. "Aye, but we have left twice that number of Lull's men on the ground. At least ten of them are known mercenaries and bandits."

Leon shook his head. "Terrible as this day is, my friends, the war that may follow will be many times worse. Our whole world may be broken. With or without us."

Derek looked at the sun. "We may not buy our lives, but we must buy time; time for Max to warn Father. The kings of Gaspaar and Averon *must* be warned of what comes."

Leon turned his charger to face the battered men. He spoke so all could hear. "If Heaven allow us die today, men of Gaspaar and Averon, I say we would die in the *best* of company."

Brian lifted a mailed fist. "And we take many of the *worst* with us!"

A trumpet blew and Derek raised his shield. "Ready, men. Remember to step back — keep the circle if a man at your side falls." He drew a deep breath to steel himself for the fight but saw three riders march their mounts toward them from the surrounding army.

Flanked by two of his knights, King Lull raised his scepter. "Knights of Averon and Gaspaar. You have fought bravely. It is not my wish that you should all die. If you cast down your arms and accept my victory, you shall have your lives!"

Derek roared back. "And you would have your *hostages* to blackmail our kings!"

Sir Leon answered also. "You will have no victory here, Lull. If we lay dead here this evening, you shall have no peace before your own grave. Know that."

Galen added, "We are not done yet. We are the very best warriors of Averon and Gaspaar. We are the heart of our armies. Think on that before you attack."

The king laughed. "When the heart dies, then your armies will wither! I will not spend another soldier on you. My archers will rain arrows until no knight stands. You may shield away a dozen or a hundred, but the rain of arrows will take you all at last. The game *ends*."

As Lull spoke, a hunting horn winded from nearby and was answered by another and another. Lull turned in his saddle, looking to the woods that bordered the field. His men shifted, uncertain of these strange signals.

A sound like hundreds of quail wings beating from cover, drummed from the forest. Lull's soldiers raised their shields above their heads, crying out warnings. Derek watched a flickering cloud of arrows arching above the field and raining down on the king's ranks.

"Catterline! Catterline!" the cry rose from the shocked troops. The king spurred his horse back from the field as his men began to run from a second flight of outlaw arrows.

CHAPTER 16

PRISONERS

"It is a retreat!" Jippit shouted and shook his chains. "I know that trumpet call."

"What does it mean?" Rhena asked. "Surely a few knights have not defeated a whole army?"

Malvern climbed up on the bars of the cell. "I see Lull's banner crossing the drawbridge." Stretching, he peered over the bottom ledge of the high window. "I can just see the edge of the town. There are men in the streets with no banners that I know. They look to be peasants with bows — outlaws maybe!"

"Do they follow Lull's troops?" Max asked.

"The last guards are running back across the drawbridge. The bridge is rising! The outlaws and knights have dropped back to the last houses of the town. The castle archers are shooting at the peasants on the barbican!" Malvern dropped back down from his perch. "Something important has happened, if we only knew what it means."

"The farmer got word to Catterline," Max said.

"What?" Jippit raised his head.

"When the knight tended my wound, he sent me to the farmer's house to tell him of this plot. He said that he would get word to Catterline. What else could bring serfs to fight?"

"It has done little but buy time, unless Lull himself —" Jippit stopped.

Rhena's face was white. "If father had been killed. It would have ended everything."

Rising from his bed of straw Max put a hand on Rhena's arm. "There may be other ways, Rhena."

Malvern shook his head. "I would like to know just what this Catterline is about."

Jippit agreed. "I would like to know just *who* this Catterline *is*."

Rhena looked from face to face. "I know."

Everyone stared at the princess.

Max licked his dry lips. "If it is something you can share, Rhena . . . we all want to know."

"No secrets among prisoners," Jippit added.

Rhena turned to Jippit. "I am surprised you do not know some of this, Jippit. I think you might have some memory of Sir Leon de Leorna. His fame is certainly wider than our kingdom."

Jippit nodded. "Yes, the tales of that brave paladin are known among the elves and the sad story of his heart-broken quest. Are you telling me that Sir Leo is Catterline?"

"No." Rhena smiled. "But you cannot understand who Catterline is without knowing the story of my uncle."

Max frowned. "Enough of what Jippit might or might not know. Tell us, Rhena. We have time for it."

"Very well, I will tell it to you as best I understand it, for Catterline has told me of what happened before my time and reminded me of what happened when I was young. And even now has told of the way of things as they are."

Malvern was astonished. "You have met this Catterline, yourself?"

"You must learn not to be surprised by Princess Rhena," Max said. "It becomes expected."

Rhena rubbed away a tear and began the tale. "Many years ago, King Orman, my grandfather, had twin sons, Leon and Lull. It was only the chance of fate that Lull was born a moment before Leon and, by our custom, became the heir to the throne."

"Did the brothers become rivals?" Malvern asked.

"No. They were close friends and shared many adventures. It was said that Orman considered splitting the kingdom in half, but the brothers insisted this not be, for their bonds were deep. Over time as they grew to young men, the two brothers met the two beautiful daughters of the Duke of Baronon. The older was the lady Lynette and the younger was the lady Caroline."

"Lynette was to become your mother, the queen of Leorna," Jippit said.

Rhena nodded. "Yes. As it happened, both pairs of brothers and sisters became very close. Falling into love. Lull with Lynette and Leon with the young Caroline, though he did not declare it, for Caroline was not much more than a child herself."

"What happened then?" Max asked.

"Lull and Lynette were married. It was a wonderful wedding and is remembered even now as the grandest occasion of Leorna. I was born but a year later."

"And did Leon marry Caroline?" Malvern asked.

"No. She was too young, but they had secretly pledged their love. It was when I was but three years old that word reached our kingdom of the Viking raids on the towns and monasteries in faraway Camelot. Leon felt it was his duty to go to help repel the raiders. Orman agreed to his request. Leon declared to both Caroline and her father the duke that he would take her hand in marriage on his return."

"How long was he gone?" Max asked.

"It was two years before the peace was made with the Viking chiefs." Jippit said.

"And when Leon returned, did he marry Caroline?" Max asked.

"While he was gone," Rhena continued, "the duke of Baronon thought of a cruel plan. One of his daughters was married to the future king of Leorna and this promised much power to him. When he learned that in the land of Galadan, King Yorn's wife had died, the duke had an idea. If Caroline should also marry a king, his own influence and riches would be much greater."

"That is terrible," Max spoke in disbelief.

Malvern asked. "What of Caroline? How could she agree to marry while Leon was gone?"

Jippit spoke. "There was a story that Leon had been killed. His letters sent to Baronon's castle were secretly kept from Caroline by her father. Broken-hearted, the young lady agreed to the match her father had made."

Rhena's words were bitter. "And when Leon returned and all came to light, he went into a fury. He would have killed King Yorn."

"Why did he not?" Malvern asked. "I would have killed both him *and* the duke!"

Rhena closed her eyes. "Caroline begged him not to. Yorn was not to blame, he had not known the lie. He was a good man and had tried to make the princess happy. She could not wish him harm. Leon knew that if he killed the duke, he would kill the love of Caroline as well. They say he went mad for a time. He renounced his title and swore an oath to become a paladin, devoting himself as a wandering defender of the weak and set his horse away from Leorna."

The boys and the elf all looked at each other. Their eyes were sad yet stirred with anger.

"In the years that followed, Leon finally visited our court, sometimes at Christmas — sometimes Easter. He spoiled me with gifts but always quickly left. Once he turned away at the gatehouse when he learned that Yorn and his queen were in attendance. I remember watching his horse riding away in the snow, the sky was dark. My mother and her sister cried together that night and I wondered at the cause. I was too young to know the story."

"It is the saddest story I have heard," Max said. "Broken promises and lost hopes."

Malvern cleared his throat. "But Princess, what has this to do with Catterline?"

"Catterline comes into the story later. What happened after my uncle left was the worst thing that ever happened to me, until now. My mother Lynette became ill and died. All Leorna mourned her. I have memories of this. I was eight years old and within that same year my grandfather, King Orman, died as well. Some say Lynette's death and Leon's distance had broken his heart. My father became king while grieving for his wife and for his father. I hardly remember a day he smiled after that time. He tried to make the palace a gay and happy place. I had ponies and maids and parties and even a jester," she looked at Jippit, "who was not so funny."

Jippit frowned. "I was appointed, a mere slave. The physical nature of the smaller peoples seems humorous to the dull wits of certain tall ones. I bid my time for escape. Even with the friendship of Princess Rhena I could not bear the confinement of this court, despite its luxury. Even so, I regretted to leave one so dear in a palace without compassion. I hope the princess has forgiven me."

Rhena closed her eyes. "I missed you, but you must never be sorry for leaving. If you had not, would you and Max and I have ever become friends?"

Jippit coughed. "Or prisoners?"

"But what of *Catterline*?" Malvern pleaded.

Rhena nodded. "My father, King Lull, passed from grief to bitterness. There was nothing I could do to bring him joy. I was the only one left he would even allow to speak freely with him. And I came to see that he did not truly see or listen to me. I was just a mirror of his lost Lynette. He only saw her in me. And slowly I have come to see that building his kingdom, increasing his wealth, raising his power — somehow it is the way he is filling his empty heart."

Max shook his head. "Those things can't fill a heart."

Rhena nodded. "No . . . but I think they can destroy it."

Malvern spoke again. *"And . . .?"*

"Yes," Rhena said, "Catterline. When time had passed, old King Yorn died, and his oldest son took the throne. His queen quietly vanished. Some said she had taken a nun's vows and was serving in some mission far to the west of those lands. Yet she had secretly returned to the one place she had learned to love when Leon had courted her long years before. Leorna."

"To her sister's court?" Max offered.

"No, for after her sister had died, she came to know that King Lull had changed. This she learned from all those she met in Leorna's villages and farms. She had been trained to use the bow by Leon when she was young and had never lost her hand for the hunter's skills. Now she turned to them to survive in the wild. Yet as time passed, she sensed that much more was desperately wrong in Leorna. She knew somehow that she must do something. The man she loved had devoted himself to righting wrongs. Now she also took this vow . . . to save his kingdom."

"Catterline is *Caroline*?" Max stared at Rhena.

"It was I that named her. As a child I had called her by that name. 'Not cat or lion, little princess,' she would laugh. 'Only your aunt Caroline.'" A tear ran down Rhena's face. "I did not remember it."

"But why the name?" Malvern asked.

"Men do not follow women into revolt or battle," Jippit replied.

"A woman could not do this without an army," Rhena agreed. "And no army would follow a woman. She told me she had had to become as quiet as a cat, and as forceful as a lion."

"And so, she became the mysterious outlaw chief." Malvern was amazed.

"This uncle of yours," Max asked, "did he wear black armor and carry a black shield?"

Rhena stared at him.

CHAPTER 17

THE SECRET OUTLAW

The retreat of the king's troops before the arrows of Catterline's archers had been a wild and fast business with few orders given. As the last of the king's men had rushed under the barbican gates onto the drawbridge, Derek and a handful of the outlaws had followed them. As they came near to that small stone fort which guarded the drawbridge landing, the prince saw that the astonished guards positioned there were torn between retreating with the army to the castle or attempting to stand their ground. This hesitation had let Derek and several of the outlaws rush inside the barbican, break into its unguarded hallway and capture the small fortification outright. However, it was too late to cross the drawbridge itself which was being drawn up from the castle side of the moat.

Still, with the gatehouse captured, they could resist with good strength any attempt by the king's soldiers to lower the drawbridge and try to re-enter the town. Now Derek had left the barbican in the care of several outlaws and two of his best knights to make his way back into the town.

Derek saw that carts had been overturned in the streets to form barriers for protection from the castle archers. He signaled to Galen at the edge of the village. Here the mixed rabble of Catterline's men and the knights and squires had paused. The princes walked to stand behind an overturned wagon. From here they could view the drawbridge which had been drawn up against the front gate of the castle itself across the moat. Its wooden bottom was peppered with a fringe of arrows.

Galen nodded. "How is your arm? I saw a blow that nearly threw you from your saddle."

Derek had pulled his helmet off and wiped his brow. "It hurt enough to make me forget my other pains. Hard knocks on all sides, Galen. This was some battle we fought, my friend."

"Not just us, Derek. Here is our comrade, Leon the black knight. He fought as fierce a battle as I have seen."

"Well, sires," Leon greeted the princes. "Despite our skill, without these good outlaws of Leorna, we would have been prisoners or dead men. We owe this forest chieftain a boon we cannot repay. I would offer my pledge of honor if Catterline has survived this afternoon."

"I think you will have your chance, Leon," Derek said. "Unless I am mistaken that fellow across the street is the leader of this band."

A small group of the outlaws dressed in forest greens and browns were helping friends limp into a tavern house. Inside, the barber was busy dressing wounds. Noticing the princes, a figure in a wide brimmed hat with an eye-patch across his bearded face stepped forth. The fellow's cloak fluttered in the breeze and revealed a slight but wiry frame.

"This outlaw keeps a hard diet," Galen said. "He could hide well in any slim shadow."

Derek shook his head. "Such a wane fellow must be hard pressed to draw that great bow."

The outlaw laughed. The voice high and light. "Is that why my arrow hit the tree instead of your head on the forest road, Prince Derek?"

Derek colored. "I meant no disrespect, my good man. I bow to your skill as well as your courage. I thank you now for the warning arrow that you sent."

"Yet it took the black knight here to make you see the danger. Without Leon's return, you would have slain your friend and dashed all the lands into war."

Derek bowed. "I and my father's knights are at your service, brave Catterline."

"That is a strange title," Galen said, also bowing. "Though I offer my allegiance to you, sir, under any name."

"Names, titles, and even faces, are sometimes altered, sires. Loyalty is a fine thing and must be guarded with care. Remember that an enemy of your enemy is not always a friend."

Leon was smiling. He had been studying the shaded face of their new comrade. "I was uncertain of your disguise before, even with what I now recall of your secret title. Yet even your altered voice has undone all at last. Though I no longer wonder at your disguise, dear fellow, it is perhaps good that you reveal it to these fair knights. Is there further need to retain it?"

Catterline laughed and the laugh was light and high pitched. "Not now, my lord, for my men will have the true leader they have waited for. No longer need they follow a shadow."

"What is this?" Derek asked. "What riddle do you speak?"

Galen stared at the shaded face beneath the wide brimmed hat. "What trickery do you work, brave Catterline, if indeed that is your name?"

"*Catterline* was a title I was given by a child long years ago. She could not manage my simple name. I release it now, for its need is past. Still, it is only proper I inform those who have followed me these last months." The leader turned back to the pocket of outlaws guarding the street. The bandit chief raised a hand to beckon the men who moved to their gathering.

"What is it, Catterline?" they asked, "Do we march against the castle?"

"That will be a decision for your new leader."

"Our new *leader*?" The men looked to each other in surprise.

"What do you mean by this?" the tallest bowman asked. "*You* are our leader!"

Catterline shook her head. "You needed someone to rise up when there was no one for you to follow. Your true leader has returned. Sir Leone de Leorna has returned to us. I will follow him with you all, but not as the Catterline you have known. That person ends now. I give you my true self —" The outlaw chief pulled off the eye-patch and peeled away false whiskers. While the men drew back in surprise. Catterline vanished as the outlaw drew off the wide brimmed hat and shook down her long red hair. "I give you, Caroline of Fief Baronon, widow of Yorn, king of Galadan. Friend always to Leorna."

The oldest of the outlaws bowed with a cry. "Lady Caroline! By the saints, it *is* you!"

The other two men stared first at the lady and then at each other. They then bent their knees and bowed alongside their comrade. "Hail Lady Caroline!" They joined the cry.

By now the word had spread down the street of the outlaw's identity. The men of the forest band pressed forward to see for themselves the lady who had rallied them all against their cruel king. They came also to see the brother of Lull himself who stood beside their lady. Alongside these green-clad outlaws were the men of the town who had joined the fight. They were arm in arm with the bandits and knights of Gaspaar and Averon. With the growing commotion in the streets the windows above opened. Women and children leaned out to see the throng and hear what was spoken. Leon mounted an overturned cart and helped Caroline climb up to join him. The women shouted and waved as they learned the identity of the lady with the copper tresses.

***

Lull

In the castle Lull paced back and forth before his throne. "Leon! Leon returns!" He spat the words out with fury. "I can't believe it! My cursed brother — this phantom knight — has come back to wreck my plans. Just as everything is within my grasp, Leon and Catterline — curse them. Curse them both! My army retreats. I — I am prisoner in my own castle."

Sitting in a chair near the throne, Darkcloak waited for the king's anger to settle. Now he spoke in a calm assuring voice. "If the king rests himself, he will see that he has slipped, but not fallen. Little has been lost but pride, and perhaps a day's advantage. You have still the army and now we know where our enemies are and will soon know their full number. I suspect we have the true advantage when the dust has cleared. "

Lull fumed. "We ran before them like beaten dogs!"

"It was wise to retreat. They might have had a great army in the trees and cut us off, but they did not. Now we know they have little more than farmers and hunters beyond the few knights of Gaspaar and Averon. A wise king makes certain of all before he commits his strength. Battles are won in the mind before they can be won in the field, highness. And we still hold an even greater trump."

A scowling figure in crude armor barged into the room. He was followed by a half dozen ruffians wearing arms stolen from a score of victims. "Lull!" the leader shouted as he spied the king. "What is your plan? My men did not hire on to be held like sheep in a stone pin by a bunch of shepherds. We came for plunder. Honor our bargain or we take it from your treasury!"

Lull glared at the mercenary chief. "Still your tongue, Garm. You are my paid servant. You do what I command you to do. Nothing more and nothing less. You will have your blood

137

money only as long as you earn it by following my commands."

Darkcloak had risen and moved beside the king. "I should wait until we are certain where alliances among Averon and Gaspaar with Wotterham lie before we make a move we might regret. Prince Linus' troop did not join in the fighting. Imagine the strain the peasants feel as they bury their dead, tend their wounded and wonder if Linus will bring his army to join with us against them. Long ago Wotterham fought alongside Leorna against Gaspaar in a great war which it lost. The bitterness of that defeat has lived for generations. As for Catterline — I told you, my lord, that I set a spy in the outlaw's camp days ago. This morning I learned that he has gained access to the outlaw. If I but send the signal, he shall seek a moment soon to take the outlaw's life. Perhaps today, perhaps tomorrow."

The mercenary stared at the cloaked figure. "Is this a man or a demon?" Garm asked.

Lull smiled as he answered. "I am not certain. Though his words will prove true, or he shall die soon. Perhaps tomorrow."

Darkcloak bowed. "With your permission, highness, I go to send my signal."

CHAPTER 18

UNCERTAIN HOPES

There was much celebration in the town as many "outlaws" had now returned to the homes and families they had left behind, yet set against this was the grief of those who had lost sons or husbands in the battle. Sentries gathered around bonfires set in a wide ring around the castle moat, far from the arrow range of the towers. Leo had given a command that all walls of the castle must be watched.

Derek, Galen, Leon, and Caroline sat at a table in the baker's shop near the end of the street, considering the situation. The day was drawing darker and no more action had been noted on the castle walls. Only a single plume of smoke drifted from a tower.

"Probably they are preparing boiling oil in case we try their gates," Galen said. "They fear us for the moment. Soon they may realize we do not have the numbers to mount a full attack."

Leon nodded. "We are at a strange place. With all the hired warriors Lull has along with his own guard, we hold no great advantage in numbers. Only the surprise of Catterline's archers confused the king and began the retreat. He will be angry to have pinned himself inside the one place we *can* hold him. Without boats, the drawbridge is his only way back to battle. We must keep our best archers ready in the barbican."

"And we should keep a dry barricade we can set afire if he tries to advance," Caroline added. "Mounted on a wagon, just this side of the barbican gate. We could roll it ablaze onto the bridge if it is lowered. A fire and a manned barbican would be an obstacle any soldier would fear."

"My lady, you know the art of war," Derek said. "It is strange to hear such from a woman."

"Not an art, a deadly skill. I learned it from an old general who had left Leorna's service for a simple forest home. One who served as a hunting guide for Prince Leon in his younger days."

"General Goosell," Leon said with a smile.

Caroline continued. "He has been a farmer now many years, but cannot forget the 'terrible craft,' as he calls it. Without his lessons, Catterline would have been of little use. Indeed, today he rode to my sentries who brought his words to our camp that Lull was to move against Gaspaar and Averon at the lists. We just had time to arrive in strength."

"How did he know of it?" Derek asked.

Caroline shrugged. "I know not. His message was very short. Only that a lance and shield of the two princes were false, to yield a murder. Goosell knew this would be war."

"No doubt your young brother reached him," Leon nodded. "I made his acquaintance and treated his wound. He made for Goosell as I made for this field. I knew the general must have a way to warn Catterline. I am certain he continued on his way; the wound was easily treated."

Derek was frowning. "Max was wounded?"

"I am sorry, Derek," Leon said. "In the heat of battle, I have lost my thoughts on this. He had a clean arrow slice the skin along his thigh. It was a very lucky wound for him. Also, I learned treatments from an elf."

"Not a Jumpjilter, by any chance?" Derek asked.

"It is indeed a small world," Caroline said. "Our old jester."

Derek laughed. "Thank heaven for small blessings. If Max is safe and headed for Gaspaar, then all our hopes are still alive."

"But they are only hopes as yet," Galen said.

Leon nodded. "By now Lull has made a study of the situation. He may have his own spies as well to signal him. He knows most of our outlaw friends are only farmers, and not a match for hardened mercenaries and his soldiers." The paladin frowned. "The question is — what next?"

"I do not think time is on our side," Derek said. "If Prince Linus returns with a full army, we have little reason to believe he will not pinch us between his troops and the moat. If Wotterham joins with Lull, we would not be able to stand. Yet, if we retreat now, the two may join unhindered into a single massive force. They could move quickly to attack either of our lands."

"Are you so certain of Wotterham's siding with Lull?" Caroline asked.

Galen frowned. "I am certain of nothing, my lady, but Prince Linus chose to abandon us to Lull's attack. I think *whoever* he finds in control on his return may well decide where his loyalty shall be. Wotterham has a history of siding with the victors."

"What of your own kingdoms?" Leon asked.

Derek shook his head. "Max will likely have lost time with his wound. Our party reached Leorna on the third morning from Gaspaar though we did not press. Assuming Max rides hard, he will perhaps reach Gaspaar within two days. If then, our king summons and mounts five hundred soldiers in a full day, which I doubt — as our camps are set wide about our borders — he could hardly march such a force the distance in less than two days. To expect his army in four or five days from this morning would be nearer magic than a true hope."

Galen frowned. "We sent a messenger after the battle. It is further to Averon than Gaspaar, even if our man got through. We saw several patrols on our way here. They said they were looking for the outlaws." He nodded to Caroline. "Now they would surely guard against messengers also."

Leon tapped the table. "We are not strong enough to mount a true siege, and if we leave, we let Lull's army loose. It seems we can neither go nor come. If we had a great catapult, we might knock down the drawbridge tower with its chains and pen them up for at least enough time for our help to come. Yet it takes days, perhaps weeks, to build such a device, even with a skilled crew. Still, seeing us preparing might force Lull into making a foolish move against us while we have no other enemies to fight."

Derek leaned forward. "Could you direct the construction of such a device here? Surely there are no military supplies within the town."

Leon stood. "We will have Goosell, who knows fully what needs must be. We have blacksmiths and many skilled carpenters among our people. We will need them all. We will put every back into it. It will be a race, but we will work day and night. Caroline, you know your people. We will need strong rope and strong men."

"Don't forget the women," Prince Galen said. "They double our number."

Caroline smiled. "You are learning, Galen."

"You are an excellent teacher, Ma'am."

A woodsman was plucking arrows from the front wall of the baker's store and slipping them into a quiver as the leaders spoke their plans. Looking away he noted a curling white smoke that rose from a tower on the castle wall. The smoke broke and puffed twice more. The man rubbed the cruel scar that ran along his face as he stopped to read the silent signal.

***

The fox was tired, he had run for hours, and twice had had to run away from dogs, putting him off his path. His paws ached and his tongue drooped. He dropped down on the path and let loose the paper he held between his teeth. "Truly, I am not the pup I was," Fanzig gasped. "I must find water or run no more. Forgive me, Max, when every moment may mean a life lost, even the fox must rest . . ." Laying his head on the cool grass his vision dimmed and he did not see the shadow flickering near him.

High above, a hawk circled and wheeled, searching out the tiny movement he had tracked below. The fox had staggered, then dropped to rest. The hunter's eyes had taken it all in and the hawk's brain tingled with anticipation of the rich meat that waited. She ducked her head, steadied, and tucked her wings tight against her body to fall fast as a stone through the air.

Fanzig was uncertain of which he was aware of first — the tumbling crash of bodies in the brush, or the high-pitched call shrieking loud in his ears. Jerking his head up from the grass, the fox saw two sets of wings beating as if tied together, then breaking apart into two bodies, talons and beaks striking out as dust and feathers scattered in a sudden cloud. Then it was over as quickly as it had begun. A pair of steady wingbeats pushed out curling plumes of dust as the hawk streaked away. A larger bird slid back in a steady banking glide, drawing up to land a few feet away. The owl shook out its feathers. Its great eyes narrowed back down as it studied the fox.

"I trust you have rested well, young fox?" the great bird said.

Fanzig's laugh was feeble. "An unending rest had you not been near, noble Fletcher. I am not so young that I might have dodged the hawk's talons."

"The air is troubled. The birds of prey fly with it in their nostrils. I sense the war wind."

"There is dark evil in this thing, great owl. I run to

Gaspaar with a message for the king, but time is against us — and Max is in grave peril. War strains to be let loose."

The owl bent to look at the parchment. "Is that the message? It is a light thing that I might carry. My wings can outstrip even your legs for time to Gaspaar."

"I will not argue that. It may prove easier for you to approach the king than I. Though I have seen Randrew from a distance with Max, I was much pressed and spent most of the time staying clear of dogs and the rough crowd. I am not sure if Max's stories of speaking beasts were believed or seen only as young imaginings from his time in the wild. I might be seen as a trickster spirit or demon shade, where you might cross the palace walls with little challenge."

Fletcher twisted his head to his right. "There is a creek in the vale beyond those trees, and the shade there is thick, even for a hawk's keen eyes. Max may need you yet, and I shall return as soon as I might. I shall follow the war winds." Saying this, the great horned owl stabbed a talon into the message and tightened its claw. "With the wind behind me I shall race the sunset to gain King Randrew before the moon. Now let us fulfill our purposes."

The owl opened its wings and beat down the air, lifting itself upward and away, drawing into a small black dot above the trees. The tired fox rose and padded slowly down the hillside toward the refreshing stream that waited beyond the trees.

***

Darkcloak

Returning to his chamber, Darkcloak bolted the door behind him. There was much to consider. He knew Max and Rhena and Jippit were all secure. He had only to hold his cards until they could best be played. If Catterline, the rebel traitor, should die with a stolen dagger of *Averon* in his back, his angry outlaws would turn against Averon's knights. In that moment of furious suspicion Lull would drop the drawbridge to storm the town. Garm's bloody band would be at fever pitch after two days penned up in the castle.

And what of *Wotterham*? Wotterham's Prince Linus thought himself clever, but his pride masked his fear of failure. He had pulled away, doubtless to see which side was strongest. Darkcloak grinned. Well, soon it would be clear to all that Lull would win. Wotterham must join him because it was the only *clever* thing to do.

The king's counselor stepped to settle in his chair but, sensing a movement near him, turned to face his own image in the mirror that stood in the corner of the room. He studied the hooded monk with piercing dark eyes and a thin black beard. Gerald raised his palm to the mirror and stared at the faint tattoo that appeared. Its green eye gazed outward from the glass. He glanced up to stare into his own mirrored eyes and — for an instant only — they seemed also to be glowing green. With his blink, all color was gone and his palm, as he turned it back from the mirror, showed only his own fair skin. For a slender moment, Gerald felt the prick of fear he had known once under the hills at the council of the Green Fire. That fear had left him as he listened to the incantations and repeated them. The cold words had echoed inside his mind as he turned his back on all he had known to step into a greater reality. He had willed away the ties that bound him to his weak human nature. Now he approached another unbinding. Severing this tie would release something more than himself. It might demand a sacrifice larger than he had considered before. Like the enchanted map the Duchess had given him once to follow, it had let him see only a little way ahead until he reached a turning. Already there had been death he had not seen, and now there would be more.

He sank into his chair and gazed out the window of the tower. Beyond the lower walls he saw the wide moat lake and the far boundary where the peasants sat at their sentry fires. He reassured himself, but did not smile, at their illusion of victory. There would be little time for them to imagine they had defeated their superiors. Soon their small revolt would crumble as the first example of the power of the new empire. Such people needed an empire. Life was too chaotic without order. The final order would be the most true. It was more important than the lives that had been lost. Only the emotional resistance of the ignorant peasants and the prideful arrogance of the nobles had caused the war that began this day. In the darkness of the night before the tournament, had he not placed protective spells on both Galen's and Derek's body armor? None would have died had they met in the tournament — only an attempt at assassination that would have been seen as he had planned. It could not be helped now. It was an empire he would build, with or without King Lull. There could ultimately be only one ruler. That was true here as well as under the hills, Gerald reminded himself. He must be strong to see it through. The ends would justify the means.

CHAPTER 19

DANGEROUS MEN

Fanzig felt drawn from his path after his recovery that afternoon. With water and rest he soon turned again to Leorna, yet something felt wrong, mistaken with each step of his paws. The fox raised his eyes. Gazing at the rising moon overhead he saw clouds scudding across the stars and barring the moon with thin drawn lines. Fanzig pondered the sign. He was drawn with the wind, the wind that moved the clouds, pointing his new course. As he turned into the brush, the way began to open to his mind. He felt the speed of conviction returning. He must meet another prince if he were to save his own Prince Max.

***

Selas, the mounted squire of Sir Castor dropped back to retrieve the helmet that had slipped free of his saddle pack and fallen in the road. Bending to lift the knight's armor from the path, he looked back up the column of knights to the banner of Wotterham trailing ahead. This march was hard. With no time to pack, the knights and their squires had been long with no food or drink. The battle in the morning had been a confusion and truly none of the men knew what their course home meant. Many had wished to rush to aid the men of Gaspaar and Averon, even if they were old enemies. Only the call of their prince's trumpet had held them back from the fight that began. Prince Linus had hardly spoken a word to the queries of his knights, though they knew well to speak little to their leader in such a place as this.

Selas saw another squire returning to the path with a rabbit hanging from his belt. He was cleaning an arrow with a rag.

"Hail, Goss," Selas called. "At least you have hope of a meal tonight!"

"Aye, Selas," came the reply of the hunter. "Sir Marsten bid me take game whenever I might sight it. Now if only the prince will allow a camp so we may build fires."

Selas shook his head. "I am not certain if he shall. He is in a black mood. Never have I ridden so long with only short resting of the mounts and but grazing as we walk them."

Goss moved to his horse which was tied to a tree limb on the other side of the path. "It is never wise to travel without food. The body needs strength to fight, and the mind needs power to think beyond want. I have no idea what this steady ride means, but I do not like it in any way."

Selas tied the helmet to the pack of his horse. "It is not ours to like or dislike, only to ride. Still, it galls my master to ride away from a battle! He cursed under his breath all morning, though he would never speak to the prince in such manner."

Goss clicked his tongue and urged his horse onto the path beside his friend. "I think there will be plenty of battles soon enough. I imagine the one we left behind is only a small skirmish — hardly more than a shoving of shields. Sir Marsten thinks Prince Linus is saving his best knights to lead back his full army to Leorna."

"That may well be, for I do not believe the prince to be a coward. The question is, when we return, which side of the fight will we join? I know in times past all three lands have had their wars against Wotterham. I wonder who is our friend back there and who is our enemy?"

Goss shook his head. "Those are questions for the prince and the king — not for two tardy squires. We'd best catch up, or we'll be called deserters." Saying this, the squire brought his reins down on the shoulder of his horse and galloped ahead. His friend followed with similar haste.

*****

Max

Max gently probed his bandaged leg. "Truly your uncle knows the healing arts," he said to Rhena who sat across from him on a wooden stool. "It is hardly more than a soreness now."

Rhena raised a hand and glanced up at the door above the chamber and whispered, "Let us keep that a secret, Max."

Malvern shook his head. "Better or worse, we are all still locked in this dungeon. I don't see what point there is in secrecy in such things."

Jippit snorted. "Master Malvern, you have a good heart. Keep your thoughts to yourself and others may think you have a good mind as well."

Malvern did not reply. Even a short time with the elf had taught him that argument with Jippit was a pointless waste of energy.

*****

Lull frowned as Garm scratched a dagger point across the wooden table between them.

"As I see it, King Lull," the mercenary chief scowled, "the rebels are all spread around the moat to watch for any boat we might try to send. They cannot match in fight with us on even ground, sword to sword, but they have archers among them who can plague us plenty. I think we would likely lose two dozen of our best fighters before we could reach the shore and then it's *uphill* on the banks. It is best to slam down the drawbridge and storm out with a rush yelling murder."

Lull nodded. "Yes, yes, we know all that, Garm. The drawbridge can only give room for a narrow rush, and they have captured the barbican and barricaded it. It will allow them to again pick off many of our best fighters . . ."

Garm chuckled. "So we put twenty of your loyal yet least-trained lads in the front rank. They'll soak up the arrows and my boys will well avenge their wounds when we get our hands on the rebels, young and old."

Darkcloak spoke from just beyond the lamp, his hood shadowing his eyes. "A day's wait makes us stronger my lord. It gives our spy time to deliver the death of Catterline. As I have said, the wait is heavier on those outside. They fear the return of Wotterham. The wait will become especially heavy if Catterline is suddenly lost to them with ugly suspicion. The first heat of battle drove many to bravery. That kind of bravery will slip away with time and doubt."

Garm slapped a hand on the table. "This fellow speaks of treachery and doubts. I say power is only good if it is *used*. What must be done must be done soon."

Kenelm, the captain of the guard, coughed. "Sire, may I speak?"

The king looked up at his first soldier. The man was in some ways even less familiar to him than Darkcloak, for the king always doubted the loyalty of those close to him. And the closer, the more doubt he felt. This steadfast soldier had served his father before him and had never given the king cause to question his loyalty; therefore, Lull always viewed him with suspicion.

"Captain, your men did not acquit themselves very well today. What brilliant advice do you wish to add that my councilor and the eager chieftain have not divulged to me?"

Kenelm pointed to the center of the scratched ring on the table. "Sire, it is true that our enemies may hold us here if they control the banks of the moat and barricade the barbican gate where the drawbridge lowers. It is also true that my men have observed activity in the wood near the village, trees being felled and hammering on wedges. Much activity. We have also used the wizard's old glass to search their camp as close as we may, and we see what can only be the construction of a siege catapult begun."

"Then we must rush them!" Garm shouted. "The devils must not have time to batter us down in this great stone pen."

Kenelm held up his hand. "Sire, it is also my knowledge that your father's first soldier, General Goosell, once caused such a catapult to be made for defense of the realm. Its parts were packed away in the storage sheds behind the soldiers' barracks. Much of it was fashioned of iron, and as the stories have it, it could hurl a great stone beyond two hundred meters."

Lull stared at the captain. "And you have known this and never told me before?"

Kenelm shook his head. "I did not know, sire. I have done an inventory of our situation since we have redeployed inside the fortress. It was only a conversation I overheard between our old armorer and a young archer that caught my ear. It is always wise to hear what the men are saying among themselves, especially in war time."

"Have you seen this device? Is it truly there?" Garm squinted at the man.

Kenelm nodded. "Goosell had seen to its best packing. The oak supports and throwing arm are well preserved. Rats and weather have had effect on the leather lashings and the ropes must be replaced, but we have that in plenty in our stables and stores. The old armorer himself knows the way of its fitting, and there are writings carved on its bucket that give weights and distances, I believe."

Lull laughed. "The moat is not two hundred meters in its widest measure. The barbican must be less than fifty. We could smash its walls to bits along with the archers manning it. We should drive the rebels back and charge after them before they could even plan a retreat."

Garm stood up and slapped the soldier on his back. "Here's a soldier worth keeping, King Lull."

Darkcloak crossed his arms. "Captain, how long will it take to set up the catapult?"

Kenelm looked at the king. "Perhaps two days, less if we have enough men working through the night . . . It is impossible to say."

"Then it is a race," Lull said, "Who will finish their machine first? The rebels or us?"

Kenelm nodded. "I do not think that the outlaws would be able to construct a true war weapon inside a week if they must cut and fit their device together, even if they have a studied armorer amongst them who might know the plan."

Lull frowned. "That they even begin shows they must have someone of such knowledge within their camp. No, we must take no chance, we must hurry to achieve our triumph. The side which finishes first may well claim victory here. Perhaps, Darkcloak — perhaps your advice to wait on our charge is wise. The loss of their hero and our sudden attack behind a rain of stones shall be an *unstoppable* force."

Darkcloak nodded. "Yes, sire. It seems that fortune smiles on you even in a dark hour."

Garm laughed. "Blood and fire. Surely you have some prisoner in your dungeon we could behead and throw at the serfs in the catapult's first volley. They'll see what we think of them then. Horror works magic on peasants and serfs. They don't understand it, and they fear those who love it!"

Lull, remembering Rhena's imprisonment, rubbed his bearded chin. For now, her place there was best. It would not do to have her hearing such talk as Garm's. "We are not yet so desperate as that, Garm. Not yet."

Darkcloak felt the twitch of disgust at the mercenary's grin. Garm was dangerous — quick to turn like a wild dog on a leash. If Gerald had time to bring all the pieces together, a strong throne of rule might be fashioned here. Yet how deep did the mercenary's delight in terror run? Such anger must hide some inner fear. Did not all anger come from fear? If he could grasp that secret then Garm himself could be made a tool Gerald might control. The lessons of the council of the Green Fire were always there, flickering in the back of his mind, and more than he remembered, something else . . . not quite visible behind his thoughts.

CHAPTER 20

RANDREW'S VISITOR

Squire Selas thrust his head into the stream as the riders all dismounted around the water. Man and beast alike shared the cool current. Moonlight bathed the valley around them and the moon's reflection shimmered in the water as the men filled their flasks. A flicker to his left told Selas that someone had scraped a flint to light a torch. He hoped this meant they would be setting up camp, though he doubted it. The squire rocked back on his knees and shook the water from his hair. He heard his knight, Sir Castor, call to him.

"Do not drink too much, Selas. We must pace ourselves for the journey. Prince Linus thinks we may reach the outer wards of Wotterham by the day after tomorrow if we can keep hard at it. Take time to scout for food. There should be berries near this stream."

"Aye, sire. Though a rasher of meat is what a man needs to ride or fight on. Do you suppose the prince imagines we shall do both? And without sleep if I may make so bold?"

Castor gave a gruff laugh. "You may not. Linus is a hard leader, but it has made his army hard as well. You are spoiled by all the finery at Leorna. Remember that a knight's first duty is to serve his king in war."

Selas nodded as the knight turned away but mumbled to Goss, "Fighting a battle is not winning one. The side what eats and sleeps best, is the side I like to fight on."

"I'd like to know just whose side we *will* be fighting on." Goss shook his head. "It was all up in the air when we left. I hear Lull has a hired army along with his own, and that Garm of the renegades from the western reaches is their leader. He's as bloodthirsty as a lion — takes no prisoners and fears nothing in this life or the next."

Selas made a face. "Wouldn't care to share a meal with that kind of chap, but then, it might be better than facing him in battle. Any rumor how Prince Linus leans on this question?"

Goss opened his satchel and began plucking dewberries from a low bush. "I'd rather ask Garm than Prince Linus. What I've seen of him, the prince looks grave, dark, and speaks only short commands. No one rides beside him and he has thrown down all save his armor to save weight as he commanded us all. So if we do make camp, you'll need your horse's blanket to make a decent sleep."

***

Randrew

King Randrew stood on the eastern lawn of Gaspaar's palace. He was arguing with the gardener about the best kind of bait for fishing mountain streams. It was known that the king worried with all his sons away and when he worried, fishing was a relief to his senses. His arguments on the merits of certain flies and worms and the best way of slipping a line over the surface could go on for hours if he were inclined. The gardener knew well what prompted the king's intense interest in the angler's art, and while he also worried for the missing princes, he was glad to favor his sovereign with this small pleasure.

"So, my good man, a bright wing wiggled on the surface is two to one, a better lure."

The gardener was not convinced, and it seemed to the king that he always took the most obstinate opinion on any matter they discussed.

"Begging your pardon, sire, but a fish is a small brain. Less imagination is found in only the tiniest of nature's creatures. A full belly is what drives the trout's dreams. A great wiggling worm, bursting with sweet juice and salty as sausage — that's what a trout would hunt for if he were granted feet for a day on the ground, not leaping for colored butterflies and such."

Randrew rolled his eyes. "Fish are not the only ones who lack imagination, gardener. If but one in a dozen trout were inspired to go after such a flitting of colors above, I am certain that he would be the very prize trout, the highest of his order, with bigger brain and more meat than the other eleven all combined."

"The king is a poet, but facts is facts, sire. I'll lay out my eleven fishes alongside your one on our trip to the mountain streams and I'll have good eats and plenty of it. You'll have your dreamer laying there just as dead and no more plump than my Ned, Fred and Bob."

At the mention of the three fish names, the king grew quiet. "Aye, gardener. one wonders what happens with one's own Neds and Freds and Bobs. . ."

The gardener knew the king thought of Derek, Gerald, and Max, his three missing boys. "Sire, you need not fret yourself. There's no surer knight in the lands than your Derek, and Max with him is having the time of his life. Prince Gerald is too wise to be taken unaware of any traps upon his roads. He'll return to us, no doubt with tales and tricks of other lands. My wife says there's never been a lad more for learning than your Gerald — why he'll be an ambassador to treat with monarchs for Gaspaar one day, or maybe a great scribe and write down all his learning in a fine library."

The king smiled. "Be it that you are right, noble gardener. Still, like fish — there's baits and hooks for every man, for some hunger drives us all."

"Sire talks beyond my thinking and my supper waits even if yours does not."

Randrew laughed. "Yes, for I hear an owl searching for his supper even now, do you not?"

The gardener turned. "Majesty, I have seen no owl hunting here in some months. We keep our lawns cut clean and mice are found in plenty beyond the town walls. Perhaps this fellow is chasing a sundown bat."

Randrew squinted his eyes in the sunset. "Indeed. That is as large a bird as I have seen. Were I a bat I would be frightened of such a hunter. Strike me, I believe that the creature is making its way to this lawn."

The gardener glanced to the nearest cottage, which was his own. "We had better to watch from inside my house, sire. This bird may carry sickness. Men have died from bites of stricken fowl."

Randrew shook his head. "Go inside, gardener. I sense a mystery here."

The gardener hesitated but made for his cottage door. He would get his fishing net and return in case the creature approached too close to his king.

As Randrew watched the owl glide slowly around the edge of the lawn, he saw it make a sudden twist and swoop down toward him. He seemed to remember this creature from some other encounter. Yes, it was the same great bird that had returned with Max in the courtyard a year ago. Max had told them all stories of the beasts who spoke with him on his adventure, yet the bird had only made strange sounds he could scarce hear over that crowd and had departed as the curious ones had drawn close upon the prince and his odd collection of friends. The feathered visitor now alighted on the gardener's cart at the edge of the path and it truly spoke, for the king heard it clearly.

"Whooo Randrew . . . are Randrew you?"

"I am the king. Are you the one who came before with my son to Gaspaar?"

"Who is a friend to young Max still . . . and brings his message, if you will." The creature's words were somehow birdlike, though Randrew had never imagined the voice of an owl, except for the haunting *whooo* he had heard called in the woods before.

The owl waited, it's great horned feathers tall and straight as it eyed the king in silence.

Randrew coughed. "Yes . . . I am anxious to hear any word of Max. What does he say?"The owl blinked. "To me . . . nothing. It is written."

The king looked at the powerful talons resting on the wheel of the cart and saw a tattered parchment held fast in the sharp claws. He paused a moment then stepped forward to hold out his hand, wondering at how easily those talons might rip and sever any flesh they fastened on. He swallowed as the owl lifted a claw and extended it to the king spreading the tips wide for Randrew to slip the pierced paper free. The bird re-balanced as it brought the empty claw back beneath it.

Randrew was in deep study as the gardener called from the door of the cottage. "Majesty? Is all well?"

"Nay, gardener," the king said without looking up. "It is far from well. We must call together the *One Hundred* this hour, and ride hard for Leorna. Others may follow as they can, but we must raise the alarm and set the signal fires and pray that they are all that burns tonight."

The Gardener came out to the king. "Sire . . . is it war?"

Randrew looked at the bird. "You have a name, owl?"

"I am called Fletcher, highness. Fletcher Longwing of the Runruggel Heights."

"As you are a friend to my son and a true friend to Gaspaar, Fletcher Longwing, I will ask you to carry a letter from me to Max if you will take it."

The owl blinked. "The air is not so free as it was. Birds of war claim much of the sky. The air is thick with anger and fear. Fly as I may, I can promise no sure passage of your letter."

***

Gaspaar

The royal gardener's wife was upset. "What has gotten into you? What is your hurry? The supper is ready."

The gardener lifted a long pole off hooks above the door. "Have you seen the pike's head? It's not attached to the shaft."

The gardener's wife frowned. "And far less likely to cause damage that way. You were sharpening it as I remember last spring. I think it likely left in your shed. What's the haste to find it now? Is there to be a parade?"

The gardener tried to smile. "There is a call for the *One Hundred.* We must be ready at the castle gate with provisions and a horse if we have one within the half hour. Where is my helmet?"

His wife had risen from the table, her face pale. "The hundred old men and servants who man the walls? Is there to be an attack on the town?"

"No. We do not man the walls. We are to ride tonight for Leorna."

The woman moved to stand before her husband and hugged him as he turned to look for the helmet. "War?" she whispered. "Oh, husband . . . is it truly war?"

The gardener saw the helmet upside down by the window with flowered vines growing out of it almost hiding it. He had near forgotten potting the vines in the fall. "Perhaps not. Perhaps a parade will be all that's needed."

"If you're to travel so far, you'll need a bedroll . . ."

***

Max

Max ate the dungeon bread. It did not taste good, but he had learned to eat when food was there on an adventure. Whatever else, you needed your strength.

"Prince Max," Malvern said, looking up from his untouched supper. "You are son of a king. Surely you can make some deal with King Lull. Whatever has happened, they must take care of you, if for nothing more than ransom or bartering."

Rhena threw a chunk of her uneaten bread at Malvern. "You really are a marvel. Max's brother has just fought a great battle against . . . my father, and we, neither of us, know they are safe or even alive. How can you sit there and wheedle on about such things?"

"I'm just thinking out loud," Malvern replied. "I think we should all be doing some thinking if we are going to see our way through this. I am certain my father will be speaking with the king about my unfortunate imprisonment and that should be cleared up soon, but with what might come, and not a word from these stone-faced jailers, I — I begin to wonder."

Jumpjilter coughed and pulled something out of his mouth. "Bit of extra meat in this bread, I'm afraid. At least it wasn't moving."

Malvern started to gag and Rhena giggled. She was no fonder of the wretched meal, but she was irritated with Malvern.

Max shook his head. "Thinking out loud may give us some help. Sitting here with no idea of what to do but wait, is making me crazy. But even if we could get out of this dungeon, we'd still be trapped in the castle. We'd be caught in minutes and punished badly if I know jailers."

Jippit licked his fingers. "Well, now, as to that — as to that . . ."

They all turned to look at the elf.

"We might not get out of the castle entirely, but I know a way to stay hidden for quite some time." Jippit smiled. "Like mice in a mansion."

Max rubbed his greasy hands on his tunic. "Go on, Jippit. What are you saying?"

The elf grinned. "I've told you all how I followed a spy into the castle and was caught. I didn't mention that I followed the spy through corridors within the walls of the castle itself."

"What?" All three of the young prisoners gasped.

"I'm saying that this old pile of stones was built with secrets, my lads and lass. Secret tunnels running all through it like a honeycomb. It's known as a solid fortress with walls thicker than any in the lands, and true that is . . . but that thickness also let secret ways be covered in and hidden well. I do like secret ways, and this mighty fortress is a temple of them. I think of the old kings listening in on private talks and checking on the comings and goings of servants and nobles alike. Imagine, a simple chat with your chum might be within inches of the king's very ear. I don't think King Lull knows of it though, or they'd have caught the spy herself before this day."

"Herself?" Malvern asked.

Rhena smiled. "Lady Caroline."

The elf nodded. "Your Queen of Lost Hopes and Friends would be my truest guess, my princess. I went a ways following her but there were many tight turnings, and as I've been sitting here, I've been wondering that like as not, there's at least one passage that moves near to us here."

"In the *dungeon*?" Malvern asked.

Max was looking around. "It only makes sense, Malvern. Who would you rather hear talking in private than a prisoner? I wonder if anyone has been listening to us?"

Rhena frowned. "Not Father, if that's what you mean. I'm sure I'd have known of it long before now, and I doubt that Darkcloak would have allowed Caroline to use it so freely if he had known of it."

Max ran his hand over the nearest bricks. "But how could we possibly find it?"

Jippit grinned. "We'll need something sharp to scrape around the stones, and we'll have to keep an eye out for the jailer."

Malvern looked down at his chains. "We still couldn't leave with these chains on us."

Max could," Rhena said. "They haven't chained him yet."

"Or you, Rhena," Max nodded.

"Well, they took away even my metal buckle," Malvern

said. "They went over Jumpjilter rather good too. I think Prince Max has been searched as well."

Rhena smiled and reached up to her hair. "I think I can spare two jeweled hair pins. Being the king's daughter has advantages."

***

Kenelm

Kenelm frowned as the men lowered the long beams from the storage shed's loft. "Easy with those levers and wedges, men. We need every beam intact. If we crack the wood before it's aligned to the catapult plans, we'll likely send the first stone into our own walls."

Old Beasley, the armorer, was rubbing his nose. "If we had a week I'd put a weapon up that would send that bunch out there running. We'd throw oil-drenched hay burning like a comet down on them all. They'd think we had a dragon on our side."

Kenelm's frown didn't change. "Burn up the town, Beasley? That's a bit on the wasteful side wouldn't you think?"

The old man's laugh was wicked. "You chivalrous boys got too many rules for me. Now Garm — I hear he's ready to swim the moat and bite the heads off any farmer that dares to shoot arrows at him. His bunch is ready to fight. That's all they talk, that and what they claim they'll do with the spoils. You should realize that all's fair in war, captain!"

The soldier nodded. "I've heard it said all my life, armorer. Maybe nothing's fair in war, is a better way to say it. Still, the sooner this one's fought, the sooner it's over." He looked away at the towers on the wall. "I have friends in the town."

Beasley laughed. "Well, when we're done, you might have to count them again. Still, I guess you can go in the little church and get all forgiven up by the priest."

Kenelm shouted at one of the soldiers. "Hey! Lurken! Watch your grip. You'll ruin your back lifting like that. That's a *lever*, not a *handle*. Lift with your legs, you dimwits. We need

163

every man of you to fit this beast together."

"And to fire it." Beasley laughed.

CHAPTER 21

DARK VISIONS

The rising sun lit the castle walls across the moat from the town where Sir Leon had just greeted an old friend. Goosell the farmer, who had taken Max's message, took the cup of water handed him by the king's brother.

"Thank you, my prince. It is good to serve you again. I came as quickly as I might, but my horse had been seized by the guards who took the young messenger."

"What messenger?" Derek asked as he and Caroline approached from the barricade.

Leon turned. "General Goosell, this is Prince Derek of Gaspaar, who we fought with yesterday."

Goosell bowed to the nobles, but Caroline had stepped forward to embrace him.

"Dear Goosell," she said, "your warning came just in time. Though lives were lost, they were few because of your warning."

"Not mine, my lady. As I said, the brave lad I spoke of gave me the warning. He had an arrow wound in his leg that had been treated —"

"By me," Leon said. "That was Prince Max of Gaspaar, Goosell. He was on his way to Gaspaar to bring back his father's army."

Goosell closed his eyes and sat at a chair pulled from the barricade. "Then much is lost, I fear."

"What do you say?" Derek bent down next to the old man. "What has happened? Is Max hurt badly?"

The old general looked up to Derek and then to the others. "No, but he was captured. He was brought to me by a patrol of Leorna's soldiers. They were taking him to the castle."

"Lull has him!" Caroline gasped.

Derek sat on a stump to steady himself.

Goosell shook his head. "I do not know, but the soldiers were sent by one they spoke of as *Darkcloak*. I took their meaning that it was he, not Lull, who was searching for the young messenger."

Derek turned back to stare at Goosell. "Darkcloak? The robed counselor that skulks about the king's court? He dared not show his face to any of us, though I did not seek it."

Caroline nodded. "Yes, he has been Lull's right hand for many months. It is rumored that he is a magician or sorcerer. They say he caught Lull's attention with an evening's entertainment and was invited to stay in the court. There is something evil about that one."

Galen put a hand on Derek's shoulder. "If Lull knew he had Max in his power, I think we should have heard of it by now. Forgive me, Derek, but I think we'd have been offered a hard bargain for his life, perhaps even a demand that we surrender."

Derek shook his head. "What can be this sorcerer's plan? If he does not boast of his capture, what terrible thing does he intend?"

Goosell rubbed his beard. "There may be a glimmer of hope in this, but I suggest we move quickly. I would not put anything beyond Lull when he is upset or frightened. Your fortunate route of his forces from the field yesterday has raised his fears."

"What can we do?" Derek asked. "There must be something . . . perhaps if we could make contact with this Darkcloak, we could make some barter in secret. I would trade places —"

"*That* we could not allow." Leon looked to Galen.

Caroline crouched beside Derek and gripped his folded hands. "There is perhaps one thing that might be done. It will be dangerous."

Everyone turned to Caroline.

"General Goosell taught me of a secret way within the castle walls. I have used it as a spy more than once in the last months."

Leon stared at her and then at Goosell. "I have never known of such a thing! What is this?"

The old general pointed to the castle across the moat. "There is a series of passages within the heavy walls of the castle and the keep. Old King Lemond had them built in from the beginning, keeping the secret from all. I will not say how the secret was kept so well, but it would be likely that the workers who made the channels did not live out their full lives. The kings of Leorna used these passages to listen to the conversations of their guests, servants, and soldiers. The secret of the passages would only be passed to the next heir when he had become fully enthroned. Your father entrusted me with the secret to give to which of the brothers ended upon the throne. He always hoped you would return to wear the crown, Prince Leon. I chose, of my own vanity, to withhold the secret from your brother Lull. When Lady Caroline returned and I saw her heart's great desire to restore honor to our land, I entrusted her with the secret. It is a defiance of the king's command. If Your Highness choose, you may have me beheaded for this offense."

Leon shook his head in wonder. "I have never been so glad to hear of a treason. If ever I am king, faithful Goosell, I will grant you pardon. Your loyalty has been to more than the king."

Derek was staring at Leon. "I must go inside the castle. I must rescue Max."

Caroline shook her head. "Crossing the moat must be done in darkness, by only a few, and the chance for discovery is much greater with all the sentries on the walls. Derek, we simply cannot risk losing both princes of Gaspaar."

"Caroline speaks truth," Galen agreed. "I know you ache to free your brother, but such emotion will make the way more difficult. I shall go in your place." He laughed. "After all, my father has four sons and three daughters. If I am lost, he will need to be reminded which one I am."

Leon frowned. "No, Galen, you are needed to lead your brave knights."

"Well, I must surely go," Caroline said, "for I alone can lead the way. It seems *Catterline* must return for another evening."

Derek turned to the castle and spoke over his shoulder. "I shall go. Max is my brother. And there is a third brother who could be crowned, if all else were lost. I cannot yield to your wishes, no matter how reasoned they are."

Leon looked at Caroline. "There is a long day ahead of waiting. We do not know what may come of tonight's mission. We must press on with our catapult. We must keep pressure on Lull, for time runs against us. Now we know that no message has been sent on to Gaspaar."

Galen had turned to look back to the west of the town. "We have no great army to storm the castle. My father's army will not arrive for many days, if my messenger got through at all. Now we know we must send another to Gaspaar. We must break the drawbridge towers of the castle soon. We know not how long it shall be before allies of Leorna arrive."

"You mean Wotterham?" Caroline asked.

"I mean Wotterham. Linus and his father remember the lost wars and lost lands of times past. Averon was not always a friend, and neither Gaspaar. Beyond that, who knows what other trick or tribe Lull may have in his pay? More of these bloody mercenaries might be camped beyond the hills held for just such a failing as yesterday's defeat. If this Darkcloak is a sorcerer, we might even be facing armies of goblins or ghouls. I don't believe in such things for the most part, but I don't ignore my nerves either."

Derek nodded. "Whatever Wotterham's plans, if all these armies come close together, things may take a turn that no prince or king intends. Father says that putting armies near each other is like using a torch to inspect a dry forest; it begs to burn."

"Haven't enough died and been hurt to make Lull reconsider?" Caroline asked. "Beyond the wounded, near a dozen have died so far. "

"For a king, that is acceptable," Derek replied.

"Most soldiers are not the sons of *kings*," Caroline answered.

There won't be a catapult ready for near a week," Leon said. "It just cannot be done."

Goosell stood. "Now there I can help you, my prince."

"Time is short, general." Leon said.

The old soldier smiled. "When was there ever enough? I know the demands of the weapon well, and I have looked over your work on the way through the camp. I can shorten your task by many days. The scaffold we need not build. By good fortune we may simply use the strong beams of the roadhouse that is being constructed at the edge of the town. Its pitched roof frame is in perfect position less than a hundred yards from the raised drawbridge, and its beams will support six tons of swinging weight arm unless I have lost my eye for lumber. We can use the mill lathe to work the throwing arm from the tall fir tree at the entrance to the town."

Galen shook his head. "What of the pivot, Goosell?

Does not all rest on the strength of a sturdy axle for such a device? Have we time to cast an iron piece to take such a load and smooth enough to rock fair?"

Goosell nodded and pointed back down the street of the town. "The great wagon used to carry stone from the quarry will provide a true axle that was hardened oak. The cart body itself shall serve as a counter-weight box and saves us days of construction as well. The pulleys needed for cocking the firing arm can be borrowed from the construction work on the roadhouse site. We've horse teams enough to pull our ropes tight, and the firing peg can be pulled free in like manner. Unless I've lost my touch, I can have two hundred pound stones reigning on the drawbridge towers and even into the courtyard beyond. A hundred pounder might reach for the keep walls beyond."

Leon laughed. "You amaze me, Goosell."

The general continued, "You already have the women of the village weaving the ropes together, and these shall be better platted than many I have used in past days. With good fortune, I may have you a worthy weapon two days hence, my lords."

Derek rose to stare at the castle where the sentries were lit by fire within the courtyard. "Max cannot wait. Tonight, I must go within the walls."

Caroline looked to Leon but did not speak

.

***

The One Hundred

The royal gardener looked across from his saddle astride the horse he had borrowed from the old innkeeper in the town. His friend, the royal cook, was squirming on the seat of the supply cart drawn by draft horses. "Stay awake there, good cook, we can't have you toppling off and breaking your back. This march would be harsh if we did not have your dinner to look ahead to."

The cook yawned. "It's hard riding for a night and a morning on this wooden plank, gardener. I'm too sore to fall asleep. I do hope King Randrew stops soon, for we've ridden a full night and half a day. Eating the bread passed out while riding is hardly going to settle our stomachs if a battle must be fought."

"What sort of battle we'll make, I wonder? It's one thing to sit upon a high wall and maybe throw down a rock on whoever is foolish enough to cross a moat, and another entirely to face a trained army in the field or make a siege on the greatest fortress in the northern lands."

"Keep your doubts to yourself, gardener," the cook said. "The king rides back to us."

King Randrew had brought his mount tramping back down the dusty path along the line of the hundred men on horseback. He encouraged these common sentries, servants, and men of the town, each wondering if they might face such a war as had not been fought in most of their memories.

"Sire," the gardener called in greeting as his sovereign reigned in beside the cook's wagon and the gardener's horse.

"Well, my friends," Randrew said, stretching his back as he rode. "I would that I were twenty years younger for this adventure. I have not ridden a horse over such a length in years. My back and bottom both complain."

The cook reached down behind his seat into the cart. "I have a poultice that the barber gave me to share with any who ache."

"Barber Ronald is a good man to have on this trek. Let us hope we have no need for his skills as a physician. I do not care for bloodletting whether from wounds or the healing arts."

The gardener frowned. "What do we expect at the end of our journey, sire? A battle?"

"Let us hope not, but pray for strength if we must," the king replied. "A show of force is only convincing if we are committed to do more than stand as actors on a stage. Do you regret your place in this train, my friends?"

The gardener chuckled. "A day away from the sheers and shovel are always welcome, sire. I only hope to resume them in good health soon."

The cook nodded. "If Prince Max needs us, I am willing

to leave my kitchen to the maids and pages. I only wish I were cooking for ten times our hundred."

"As do I, cook. We sent the call for our men on the far borders to follow as soon as they receive our message. Within two days perhaps the full army will be upon its way, though five hundred in a week may be worth less than our hundred on the morrow. That is why we stop only long enough to change our horses and your draft team. Thank heavens for these clouds and a cool breeze for our march."

***

Max

It was late afternoon by the shadows of the bars in the high windows of the dungeon, but Max, Malvern and Rhena were hardly aware of the time as they pushed, pulled and scraped at the stones of the dungeon walls and floor.

"There's someone coming," Jippit whispered an urgent warning.

Max and Rhena, who had been digging at the corners of the stones along the wall of their cell with the metal hair pins, were fast to brush away the extra dust around the base of the wall.

Malvern, who had been digging between stones at the end of his chain whispered. "Hurry, even I hear the key in the lock."

Above them the door to the dungeon opened and someone stepped inside. The jailer pointed out Max and a guard followed him down the stairs to stand with his sword held ready as the jailer worked the key to the cell's lock. The guard stepped forward as the door opened.

"Prince of Gaspaar, come with me," the guard commanded.

Max stood up from his cot. "Does King Lull wish to see me?"

"Come. Make no attempt to escape. I am to tell you that your fellow prisoners here would suffer cruelly if you should try any such chance."

172

Max looked at the others then walked out of the cell where he was gagged with a rag and his hands tied behind his back. The jailer frowned. "It is on order," he explained to the prince.

Rhena rushed to the bars. "Be brave, Max."

At the prodding of the guard, Max moved gingerly up the stairs and out of the dungeon into the dark hall. Only a few doors up the hallway from the dungeon Max was shown into a room lit only by a single candle. There were no windows. Inside a figure waited, seated at a table. Darkcloak held a hand up to the guard as Max entered the room favoring his wounded leg.

"Stand outside the chamber. No one shall interrupt. What may be spoken here, you do not wish to know, guard."

Max's guard nodded a silent response and Max felt the soldier untie his hands and then heard the door close. The prince raised his hands to work the gag free of his mouth. "Gerald. What have you done? This terrible thing — this war?"

Darkcloak slipped the hood from his shoulders, revealing his face. "Sit, Max." He looked at his brother's bandaged leg as he sat. "I am glad your injury was well tended as reported to me."

"No thanks to Lull! Were you part of his terrible mad plan?"

Gerald met his brother's eyes. "It is truer to say that Lull was part of *my* plan."

"What?"

"I cannot expect you to understand things that are far beyond you. I am your brother, but I am much more than that now. I have . . . been changed since you knew me."

"What do you mean, since I *knew* you, Gerald? You are my brother. I know you! What are you talking about?" Max felt a cold fear working up his back. He wanted Gerald to stop this sober, solemn talk. He wanted him to suddenly laugh and be the argumentative, sarcastic, even rude, older brother, he had fussed with and pestered, only a few summers ago. "Stop this talk," he said.

Gerald stared at him. "Max, as *you* were chosen, so *I*

was chosen. Not by a king, but by something . . . greater. When Randrew chose you as his heir, he chose a way of weakness, a failed future for Gaspaar. I can do so much more . . . things you can't imagine."

Max shook his head. "I don't know what you mean, Gerald, but whatever has started this, people have died. Was *that* part of your plan?"

Gerald was silent for a moment before speaking. "No. Not as it has happened. Some injury might have occurred, but perhaps fate deemed that too small a price for all that is promised."

"What are you saying?" Max was more horrified than he had felt even in the giant's hand above the bubbling cauldron in the hills of Gumbor.

Gerald slid a finger across the table. I will tell you that I have gained much knowledge and power . . . but I have still much to learn, even now. The power must be carefully used, or it will use you instead. There is a price to everything."

Max wanted to demand that Gerald stop this frightening talk, but he could find no words.

Gerald was forming lightly glowing green lines on the table surface in the wake of his fingertips, like fiery trails from celebration rockets, streaks flowing into images before Max's eyes. His words were like a spell above the shifting scenes before them.

"If a power does not rise to take command in this land of small kingdoms, then another shall soon come and sweep everything away — its farms, its towns, its people. It demands an *emperor* to rule above it, to protect it and fashion it into an empire of order that will last through time. To do this, the crude ways and traditions must be put away. I know I speak of more than you dream of in your happy boy's vision of the world. You want to be a good king, but you do not understand that the very *idea* of a king must itself be destroyed."

As Max watched Derek's finger, he saw a pale map appearing of Gaspaar and Averon and Leorna and Wotterham — Empt and the Northern Reaches — the Runruggel Mountains — even the edge of the sea. As he watched he felt his vision itself going downward, down to the land of Gaspaar and the castle and the road and for an instant he thought he saw an army moving along it, eastward and north toward Leorna, but clouds slid across the table, shrouding the vision and he saw that wherever he looked strongest, the vision was weakest. Still . . . he knew those clouds.

Max blinked and forced his eyes from the table to stare into Gerald's face. "Gerald . . . I am no great king or prince to understand all you say, but this thing that has begun . . . the battle . . . the killing . . .the lies . . . this can't be right no matter how clever you are. Tell me you know this."

"Max, you are still trapped by childish longings. This is surgery. I cut the rotting arm that will kill the whole body if it is not removed. It is not for the weak. I do not care for the wild joy that some take in it, but these barbarians are only crude tools to be rid of once they serve their purpose."

Max swallowed. "What of *my* purpose here? What do you intend with me — with Rhena and Jumpjilter?"

Gerald slid his hands across the table and the visions trailed away. "You were the only one I intended to capture. You are the hostage I would use to barter a submission from your king rather than a blind war against us."

"*My* king? *Father*? He's your father too, no matter what you say. And your king also, isn't he? Or is Lull your king now?"

Gerald frowned. "I have no king. Lull is but a piece on the board, Max. A handy one, as is Garm, and Prince Linus and Prince Galen . . ."

"And Derek?" Max said. "Derek's out there fighting. You might have killed him with your trickery. Is Derek just a — a piece on your chess board too?"

"If all had gone as I planned it, there need have *been* no battle. A spell kept harm from both princes so that only an attempt at murder would have been seen — an arrest, a trial, and Gaspaar forced to submit to the court of Leorna. But events sometimes run wide of plans and fate may demand a harsh price if success is to be achieved. Who could have foreseen the arrival of Leon and the accursed Catterline breaking in upon such a carefully crafted point? It is not my fault if those who *interrupt* fate force pain and suffering where it need not be. Still, success is held for those who hold to their purpose. Deeper ways are opened. Sometimes a sacrifice is demanded for victory."

"And you would sacrifice Derek and me?" Max wondered if Gerald's argument were really with himself. He almost heard Gerald's old voice break through in his tirade.

Gerald stood. "You still think you can call me back to the old ways? I have told you; I think *differently* now. I seek clarity — sheer knowledge — final power."

Max fought for words. "Why have you called me here at all? Why do you care what I think? Do you want me to think of you as a monster?"

"Better that, than a brother. Perhaps one day, you will see my wisdom and seek my way. There could yet be a throne for you, Max."

Max could say nothing.

Gerald held a hand out to the door and it opened. The guard stepped in at this silent summons. "Bind the prisoner again and return him to the dungeon."

***

Lull

Lull and Garm stood watching the soldiers in the courtyard pounding heavy pegs into place as the arms of the great catapult were put together under Kenelm's leadership.

"You're certain this device can reach the town with its shot?" Lull asked Kenelm.

The captain turned to the king. "Sire, I can only speak of it as the old armorer has related. Upon the counterweight basket are carved the figures for the shooting. Beasley assures me that if followed properly, a small weight of perhaps sixty pounds could reach the nearer houses, though I should think our goal would be to hit the barbican with heavier shot. Something nearer two hundred pounds would certainly knock the stone walls apart. The archers would be driven back, and

176

we could lower the bridge and make our charge."

Garm grunted. "How far might a human head be hurled? Might the square of the town be near enough for that? Nothing would do better than the head of one of their own bouncing down that path! I've known armies break and run when they caught their leader's head in their laps."

Kenelm bit his lip. "I suppose some of them might fight more fiercely at such a message."

A cruel smile slid up Garm's face. "Oh, perhaps a few saucy ones fight harder, but that is good. Hot blood bleeds most easily. Sometimes, captain, these turn mad with their rage and become as dangerous to those around them as to us."

Lull grunted. "Beyond a bothersome elf, we've no prisoner worth mentioning."

"An elf?" Garm stared. "Now *that's* good sport. You're better off with it dead than resting in your dungeon. They have a way of getting loose, and there's not one born that can't fight."

Lull nodded. "We have your word that you will be ready tomorrow, Kenelm?"

"We have the pivot and firing arm, as well as the more complex pieces, all stored well, but the trestle we must fashion from stored lumber and secure . . . another day at least, sire. We try for dawn on the day beyond tomorrow."

"Are you saying you cannot meet our command?"

The captain tightened his lip. "I am saying that tomorrow would be a great achievement. Only Beasley has worked such an engine before. We've two injuries so far with slipped hammers and dropped timbers. Even three days would be a short time for such a job in the open field."

Garm scowled. "You are not in the field, captain. Your lads have all you need near at hand, with the hard parts laid out nice and neat. A lash would get your soldiers moving at a better pace."

Lull looked to the flat courtyard where the men were pounding the ends of long frames into the ground with heavy hammers. "With enough time, the rebels may gain advantage over us. We must destroy the gatehouse so our drawbridge can be landed safely for our attack. If they should manage to raise their catapult in time to break down our bridge and tower, we could be sealed up to be starved. The consequences for your failure would fall on us all."

Kenelm saluted as the King Lull turned away. He saw that Garm was studying him.

"You supply the catapult, captain, or you'll supply the head."

For just an instant Kenelm felt an overwhelming urge to pull his sword and attack this vile warrior. Though "warrior" was hardly the word he would use for Garm. He turned back to the men at work in the courtyard.

CHAPTER 22

A QUESTION

Night had fallen again, and the moon and stars grown bright and still the hammering and chopping never ceased. The echo of hard work resonated from the town and was answered by like noise from within the walls of the castle as both camps prepared their fierce war weapons.

Caroline held out a goblet to Derek. "The work is hot, quench your thirst, good prince."

Derek thanked her and took the drink. He looked up at the castle. "What will they do next, I wonder?"

Prince Galen wiped his face with a dry rag, he had been using an ax to shave limbs from the downed trees in the clearing with his men. "Whatever it is, they are probably already doing it."

One of Catterline's men stepped to the circle and bowed, his scarred cheek lit by the fire where men hammered an iron rod on an anvil forming a trigger for the catapult. Derek wondered if Lull's henchmen had given the outlaw that scar. The man's face reminded him of nightmares he had as a child and oddly, he felt himself now almost to be in a dream state. He stared at the man and concentrated as he spoke to the leaders.

The outlaw motioned to the castle. "My lords, it is the darkest point of night. Surely Lull's sentries are weary of watching our fires. As you instructed, we have let the small fires on the rim of the moat on the far side of the castle burn out. That side now is in the greatest darkness as the moon-shadow of the castle hides its water. It is now the time you wished to go."

Caroline nodded. "Very good, Liam." She turned to the others. "Good comrades, we should be better served in only our lightest clothing, and with only our swords. We shall darken our faces and arms with mud, so moonlight will not shine on our skin."

Goosell turned to Leon. "She makes you a better general now than I."

Derek swayed on his feet, and Caroline and Leon grasped his arms to steady him. Caroline frowned as she spoke with regret to the prince. "Brave Derek, I pray you will forgive me for the treachery I have done."

Derek licked his lips and her words seemed to echo in his ears. His mouth felt as if it were full of wool as he tried to answer. "What . . . what have . . . what is . . . done?"

Leon spoke as they helped lay the prince's back against a tree stump. "It is on my order. We knew with all your heart you would go on this rescue into the castle. You must see that losing both of Gaspaar's princes is too great a risk for us to take. We have put a potion in your cup. You will sleep well tonight and tomorrow we shall be back, if all goes well, with Max and Rhena."

Derek was blinking hard. "You . . . cannot . . . *my* brother . . ."

Galen steadied him. "I also shall wait with you, Derek. Our men will follow our commands best if we are here for them. This mission calls for stealth. Only Leon, Caroline, and Liam shall make the journey. We may have to stand off Linus' army, remember? Your courage and skill are needed here most. The head above the heart is the winning way of war."

Derek was trying to speak, but his head slumped to his shoulder. Caroline and Leon steadied him gently.

Prince Galen summoned a sentry. "Take Prince Derek to a bed within the village. I hope he sleeps well with that draught and that he has no dreams. I should hate to have any of *my* brothers held captive and be forced to do nothing."

***

The Road to Wotterham

A sharp blow on his shoulder brought the squire Selas awake. He gripped the reins of his horse which was moving at a slow trot. He glanced wide-eyed at his master.

"You'd have been on the ground in a moment, knave," the knight scolded. "I will not be turning back to hunt for my squire and pack horse."

Selas rubbed his shoulder as the knight galloped further ahead. His friend, Goss turned his horse nearer. Selas glared at him. "Why didn't you warn me of Castor?"

Goss yawned. "I was near asleep myself. I do not know how long we can manage such a push. In darkness these roads become less familiar; it would be easy to take a wrong turning."

Selas frowned. "I wish it were so. The longer before we arrive at Wotterham, the longer it will be before our return to battle. We could be lost for a year and I wouldn't complain."

Goss stretched, "You talk treason friend, I —" The squire suddenly stopped and pointed into the woods beside

181

them. "Faith. Did you see that?"

"What?"

"A fox running alongside us, unless I'm dreaming now, running along to match our pace."Selas turned to his left and stared. "I see no creature of any type, but a fox is an animal I would not be surprised at seeing. Why your awe?"

"Fox run *from* mounted men, not *with* them. A fox may be an omen. My gran says evil signs and evil times run together. Haven't you noticed the carrion birds always flying overhead?"

"Your *gran* sounds like an old hag telling fortunes for a coin, Goss. Pay me a tribute and I'll give you signs and omens to make you sleepless for a fortnight."

"That might be handy now," Goss muttered.

Selas shook his head. "Too bad Prince Linus takes no notice of such things . . . I'd pay a hag a fortune for an evil eye on this trek. Rest, then ride. Rest, then ride. We'd as soon walk home. We've no purpose, only a direction."

Sir Castor realized that the prince, riding ahead, had slowed and the front riders raised their hands in warning to those behind. He trotted forward to bring his mount to the side of the prince who had paused upon the crest of a ridge on the path.

"Sire? What is it? Do you wish us to unsaddle for a rest again?"

At first the prince did not answer but lowered himself from his horse and walked ahead, leading his mount by the reins. Castor, knowing his prince's manner, followed his example. Soon all the train of riders were walking their horses behind them in the dark.

"Castor, do you believe in signs?" Linus continued to walk, looking ahead, as he spoke.

The knight licked his dusty lips. "I have never given much thought to them, sire. "

"Nor have I. Signs and omens are for children and old women. Yet a thing catches my eye. Again and again. I see a fox who has run alongside us for some time, first one side, then another."

"Passing strange, but what have you?"

"You do not think that Fate is speaking to me?"

"An odd way to declare its message, sire, surely a more direct sign would —"

"The fox waits ahead on the bridge yonder, Castor. His golden eyes burn bright and he sits, unafraid of our column."

Castor stared ahead. "I cannot see anything there. The shadows are too great."

"Wait here, Castor. I will meet this omen face to face."

"Sire! It might be evil magic. It might be a sorcerer's trap."

"You give little thought to signs, brave knight. Now you fear a small creature we hunt for sport. Your nerve turns quickly. I will not have mine do so." He turned to the knight. "Wait here with my horse. Do not come forward until I call for you." He handed his reins to Castor and walked ahead, his cape flapping around him as a sudden cool night wind blew across the path.

Linus thought he had been mistaken. Perhaps he had imagined the fox on the bridge, but then the glowing gold eyes blinked open and he could see the small head turning to face him. He stopped ten feet from the creature. The prince cleared his throat, finding himself reluctant to speak, as if he were waiting for the creature to speak first, as though he did believe in such things. He almost laughed before he spoke, but his voice was not so confident as he had intended.

"You are a brave one, brother fox. Does hunger or curiosity put you in my path, I wonder?"

"Neither, Prince Linus," came the answer.

Linus gasped. "By sacred heaven! Are you a demon?"

"Neither demon nor angel, Prince of Wotterham. I am only a question."

"A question? What question would that be? And who asks it?"

"You ask it, yourself."

"Me?"

"It drives you now. You seek your army, a force to bend

the way of the days. It waits for your bidding, only hours from this place. Two kingdoms lay open to your might, a chance not offered in generations, and a taller crown than Wotterham has worn since the great wars of long ago. Only honor stands between you and the false prize that is always offered to the blind."

The prince closed his eyes and looked away and back at his men in the distance. "Am I mad? Are you some dream I have imagined?"

The voice was softer. "If you break with honor, if you grasp the blade of conquest — then I am a dream. One that will fade from your mind like forgotten promises. It is your question to answer, Prince Linus . . . Be mindful of the bridges you cross."

The prince turned back to face the fox, but there was nothing there.

Sir Castor saw Linus returning. "What was it, sire? Was the fox there?" The knight had seen the still figure of his master standing at the bridge for a long minute, he could see nothing beyond him in the dark.

Prince Linus took his horse's reins and climbed onto his saddle. Sitting still he gazed ahead at the bridge across the river. The path was open. No golden eyes watched him from the road ahead. He turned to the knight beside him. "Mount the men, Castor. We must ride hard."

CHAPTER 23

DANGER IN DARKNESS

The water felt cold as Leon slipped down beside the log near the dark bank of the moat. Behind him he felt Caroline's hand on his shoulder and looking back, could see her mud-darkened face smile as she slid down to grip the log. Across the trunk Leon could see the top of Liam's cap level with his position. He heard Caroline's whispered command to push away. As they agreed, Caroline would use a stick to tap the shoulders of the two men ahead of her to let them know which way to paddle. Leon knew that Caroline had used a small boat before to make this journey, yet it could not hold the three and would be more easily spotted. The log could float as debris and the trio could even duck their heads beneath the water if they sensed they were being watched and more people could cling to it without sinking. The moat was wide here, almost a hundred yards, and they hoped the clouds drifting above would help keep the starlight low. Leon marveled at the courage of Caroline. She had made this crossing several times, though of course there had been little watch kept before the battle. He wondered how hard it would be to find and rescue Max and knew if they could not escape by dawn, then they must wait at least until night again before trying to re-cross the moat. It was a great gamble, but he knew that if they did not return that Derek and the others would do everything that could be done to hold Lull's army until a true siege could be won. It was strange that Lull's plot to divide the countries had brought together old rivals like Gaspaar and Averon. Still, so much was unknown. What of Wotterham's intentions? How far away were they and Gaspaar's troops? Were more mercenaries marching to the aid of Lull? If only there were time — but Goosell had reminded Leon that there was never enough.

***

Max

Max and Malvern had not given up. By the low light of the torch outside the dungeon's door which lit the small square of bars the jailer looked in every quarter of an hour, the two lads dug away and tested bricks along the wall. Rhena had fallen asleep and Jippit's chains kept him from helping. He could only listen for the footsteps of the jailer approaching the door above.

"This is hard work," Max whispered. "It's worn my fingers down to the nub."

Malvern nodded. "Sorry I can't get over there to help you beyond this bit of wall. My chain's wearing a chuff on my leg too."

Jippit moaned. "I'd like to move about as you two. I can't even take a sip of water."

Max sat up on his knees. "I'll bring you a dipper Jippit. I need to stand for a moment anyway." He stood, stretching, and stepped across to fill the dipper by the bucket that the jailer had brought in. Max knew they were fortunate that Rhena was imprisoned with them. Having the princess in the cell meant they had clean food and fresh water. Rhena even got to be escorted to an upper chamber when she needed privacy. The elf and boys had no such provision, though the waste buckets were removed to be cleaned immediately so that the princess would have no ill odors to contend with. There was even incense burned in a small sensor in the corner, so the dungeon smelled more like a monk's cell than the foul prison it was. The king had commanded these comforts from afar and had no idea that he was also providing Max of Gaspaar with such luxuries.

Unfortunately, as Max stepped back toward the shackled Jippit, his foot caught on the chain that ran to Malvern's leg. He stumbled to the floor, spilling the water from the dipper. "Blast!" he shouted, then whispered. "Sorry, Jippit. I'll get another dipper."

"How is your leg, Prince Max?" Jippit asked. "You haven't opened your wound?"

Max started to answer when he noticed something.

"Max? Are you alright?" Malvern whispered.

"I'm all right. In fact, I'm more than all right."

Rhena rose up. "What's happened?"

Max was on his hands and knees staring at the floor, inches from his nose. "Rhena," he said, "fill the dipper and hand it to me, please."

The princess shrugged but picked up the spoon and moved over to the bucket. "Here it is. What are you doing?"

"I didn't want to lose my place." Taking the full dipper, he held it in front of him and poured the water out on the dirty brick and straw floor. In a moment he looked up at the others. "I've found it. The water goes down a straight line and corner of brick. This is a hidden door."

***

Garm

Garm drummed his fingers on the windowsill of his chamber as he watched the late-night work of the soldiers in the courtyard below. He had been furious that the cursed Captain Kenelm had insisted on mounting the entire catapult on wheels. They would only need to aim from the castle and leave the weapon behind, Garm had argued. Kenelm had explained that the wheels were not for transporting the *Trebuchet* as the armorer called it, but to allow the great arm to swing in a more efficient manner, that would both keep it from shaking apart and also send its stones further. He had yielded to the argument but resented the cool manner of the captain. He was far too willing to wait for battle, Garm thought. The mercenary ground his teeth as he remembered the cold look Kenelm had given him. When this battle was done Garm thought it might be good if one of the casualties were the captain. He'd make sure of it. He smiled at that and then at another thought.

"At least I shall launch some bothersome elf screaming into the far street." He crossed his arms and leaned on the sill. "I wonder if this midget might be of the saucy tribe that warned the fief of Breanna of our raid last year?" He grinned and picked up a lamp with a bright candle. A late visit to the prisoner might be useful. It was good to gauge a man before you killed him.

***

Max

It had been hard to leave Jippit and Malvern behind, but without keys to their locks there was no way to release them. Malvern had been more noble than Rhena had expected, telling them to go on, that he would certainly be released once his father had a chance to speak with the king. Jippit had looked in Max's face and nodded. "Be a good king, Max. Stay true to your heart."

188

Max bit his lip as he crawled down the narrow tunnel beneath the dungeon floor. *"I must return,"* he promised himself. *"There must be a way."*

Rhena was uncertain of their dark passage. With no lamp to guide them they had to inch their way along, and it crossed her mind that they might become lost or trapped in the labyrinth of the castle and be forced to surrender or else perish of hunger. Without knowledge of the passages, even finding a way out was a challenge as well. She had only traveled a single path, one with room to walk upright, yet here the way was so low and narrow that only by crawling on their hands and knees were they able to move. She heard Max knock into something and after a low moan she reached forward to feel him sitting still and rubbing his head.

"Are you all right, Max?"

"I have run into a fork in the way. The tunnel splits. The left seems to be going up, the right going down. I wonder which way we should go?"

Rhena swallowed. "If only we had a light . . . or if there were a draft of air."

Max grunted. "This downward tunnel is wet. Perhaps it is a drain to the moat. We might be able to get out that way."

Rhena frowned in the dark. "Must we? I hate the slime."

"Well, I suppose it's all equal at the moment. We might as well try to climb upwards. Lately I seem to keep making bad choices."

"Then let it be mine," Rhena crawled past him. "Thank goodness I dressed in riding britches when I left for the orchard yesterday. I'm sure my knees would be shreds by now."

As they climbed, they found a sudden angle that went straight on and it was narrower still. It required them to crawl on their stomachs and Max said it must be a part of a rain-drain from the top of the keep and that they might work backwards to their old way when Rhena saw a flickering light and gasped.

"What is it?" Max whispered as he felt the boot ahead of him with his hand.

Rhena whispered as quietly as she could. *"There's a light . . . this tunnel opens above a larger passage. Someone is moving along it."*

"They may be hunting us." Max replied. *"We should go back."*

"No," Rhena hissed. *"I must see who it is."* Before Max could grab her feet, she inched ahead where he saw her silhouette against a lighter square of stone passage beyond their tunnel.

***

Caroline

Caroline wiped the hair back from her face and ran her hand along the brick ahead of her. "Hold the lamp closer," she said.

Leon raised the metal lantern with its candle up in the passage. "Have we lost our way?"

"This is a part of the labyrinth I have not traveled," she said, "but Goosell has explained the markings to me. If I find one, I can get us closer to the dungeon."

Liam looked back down into the dark behind them. "My lady, I thought these passages were all near to the inner rooms and halls. Perhaps we should slip inside and make our way to the dungeon in a more open way. It is late and there will be few sentries."

Leon nodded. "Liam makes sense. I am afraid our time is near gone."

"No, we are in one of the more solid portions. There are no quick ways out of this channel. These walls are very thick and that is why we can talk openly here. One might even scream and not be heard beyond this room."

Liam looked up. "What was that?" He reached to his scabbard, gripping his sword hilt.

"Stay your hand, Liam," Leon said. "It was most certainly a rat."

"It feels like a rat trap," Liam replied. "If someone broke the pivot on the secret door we entered by, we'd be caught like rats, am I not right?"

Leon turned to stare at the man. "What are you saying, Liam?"

"Only that I wish we were free of this blasted tomb-works."

Caroline nodded. "I understand, friend, but the pivot is well hidden. We are safe as long as we do not give ourselves away."

"This is taking too long," Leon sighed. "It will surely be sunrise before we find the dungeon."

***

Rhena

Rhena had almost shouted with joy when she saw by the lantern that it was Caroline and her lost uncle in the passage below her, but as she opened her mouth to speak, she saw the third face beyond Leon's and her words froze in her throat. It was the face from the barred window in the turret. It was the face of Darkcloak's henchman. She could not forget that face and now she saw his hand on the hilt of his sword as the trio moved forward below her. She knew if she yelled a warning that it would be too late for Leon or Caroline. She must do something. Her hands moved quickly to the leather belt of her riding britches. It was her one hope.

Max knew something was wrong. The voices ahead were strange echoes, and he could see from the outline of Rhena's raised hand that she meant him to stay silent. When he saw her pulling loose her belt and gathering herself closer to the opening instead of backing away, he was confused and alarmed. If only he could see beyond her. He knew he must be ready to move to her aid if something happened suddenly.

***

As Caroline peered at the scraped sign on the chamber's forward wall, Leon held the lantern closer for her better vision.

Liam stepped back to give himself room for his deadly

blow. In silence he slipped the sword out of its scabbard and raised it over his head. He would bring the blade down first on Leon's neck and take Caroline as his prisoner. Soon he would be rewarded by Darkcloak. He might even be knighted by King Lull.

A loud cry echoed around them and Leon spun around to see the most unexpected of sights in the swinging light of his lantern. Liam thrashed with his sword above his head, his blade tangled in a strap held back by a shouting Princess Rhena above him in the wall. Leon leaped forward, gripping Liam's arm and strained to wrench the sword free of the villain's hand.

Max jumped ahead to grab Rhena's legs as she was being dragged out of the tunnel. He felt her slipping down and realized a fight was going on in the chamber below. Wild, echoing cries rang out and then a solid cracking sound. There was silence followed by a moan and the heavy panting of more than one person. Then Max felt Rhena moving forward on her own and calling to him.

"Come on, Max, it is all right. It is Caroline and Leon!"

***

Garm

The jailer was unnerved when Garm hammered on his door. "Who summons me?"

"If you do not know me, jailer, you soon shall. I am Garm, leader of your king's forces. I will be shown the prisoner elf you have below, along with any other prisoners you quarter."

The jailer frowned. "My orders come from King Lull and Lord Darkcloak, only."

Garm laughed. "I am head of your king's troops now, jailer. If you do not recognize my authority, you shall soon be begging a *new* jailer to let you out."

When the jailer opened the door at the top of the dungeon chamber and stepped in with his torch, he had to steady himself at what he saw, or rather what he did not see.

Where there had been four prisoners, there were now two. The princess and the prince were missing. Still, he could not say anything as yet because he knew Lord Darkcloak kept the nobles' captivity a secret.

Garm was already inside and striding to the barred cell door, urging the jailer on to bring the keys. In a moment he had marched in to stand in front of the shackled Jumpjilter and the startled Malvern who sat against the far wall, rubbing his chaffed wrist nervously.

"Well…well. Who have we here? An elf, dwarf, or midget of some species. Speak up, *Long Ears*, or I'll clip them for you."

Jippit stared into the villain's eyes. "Courage comes easily when your enemy is bound. Let me loose a minute and you decide what I am."

Garm laughed. "Bold. I like that in a doomed prisoner. I wish to know the name of my victim before I send him to his reward."

"Your master knows me well enough. Jippit Jumpjilter played jester for him in years past. Whatever your evil plan, know that your betters gather to break it. An elf's blood on your hands will only write your doom more certainly than any law you break."

"You talk a hard talk, Jumpjilter," Garm chuckled. "Jumpjilter — you would not be acquainted with the elves of Breanna would you? They cost me a goodsome prize last year with their nosy ways. You've no friends or relations among them, would you?"

Jippit scowled. "If they cost you a hard winter, then I claim them all as brothers."

Garm grinned. "Well, tomorrow you shall claim a good fly into town from here. We've a pretty catapult going up outside and your fine head will serve to help us find the range."

"Tomorrow is a fine time for everything isn't it? Tomorrow doesn't belong to anyone yet."

Garm gripped his dagger. "If I did not like a good beheading, I'd slice you for such cheek."

Malvern gasped and Garm turned to stare at the

cowering boy who had raised his hands over his face.

"Who is the pale wad whining there?"

"M-M-Malvern, s-sire!"

"Well, M-M-Malvern, if you've no better plans, perhaps we can let you ride the great catapult as well."

Malvern fainted and Garm laughed. "Ahh, brave hearts have these nobles. Well, I look forward to our re-acquaintance soon, Jumpjilter."

As Garm turned to leave, the jailer stared at the elf and around the room but said nothing.

***

Gerald

Gerald sat cross-legged on the floor of his chamber, slowly spilling sand from his palm in a pattern across the stones before him between five candles. As the sand traced the points of a star the hooded counselor chanted low words of a forbidden tongue. Finishing, he opened his fingers, revealing the green eye tattoo, glowing low in the candlelight.

There was a hammering on his door and Darkcloak cursed the sudden interruption. "Who disturbs the king's counselor at this hour?" he barked, twisting his head toward the locked door.

"It is Turney, the jailer, Master Darkcloak."

"What? I have told you not to seek me out."

"But sire, there is trouble. The prince and the princess are *gone*."

Gerald rose to open the door, shielding the room from the view of his visitor. "What do you mean, they are missing?" He stared into the eyes of the chattering jailer.

"I — I had looked in on them only moments before and all was well. Then when this Garm demanded I take him down, there were only *two*. The elf and young Malvern. I swear I have no idea of what has happened. I went round the cells checking but all the locks and bars were sound."

Gerald glared down the hallway in both directions. "Return to your station. Speak of this to no one. I shall come

194

see for myself in a few moments." He closed the door and snuffed out the candles and spread the sand out across the wide floor. Visions and spells must wait.

CHAPTER 24

DESPERATE MEN

Lull was waiting for his counselor at the door of the dungeon. Gerald saw in an instant that things did not bode well. For the king to be awake this late in the night and to meet him here as he moved to the dungeon was an unpleasant surprise.

"Your Majesty," he greeted the king with a bow. "What brings you to this dark place?"

Lull's eyes were narrowed under his heavy brows.

"Whatever reason brought me, I find strange things await me. I came to release and make peace with my daughter for her imprisonment today, yet she is *gone*. The jailer pleads for mercy, but the question is, who *else* must plead? I find you have imprisoned others without my knowledge. Such lodgings may prove better for you as well."

Darkcloak ignored the guards and turned to the jailer. "Speak to this matter of the king's daughter, jailer. We must think wisely and act quickly to save Princess Rhena from harm."

The jailer stared at the glaring king and looked pleading to Darkcloak. "My lords," he begged, "I am lost in confusion myself! I swear by heaven, no man left or entered this door from my last check until Garm came to speak with the elf Jumpjilter."

"At least *he* has not escaped," Lull said. "Perhaps we can get some answer from him. Let us go inside now, counselor and try to get to the bottom of things."

Jippit Jumpjilter's stare was cold as the nobles approached him. He knew that saying too much here would ruin his chances of protecting Max and Rhena. He hoped Malvern would not spoil things with his fear.

"So, Jumpjilter," Lull said, "It seems you at least were a witness to Rhena's kidnapping. I shall say that if you do not tell me all you know, I shall regard you as one of those responsible."

Jumpjilter looked to Darkcloak. "A form of magic, I would call it, sire. One moment she was there, and then gone in a puff of smoke. Something your counselor here should know all about. Isn't magic one of *his* talents?"

Lull stepped closer. "Do you mock us, elf?"

"I suppose that I care more for your daughter's safety than do you, sire. *I* did not place her here in a dungeon. If I could have aided her release, I would indeed have done so. But as you see, I am powerless . . . as is the poor lad in the corner. Tell them what we saw, Malvern."

The king and Gerald looked at the frightened youth.

"Does the elf speak true, lad? Are you not Lord Brimwick's son? Why are you imprisoned here?"

Malvern was shaking. "I — I tried to help Rhena get away. I — I shot an arrow with a note to her friend."

"What friend?"

Darkcloak spoke. "He means that your daughter tried to warn Prince Max of our plot. I believe he regrets his adventure now. What do you think of being deserted by your friend, Malvern?"

Malvern swallowed hard. "I hope Princess Rhena is safe. That is all I know."

Lull rubbed his neck. "Magic. I would not have believed it possible had you not shown me such things can be worked," he said to his counselor. "See that you solve this, Darkcloak. I will have my daughter back or many will pay." He stormed from the cell.

Darkcloak spoke to the jailer who followed the king and closed the door at the top of the stairs. The counselor turned back to Jippit. "It is well you chose not to speak of Max's escape, Jippit Jumpjilter. I do not see all that has happened here clearly. I think something besides magic was the means. I suspect you each know more of it than you say."

Jippit smiled. "Magic or miracle? You decide for yourself, Gerald. I think you have met a stronger hand played here than your own. What do your dark arts tell you?"

Gerald stared into Jippit's face then scowled. "It is true that the mind of an elf is locked tighter than most. I would lose much effort in reading it, but there is another witness." He turned to face Malvern. "You, boy, you saw all that happened here. Look into my eyes and remember it."

"No, Malvern." Jippit warned. "Do not meet his eyes."

"It doesn't matter, Malvern . . . no one can blame you for remembering . . . I only want to save the princess from the harm that might come to her in trying to leave the castle. I know Garm was here before. Surely you know that he would not be so kind toward her. He might use her against the king, himself. We don't want that, do we lad? Now . . . where is the way out?"

Malvern tried to look away, but something in Darkcloak's eyes held his.

CHAPTER 25

TRAITORS AND TRAPS

Leon tightened the knots of Liam's binding as the small party huddled together in the deep stone chambers of the castle. The spy's eyes were open and glared fearfully from Caroline to Max and Rhena. There was a sharp bruise over his right eye where Caroline's sword hilt had crashed onto his head as he struggled with Leon. He had only recovered on his ropes were pulled tighter.

"What . . . what will you do with me?" Liam asked.

Max was staring at the man. "My friend Jippit says that a sword raised against a woman should mean naught but death for its bearer."

Caroline shook her head. "Liam — why? Why this treachery from you? I trusted you deeply. Were you not a victim of the king's decrees yourself? A soldier punished for failing to enforce the cruel tax upon a poor family?"

Liam stared at them. "I was offered a choice. Serve as a spy or be hung as a traitor. My family would have lost all. I saw the sorcerer's power. He showed me a vision as clear as a mirror. I knew I was wrong, but all else was ruin. Now I am doomed indeed, but not more than I was."

"Honor is hard," Leon said. "If death is all one believes in, then honor is only a dream no more real than a wizard's spell. What we shall do with you now is in the hands of Lady Caroline."

Caroline looked around. "It seems we are all in a dungeon of sorts, at least until tomorrow. If we bind you here, then I think your punishment will be closely tied to our own fates. If we win out, then we will bring you out alive at least, wretched man. If we lose and die, then you shall perish here alone in darkness in a place where your cries will only echo back at you."

Rhena turned to Caroline. "Do you know the way out of the passages from here?"

The lady nodded. "Many of them. But, if we left in daylight, we would be seen on the banks of the moat and caught or killed before we could swim even a portion of the distance. I think our wisest course would be to stay hidden here until another nightfall comes."

Max coughed. "I hope that there are many passages, for surely they will be searching for us — and Darkcloak is very clever. He may well imagine that such secret passages exist within the walls and floors of the castle. If he sets about it, he may likely discover the entrance."

"Yes," Leon said. "This sorcerer seems almost an

inspired servant of darkness, as much to fear as my brother Lull. How do you know of him, Prince Max?"

Max looked at Rhena and then at Leon. "He is my brother."

***

Derek

Sunrise was spreading over the town and Derek stretched. It had been a long night, broken only by the blows of axes and hammers as the preparations for battle continued. The prince had walked the banks of the moat in darkness, from sentry fire to sentry fire, wondering what was happening in the great castle in the center of the huge moat. Sleep had come only in snatches. He knew it was his duty to rest himself for what must come soon. Yet his mind always returned to his brother in the dungeon across the way.

Prince Galen approached with two steaming mugs of cider. "This is the benefit of holding a town. The merchants' stores are open to us, though I suspect they wonder what their generosity will cost if we should lose."

Derek took a cup and sipped. "Not as much as we would receive," he said. "Still no word from our friends. And dawn has come. All seems lost."

Galen shook his head. "Not so. If Leon and Caroline were both caught, or Max discovered by Lull, we would have heard it blared from every trumpet in the castle. Do not be fast to despair at silence, my friend."

"You sound like Fanzig," Derek said.

"Fanzig?"

"Just a friend of Max's. A wise one I wish were with us now."

"If wishes were horses —"

"Beggars would ride." Derek finished. "That's Jumpjilter's wisdom."

Galen sighed. "Yes, it is an old saw, but it still cuts true."

"The thing is," Derek said, "beyond wishing, what to do next?"

203

Goosell was approaching them and Galen nodded to the old soldier. "I think the general will have plenty for us to do, and none of it easy."

Goosell squatted by the remains of the night's fire and gripping a burned stick, began to trace a plan upon the smooth dirt. "Sires, for the moment, Lull is bottled up, but soon he must try an attack over the drawbridge. Kenelm is too good a soldier to waste men on a charge without hope. I fear he prepares something to make their attack greater than we imagine or he would not have allowed us time to prepare defenses. Certainly he has discovered the catapult stored from my days. The armorer can manage its construction. The sounds of hammers we have heard across the water, make me believe they are constructing it to attack our gatehouse. With that defense broken, they could storm their way across the drawbridge and up the landing into town. If they hurl burning shot, they may even start a fire in the town beyond us. That would put us in a very bad position. We do not have time to build a movable catapult, nor the time to move it should we need to. It is all a matter of who completes their weapon first."

Derek nodded. "Still, they will have to travel in a narrow front on the bridge. We can hit them from both sides with our best archers. We would cost them dearly."

Goosell grunted. "True enough, but we also must be ready to defend our rear. The outer reaches of the town have only the simplest of walls. We must keep ready to send many of our troops to man the wall against Wotterham's army if it arrives soon. We could be fighting on two flanks at once. It may be *we* who will fall under siege. It may be that this has been Lull's plan from the beginning."

Derek frowned. "I do not think Lull is so wise as to foresee such a thing."

"I think his counselor Darkcloak might," Galen said. "If we only had some hope of relief."

***

Gerald

Gerald climbed the steps that wound to the roof of the tallest tower. He knew Lull and Garm waited there discussing the outline of attack and that anything he shared regarding the dungeon escape must be carefully weighed. On the one hand, he must convince King Lull that he could soon find the princess, yet without giving away too much of his own secret planning. For Garm, he must consider that, should the rogue captain learn that Catterline might be spying within the castle itself, he would tear down every stone to seize them, and this would bring to light Gerald's own knowledge of events before the escape as well. His best course was to keep his own men to hunt down the secret ways and thus keep control of the situation away from Garm. But how to explain the prisoners' knowledge of the secret tunnel? Gerald frowned. He would have to be persuasive. Lull wanted to believe anything that worked to his advantage, and Garm would not dare directly contradict the king yet, though the barbarian was cleverer than he appeared. Gerald must be careful with his tale.

***

". . . and so a fire in the first row of houses would seal the rebels escape when we come across the drawbridge," Garm was saying. "I would have been a happier warrior to have had such a catapult with me in other times, King Lull, yet I see that the device the rebels build on the edge of the town is aimed for the bridge. We must stop them from launching the first strike."

Lull grimaced. "Kenelm assures me we will launch at first light tomorrow morning."

Lull saw Gerald come up from the stairs. "Darkcloak. Have you word of my daughter?"

The hooded counselor smiled. "Your Highness, I have been able to learn much from my interview of the elf and the boy. They resisted as best they could, but they could not match a truly focused mind."

"Have you found her? How did she escape?" Lull was

excited.

"I know how she escaped, and she has not gone far. I have come to request you allow me a half dozen handpicked guards to gain her safe return."

Lull frowned. "Explain yourself!"

Garm was staring with narrowed eyes at Gerald but did not speak.

Darkcloak nodded. "The princess was bringing a dipper of water to the elf to quiet his thirst when she tripped upon the stones of the floor. When she fell, the water from the dipper ran into a narrow channel and disappeared. The elf, for all his irritable manner, is highly observant and has vision second to no living creature. He saw the pattern of a hidden trapdoor."

"A trap door! In the *dungeon*?" Lull was astonished.

"Jumpjilter guided her search for a release and soon they had opened the way to a secret passage beneath the floor."

"Incredible! But no matter, have you found her?"

Gerald shook his head. "Nay, sire. The passage splits and moves into a series of tunnels that must run within much of the castle. It would be the wisest course to send six of your most trusted men to seek her gentle capture and safe return."

Garm scoffed. "*I* should send my best *hunters* into the tunnels, Lull. I've some lads that's gone after bears in their caves and no tunnels would slow them from finding your darling girl."

"This is no matter for your concern, Garm," Darkcloak said.

Lull looked at the red-faced chieftain and Gerald saw that he agreed.

"I have sufficient men to rescue my daughter from this dark maze." He turned back to Gerald. "Do as you see fit, but do not fail me in this, Darkcloak. If harm comes to Rhena, I promise that you will wish you had suffered in her place."

As the king spoke, Gerald noticed Garm was staring at him and smiling. There was a shrewd look in his eyes that was more disturbing than his usual angry glare. The counselor bowed to the king and made his way back down the stairway.

He had a half dozen men he had put under his control over the months with secret gold for favors then spells that slid their minds within his reach. He would lead these within the labyrinth to seek Max and Rhena. And now, more than ever, he realized that control of the young prince and princess was the real key to breaking the resistance not only of the rebels outside —but also the king who commanded him.

CHAPTER 26

HOPE

Derek stood in the street before a large farm cart that men were loading with straw. He was speaking with an older serf and pointing to the empty yoke at its front. "You must bind the yoke stiffly to the front of the cart, Falan. When the hay is set afire it will allow us to shove the wagon into the enemy's path. No horse or ox would do this with fire so close. If the enemy lowers the drawbridge, our plan is to rush this in to block the way and slow their approach on the narrow landing. It will take much courage, for the wheels must be broken before it is abandoned so it remains a barrier."

The old man nodded. "It is all I can do to keep these lads from taking swords themselves, sire. But they are too young to throw against the soldiers of the king."

"You speak truly, Falan. Yet they do their part to shore the walls and set the traps."

At that moment a young girl rushed up to the prince and tugged his sleeve. "Sire *Deret* . . . Sire *Deret*."

Falan frowned. "Forgive the girl, sire. Autry is — touched — not of full mind, but a kind child who means no harm."

The prince was looking down into the upturned face with bright brown eyes and an eager smile. He bent down on one knee, "What is it, little sister? What do you wish?"

The girl's eyes were wide with excitement. "I show you a owl."

Derek smiled. "An owl, young maiden? At this time of day?"

Falan took the girl's hand. "Come, Autry, Prince Derek can see the owl another time."

"*Now*." the girl frowned. "He says come *now*."

Derek's smile twitched. "The owl *spoke* to you?"

"Sire, she is touched — she believes what she imagines."

"So do I," Derek said. "Take me to your owl now, Autry, if you will."

The old serf stared after the knight walking hand in hand with the excited girl.

The barn was dark, but Fletcher's eyes stood out like two yellow beacons when he turned his head to face the prince with the swivel that makes owls seem to have no front or back. The bird of prey was perched on a barrel with one great wing hanging down.

"I remember you," Derek said. "You were at the

courtyard when Max was chosen. I did not hear you speak, yet later met Fanzig. I listen now to such tales and to those who tell them."

The owl blinked. "Fletcher, I am called, Prince Derek. I have brought a message and Autry has brought me. She found me, outside the walls this morning. I fought two hawks and could not fly the last way. Autry was gathering sticks for her mother. Her brave heart heard my summons and brought me here and now has brought you near."

Derek stepped closer. "I am sorry for your wound. What is the message you bring?"

The owl held out a talon and blinked. In the claw was a tattered scroll. "It is from your father. I have flown a long night and a day to bring this to you."

Derek unfolded the paper and read.

"The One Hundred ride for Leorna. We rest short tonight and the next. We pray to arrive on the second day. The call for all men-at-arms is sent. That they follow within a week is hoped. You must hold Lull in check. Our prayers are with you. - Randrew."

Derek looked up. "The One Hundred. Servants and old soldiers — the guards of the castle — not much army, my friend. Yet, a hundred at the right time and place could matter much. Tomorrow or the next day? It is a hope."

"How of Max?" Fletcher asked.

"We are uncertain. He was taken prisoner, but Lull has not announced it. It is very strange. Leon, Caroline, and Liam have gone in secret to the castle to try and gain his freedom."

"It seems we shall need that prayer."

The prince stood up and slipped the message in his tunic. "What of your wing, Fletcher? What shall we do for you?"

The owl slipped his head to the side another inch. "Kind Autry will do all that is needed. She hears me clearer than any here. I shall have better care than I could have hoped. Do not worry for me, my prince. See to your men and hold firm."

Derek took Autry's hands in his and bent down to kneel before her, looking again closely into her wide set eyes. "Little maiden, you have done us much true good this day. You give heart to a knight near the end of his courage. Know you have my gratitude and are a friend of the royal court of Gaspaar always."

***

Max

Max's stomach rumbled. "I don't suppose you brought food with you, Lady Caroline? We did not dine very well in the dungeon."

Caroline shook her head. "Alas, we traveled light, hoping to be back across the moat before the morning light. I also feel hunger, but many in this land go without much more from day to day. I'm afraid I've grown used to eating better in the wild wood."

Leon chuckled. "I would love a shoulder of the king's deer myself. Waiting gives one little to do more than think of food and drink."

Rhena leaned back against a column in the tunnel. "Oh, let's not speak more of food. I think I smell fresh bread."

Liam squirmed upright against the wall. "Indeed, I think I smell food as well."

Caroline leaned to peer down the dark passage. "We might be near the kitchen or perhaps there is an entrance there and so the smell has drifted in."

"Are there many entrances?" Max asked.

"Several, some in quite odd spaces," Caroline answered. "I do not know them all."

Leon held up a hand in the lantern's pale light. "*Quiet. I hear something.*"

They all sat still, and Leon quickly moved to Liam's side and gripped a gag, slipping it into place between the traitor's teeth. "*Stay quiet, Liam, or you shall not leave this chamber alive.*"

Now there was another knock, a clear echo from the

tunnel they had traveled. Caroline reached up and took the lantern from the wall and extinguished its candlelight. The room was plunged into sudden blackness.

Max held Rhena's hand as they crouched against the wall, staring into the darkness seeing nothing. Only the sound of their breathing was audible. Max thought the danger had passed when there was a sudden clear clunking echo. Then a gruff voice bounced through the caverns.

"In here. The way divides again, but below is the path they took from the wall."

Max swallowed at the voice that replied.

"We'll place a guard there to cut them off. We'll have to check every channel. Move on, sergeant." It was Gerald's voice.

Max almost jumped when he felt Leon's hand on his shoulder and heard his whisper. *"Come. Hold to this cord and pass it to Rhena. I have it tied to my belt. I will follow Caroline. We must move quickly and quietly. If you strike stone, keep your cries in your throat."*

"What of Liam?" Max asked.

There was silence for a moment. *"We shall leave him here."*

Max felt the rope tighten and moved ahead, feeling the quick tug of Rhena and then she also was moving behind him. Just as he felt the edge of a small opening in the wall and knew they were climbing into it, he heard Caroline's whisper. *"Be careful, we travel to the king's chamber."* Then they were tugged along after Leon into the deepest dark

.

***

The One Hundred

The royal gardener of Gaspaar stretched his back as he stood on the roadside. It was amazing how riding in a line with spears made you feel that you were part of a great and powerful force. The helmets — though many were as rusty as the gardener's — gave the look of fierce warriors at a distance. Yet here, gasping and groaning, working to hoist heavy bellies

213

over their saddles, they were exposed as the make-do assembly that they were. Their real job was to man the castle walls until the soldiers of the realm could be summoned from across the land. Right now, stretched out in the cool of the evening, they hardly looked a threatening band. Here was a draft horse from a merchant's wagon, here a donkey, here a sway-backed nag. The gardener shook his head. Somehow the king buoyed them up. His confidence seemed boundless, and he was everywhere; riding up to the front, passing back down the ranks. If he saw their weakness, he did not speak of it.

Randrew did see these things, but he also saw the men beneath their wrinkles, their bellies, and their fears. He had spoken to them of the war that balanced ahead of them, and how their few days of standing at the rim might be the one thing to hold back a flood of fire and blood not known in generations. They could have their fear, he considered, but they must never see it in their king. Now he was the first to mount and nodded to his herald who blew the trumpet signal to continue their march in the lengthening day.

The gardener urged his horse nearer to the king's mount as they began to move ahead. "Sire?" he called and seeing the king beckon him closer, nudged his old sorrel alongside the king's big chestnut. "Sire, have you a sign of our omen owl? The one who carries your message?"

Randrew shook his head. "Nay. I should hope to have his return and a reply from Derek, but the creature spoke of danger in the skies. Perhaps he cannot fight his way back to us."

"I hope he got through to Derek," the gardener said. "Though I know the prince would hope to be joined by more than our lot of old men."

The king leveled his gaze at the gardener and for the first time the servant sensed a dangerous anger behind those eyes. "In a hard place, in a hard time, it is often the fight in the men that matters most, not the number of men in the fight! If you wish to turn back, you have my leave, but if you ride with me, ride now resolved. To speak of all we lack, makes a lack of all we have. If you are my friend, bind yourself to this thought. We are here. That is enough.”

The gardener nodded and reigned back. Soon he was again beside the supply cart where the cook rode and hailed him.

“Gardener, I saw you speak with the king. What do you think of our chances?”

The gardener grinned. “Chances are chances, friend cook, but where would you rather be? I'm sure whatever happens to this band, I'd never live well with learning of it back home with my helmet still a flowerpot in the window. No, I'm the king's man, for all the good or ill that may come.”

The cook laughed. “Well, I guess we're for it, then. This will soon be another long night on the road taking rest in our rolling carts and wagons and changing saddles with those who need sleep. The real stops are for the horses. I'll be passing my best ham down the line and you and the others can gnaw at it as you ride. We'll all need red meat in our bellies if we're soon to growl like the dogs of war we pretend we are.”

CHAPTER 27

TIGHTENING WAYS

Max

Max's knees were as sore as his bandaged wound from crawling through lower passages, and he nursed a bruised shoulder where he had run into a wall at a dark turning. All day, though it hardly seemed day, they had traveled through a web of tunnels and halls, climbed and descended narrow stairways leading to small rooms like the chambers in an anthill. Occasionally a small scrape of light from a chink in a wall or a drain above gave some relief from the nightmarish blindness. They had not gone to the king's chamber high in the keep. That had been a false clue left for Liam to share with the guards who searched for them. Many times they had heard soldiers in the tunnels near them and thrice seen the glow of their torches, but so far Caroline had found turnings or branches that lead away though she hardly knew them. Now, as his stomach ached from hunger, Max felt Leon's hand reach back in warning. He waited for the hissed signal that always came when the search party was nearby. This time, however, there was no such warning or quick change in direction. Instead, they stayed still, straining to listen. Max heard voices nearby, but not the short commands or signals of Darkcloak's men. This was a conversation. Then Max saw a sudden slender beam of light falling directly on the eye of lady Caroline ahead of him. She had removed or pulled aside some piece of the wall and was looking into a chamber of the castle.

***

Garm

By the lamplight of his chamber, Garm sharpened his blade. He looked to Norda, his second in command, as he honed the fine edge of his sword.

"Tomorrow will be a day to remember, Norda. Much may hang on how the first cards are played, *and* who plays them."

The barbarian lieutenant nodded. "I believe our men shall be more than a match for the rebels and knights who guard the town."

Garm grinned. "Yes, we are a match for those knights of Gaspaar and Averon, and we outnumber them as well. No, the trick will be in how the Lull's men are used — and how the king's nerves hold. Mark me, Norda, I do not like the look in

218

Lull's eyes when we talk of destroying the enemy. He speaks a great game, but I think he fears the damage we may do his pretty town and subjects — though rebels they have shown themselves to be. And there is some other thing here that concerns him, some secret thing I do not know. I do not like this Darkcloak and his charms and quiet words. I see no fire in him at all. Such an odd fish disturbs me. I think a moment may come when, in the rush of battle, the king might fall, and his *counselor* perish also. Do you think that would be such a blow to our fortunes, Norda?"

"What do *you* think?"

"*Ah!* You have learned to listen, Norda, that is good. Yes, I should think at the *right* moment, there will only be need of one leader. And why not *Garm*? Here I would have a castle with rich land and army feared by their own people. And if my guess is right, I would have the friendship of Wotterham for bringing down one of her old enemies and dealing two others a deep wound. We gain wealth and power beyond our *dreams*. I tire of raiding and running. Here we would have our own kingdom. We could gather raiders and brave plundering rogues from all the lands. We would raise an army of a fierceness never seen. None would dare oppose us."

Norda smiled. "I will await your signal, *King* Garm."

Garm laughed then stopped. "Did you hear something then?"

"Perhaps a mouse or rat?"

Garm moved to the door and threw it open. After looking down the hall he turned back to Norda. "There are too many rats about. I'd forgotten that dratted princess is playing games within the walls. *I* would have the dogs after her. Lull is too soft. He cares too much for his child. We'd do well to track her down, Norda. Send Skinnard and his idiot brother to the dungeon to join the hunt. Skinnard needs only a whiff of some bit of her perfumed clothes and he'll track her through a bog. He's more hound than human."

***

219

Derek looked around the tired faces. Here, resting on the barricades at the end of the street were the defenders of the town. Only Goosell and his workers toiling at the trestles of the catapult nearer the gatehouse at the end of the landing were not here. Inside the houses, women cooked and tended the wounded while children stared at every scene that these days of conflict brought before them. Derek caught the eye of a small boy hanging over a window with a thumb shoved in his mouth. What lesson was the child learning today, he wondered. What lesson was he teaching? The prince straightened and braced his hands on his lower back. He saw Sir Brian rest as a squire re-wrapped his bandages. Brian had certainly learned something for he was far quieter now and even Sir Quinn had nodded to him as they worked at the barricades. Quinn had become much friendlier as things had gotten darker. Maybe when things were really terrible, he felt more at home, as if he never trusted happy times in the first place. Sir Claire had returned from the last burials for those whose wounds had been too great. Claire had been Derek's mentor, whom he had served as squire. Good or bad, all times were as one to Claire, Derek thought, though perhaps he had been different in the court of Camelot. Whatever their differences, each of his band, the knights of Averon and the outlaws of Catterline had all blended together in this sweaty, tiring work. It had kept fear from closing in on them as they braced the town for the coming battle. Wotterham's army was rumored to be a thousand strong. Derek prayed his father's Hundred could get inside the town before the host of Linus arrived.

Derek raised his arm to gain attention, and when silence fell, he began. "Fellows, brave friends . . . we have done what we may do. I will tell you now, what cannot be hid. I believe it is wrong for any to stand in battle who have no true knowledge of what they face or what to expect upon their own side. I will have none die for a lie on my tongue. You have wondered today where are Sir Leon and Lady Caroline?

Where is Liam? Where is Prince Max, and what of Randrew's army, or Averon's or Wotterham's? I hold little good news to tell you, but I will tell you true what we do know. Prince Max is in the castle of Leorna, as are Lady Caroline and Sir Leon."

At this there was much commotion and Derek raised his hand again and waited for quiet to return. "We do not think they are prisoners. The Lady Caroline, Sir Leon, and Liam all journeyed in secret last night to rescue Max and any other prisoners held there. If they had been discovered surely their ransom would be our surrender, yet no such demand has been made. There has been no taunt of their capture. We believe they remain hidden. Of Gaspaar's army, I have received word that the first hundred men may join us on the morrow. They come while a call for the full army is sent throughout Gaspaar. That army will take many days to reach us, but it will come. We wait on word of Averon. We pray that help marches from Prince Galen's father." Derek saw Galen's determined nod and went on.

"As to Wotterham and Prince Linus . . . we are uncertain. None know the mind of the prince or his king on this matter. Some warn that he rushes to bring the full army of Wotterham to Leorna. It is said to be the largest in our lands. That army might be our enemy or it might be our friend, we cannot know. But we shall hold our place, here, between the town and the roads from all the kingdoms." There were many worried looks and more murmuring. Again, Derek spoke.

"Yes, we know that Lull works to launch an attack. He puts together a catapult as we build our own. As soon as we are ready, we shall hurl stone on stone to smash the drawbridge towers and seal the enemy inside. This will allow us to defend the town walls as we soon must. However, if Lull's great war machine breaks our gatehouse defense, and lowers his bridge, he may charge through. For this we must be ready to meet them on the landing and keep the enemy from the streets of the town. This we can do if we face but one foe at a time. If we are attacked from the rear by Wotterham and also from the castle, then we must be as the Spartans of old at Thermopylae. You must all know that we fight for time

Time for the lives of our peoples. I have told you all I know. Now, any who believe they cannot face the worst of what may come, any who fear they might not stand by their friends on such a day, I ask to leave us tonight. You will be given food and passage and our blessing. Those who stay with Derek and Galen are our brothers and sisters, and we pledge ourselves to you until we are free of tyranny or free of this life."

***

Lull

King Lull lifted his empty wine cup from the table and stared at it. Everything seemed empty to him now, like this cup. No family, no friend, only servants and counselors whispered advice, loud laughter at his whims . . . all purchased with power and fear. But what was that noise? Some odd sound outside? He stood and moved to the window of the hall. In the streaks of sunset, he could see the glow of campfires and lanterns in the town. "Guard!" he called and in moments a soldier ran puffing to stand before him.

"Sire?"

Lull pointed to the town. "What is that sound? What happens in the town?"

The soldier swallowed. "It is cheering, sire. They clap and cheer at something. Must be most all of them for us to hear it so clear."

CHAPTER 28

WHAT IS SEEN?

Kenelm listened as Beasely spoke with the men around the base of the catapult. For the first time in two days no one swung hammers or worked saws or hauled at ropes. As the armorer pointed out the tasks the team of soldiers were to perform, Kenelm eyed the great weapon that had grown from a stack of timbers, wheels, and metal rods, into a towering figure silhouetted by the moonlit sky.

"So, you see, this trebuchet must roll upon its wheels back and forth as the counterweight box drops down. This, of course, will balance the long swing of the throwing arm and send the sling with a great stone out with a smooth, powerful motion. Ah, it is a thing of beauty to see, lads."

One of the soldiers grunted. "But what if we miss?"

Beasley nodded. "Yeah, that can happen, and we'll be plenty glad to have those wheels you complained of mounting then. We can turn our weapon to left or right with a few minutes of heaving. The rebels in the town have taken a short cut using the structure of that roadhouse for their machine. They can't turn it much. If they're wrong at all, they'll hurl their stones to left or right and we'll smack them at our leisure."

A hand went up. "Well, I don't fancy trying to haul that weighted box up to set up the shot. That's a couple thousand pound of rock and sand we've shoveled into the blasted thing."

Beasley laughed. "You have to do something to be worth your keep, Wooster. Besides, once we shoot, it's only a matter of a few shovels this way or that to get the range. To pull the counterweight back up for each shot, we'll use a team of horses, though I think you'd do well to strap on a harness yourself, for all the loafing you've done."

Kenelm clasped his hands behind his back and strode back toward the keep. Nearby he saw the mercenaries sharpening their swords and battleaxes. There was coarse laughter and back-slapping among this brawny band of men as they prepared for the morrow's attack. Several nodded to him as he passed but laughter followed and he knew Garm's men held little regard for the common soldiers of Leorna. He wanted to forget his troubles, forget his doubts. He was not sure if he were more fearful of defeat or victory, for victory would mean crushing his own people and the triumph of these foul mercenaries of war. Perhaps a cup of wine would mellow his thoughts. Returning the sentry's salute, he entered the keep and chose a dark hallway to the great kitchen. A low fire burned in the vast fireplace and baskets of bread stood covered by towels on the tables to his left. The kitchen cat quietly guarded the morning's meal. Along the wall he sought a tapped barrel of wine. He would have punished any of his men for drinking on the eve of a battle, but now he was searching for anything to soften the distress in his heart. Taking a goblet from a pantry shelf, he pulled the plug from the cask and tilted it so that the wine spilled into his cup.

Raising the vessel in shaking hands he shuddered and made a prayerful pledge. "May the fates save what is good in Leorna tomorrow, even if I die." As the cup touched his lips he gasped and dropped it to the floor. Facing him in the half-light of the fireplace stood Prince Leon.

"If you meant that pledge, Kenelm, you will not call for the guard. That is my pledge also."

***

Darkcloak

Darkcloak glared at the two swarthy men in hunter's garb that stood before him at the entrance of the opened tunnel inside the dungeon cell. "Who sent you within the tunnels?" he demanded.

"Beggin' your grace's pardon," the slyer looking of the two replied. "We are Garm's hunters. He sent us to help find the poor princess lassie what is stuck in the walls." The other man snorted beside him and the speaker swung a hand to smack him on the ear. "Watch that, Gee. The gentleman wants none of your sass."

Gerald's hands tightened to fists. "The king has told Garm that his help is not wanted here. I have my own men searching for Princess Rhena now."

"Well," the grinning rogue replied, "seems to Garm that your nice lads have had a turn and nothing much to show fer it. Wouldn't do to have the gal starving in the walls like some poor mousey. Me and Gee'll fetch her out quick. Why, her maid give us this bit of the princess' cloak all perfumed like! That scent is clean and true as a thread we can follow to its end. The strange thing, if you don't mind me sayin' so, is that there's plenty other perfume down this tunnel too. We didn't get in far 'til we smell another scent down this way. Is there may be a pair of princesses down the holes or are some of your pretty boy soldiers as keen on smellin' nice? We only come back out to tell Garm that there's more than one pretty rabbit to be chasin' in this warren. We figure he might want to know that right away, don't you think?"

225

Gerald raised his hand and spread his fingers wide. "Fools. You dare to taunt the counselor of the king? You dare intrude on my business — interfere with my purpose? Look, look at my hand. Do you see the eye upon my palm? Yes. That's right. Look, both of you. You can see it looks into your own eyes and draws you in, doesn't it? See the dark at the center? See the darkness swallowing up all the light in this room? On your knees now or I'll crush the last light from your minds.

The two men fell dumbly to their knees, quaking before the cloaked figure in the torchlight of the dungeon.

***

Max

Kenelm stared in disbelief at the faces that his candle lit in the back of the pantry closet. Here was Princess Rhena, Lady Caroline, and the young Prince of Gaspaar. He dropped to a knee.

"Forgive me, Princess Rhena, for all that has happened here. I have done much wrong."

"It is not you that caused it, Kenelm," Rhena said, wiping a tear from her soot-covered face. "It was not you who betrayed Leorna and her friends . . . it was my father."

Kenelm licked his parched lips. "What . . . what would you have me do?"

Leon held his hand up for silence and turned his head to listen. "We cannot stay in these walls and tunnels. Three times we have almost been caught and soon will be forced into the open. Kenelm, we must find a way to protect Rhena and Prince Max."

Max blinked in the lamplight. "But surely the king would never allow harm to come to his own daughter?"

Caroline shook her head. "He would not wish it, but there are others here of more evil spirit and we have heard their treason, Max. They would not shrink from anything to cast terror into the people who oppose them."

Kenelm nodded. "Garm. Yes, I've seen the blood lust

226

in his eye. Hate comes off him like heat. He speaks terrible deeds."

"Could the king stop him?" Max asked, his hand closing on Rhena's.

Kenelm shook his head. "A week ago. Even two days ago, perhaps. Now, the king seems confused, uncertain. The men sense it. Garm sees it. It is clear who will lead the charge tomorrow, and who will reign if the victory is won."

"Then there would be no mercy if we are taken." Caroline said.

Kenelm gripped Leon's shoulder. "I need to speak with you alone, Prince Leon."

"We have no secrets here, captain."

The soldier turned from the children. "Hear mine, sire, I beg you."

Leon leaned close to listen to Kenelm's whispered words.

"Garm speaks of hurling the heads of prisoners into the town on the catapult's first launch in the morning. He wishes for a leader known among the people to strike their hearts. He would send each of your heads with not a second's thought."

"My God!" Rhena gasped.

"I am sorry, my princess. I wished you not to hear." Kenelm turned back to the young nobles.

Caroline crossed her arms. "Kenelm, how far did you say the heads would be thrown?"

Kenelm stared at Caroline. "My lady? Uh . . . Beasley says a head would travel easily into the end of the landing. He intends to send stones of 200 pounds to strike the gatehouse at the edge of the moat."

Max swallowed at the image of their heads sailing through the air and tried only to picture the heavy stones flying instead. He saw that Caroline was also thinking yet frowning as if weighing thoughts very carefully.

***

Sergeant Nef set down his lantern and whispered over his shoulder to the men behind him in the narrow passage. "It's a door, fellows. I think they've finally gone outside. When I count three, we'll smash it open and be on them. Remember — we're not to hurt the princess or the young prince, but we can't let them get away. And Darkcloak says there's others with them. Be ready for a fight." The men nodded as Nef counted, "One . . . two . . . three!"

The wooden pantry door smashed outward and Nef dived through the opening with Magus and Jelick rushing out behind him. The party of guards drew to a sudden stop as they confronted, not the prisoners they pursued, but their own captain of the guard sitting at a table carving a slice of cheese for a loaf of bread. They stared about them to see they stood in the kitchen of the castle.

"Sergeant, what is the meaning of this," Kenelm demanded. "Have you gone mad? Are you raiding the pantry?"

"Sorry, Captain Kenelm," Nef said, drawing up to salute. "We were under counselor Darkcloak's orders. We've been hunting the Princess Rhena in the way between the walls."

"All three of you?"

"There's another three back there too, sir. You would not believe the maze of tunnels and turnings all through this castle. It's an anthill, it is, and the little lass has been quite clever, though I was certain she'd come out here. You wouldn't have seen her coming through, sir?"

Kenelm stared at the sergeant.

Nef swallowed. "Sorry, sir. Of course, you'd know that right off. Uh, I guess she's give us the slip again. Still, I'm thinking she's loose in the rooms now. We've sealed off most all the tunnels, we'll find her soon enough now. Daylight's all but on us."

Kenelm rose from the table. "Sergeant, there's a battle to fight in the morning. I suggest you would better serve the king by preparing for that than playing at such foolery. That is a better use for six soldiers."

Nef bowed. "Begging your pardon, sir, but the king his-self give us over to the counselor Darkcloak for such things as he wishes. We're his bodyguard you might say. We'd a sight rather be under your command, captain, that we would, but it's not ours to say, is it, sir?"

The captain frowned and went back to his cheese and the three embarrassed soldiers filed back into the pantry, closing the secret door behind them. Kenelm tapped the table and sighed as the fugitives all slid out from beneath the wooden benches along the wall. "Nef is right," he said. You can't stay hidden outside the maze in daylight for long."

***

Darkcloak

Darkcloak stood before the king. "You sent for me, sire. Is your mind troubled? You should be sleeping soundly, for surely you need your rest for the challenge of the morrow."

Lull glared at the counselor. "Do not be telling me what I need, Darkcloak. I need many things. I need my daughter safe, and you have not delivered even that simple task. How am I to trust you with my counsel for a battle? Nay, between your fumbling and that detestable barbarian chieftain I have more trouble *within* my castle than outside it. Now, I call on you to use your power of vision to let me see the true way of the lands. Does Wotterham approach? Is help for the rebels nearing us? Though it strains your cunning to open such a sight, I demand you show it now."

Gerald frowned beneath his hood. "Sire, it is night. Such a view is hard at all times, but daylit paths hide less truth."

"Yet you said that the clouds had blocked the way yesterday. I see a moon breaking free of cloud. Look now and let us see what may be seen. All may hang on what comes toward us."

"As you wish, sire. Know that your servant only wishes

229

to use his gifts to best serve you. I shall lose some strength for such a vision as you request . . ."

"Yes, yes, let us have it now," the king demanded.

***

The One Hundred

King Randrew walked beside his horse, letting the mount rest after the hard ride they had taken and the hard hours to come. The stars overhead had played tag with the clouds all night, there had been little help to the torches the riders carried. The column had strung itself out far longer than the tight band it had been at the start of the journey. It would be some time before his friend the cook would catch up with the main body. He turned to look back from the crest of the hill he was crossing and saw the torches far apart like a flickering stream of fire dotting the winding way behind him. Soon they must gather up again as they rode into Leorna, for there they might run headlong into battle. They must be a united front, ready to fight side by side against whatever foe awaited them. He looked up at the moon breaking out free of the clouds. "At least we have a clear day coming," the king said to himself. "A fine morning, though it may be our last."

***

Lull

King Lull watched the eyes of his counselor beneath the hood. The glow of the candles around the room flickered in the black pupils. Darkcloak sat at the round table whispering some words of a strange tongue. He brought his hands together above the disc, the fingertips touching each other as if the hands held a ball. Such ritual show as this made the king both uneasy and angry; uneasy because he did not understand it, and angry because he could not control it. He tried to keep his eyes on Darkcloak's but his vision was led to the table as the hands splayed out and the fingers ran lines and circles, cutting first one way and then another as the

230

counselor spoke more strange commands. And then there was something. A green glow seemed to work around the edges of the table, but it was the edges of his vision as well the king realized, and he would have been afraid if he had not seen below a dark map of hills and forests and the lights of Leorna far along. A winding path of lights was working through the darkness. As his eyes stared at the flickering lights, the king knew they were torches carried by riders spread down a long, long road. Though he could not see the horses or men, he knew the way they traveled, and he knew the torches covered over a mile from first to last. "This is the road from Gaspaar," he heard himself whisper. "They shall arrive soon . . . so many . . . so soon." He glanced to Darkcloak and saw the eyes of the sorcerer glowing with the green light. "What of Wotterham? What of Linus?" Lull demanded.

The counselor shuddered and slid a hand across the circle. The image of the table rippled like a pond and now other lights pricked up from green darkness. There were fewer lights and these seemed closer together, not nearly so long a track.

"What is this?" Lull whispered. "Does Linus bring a smaller army than Gaspaar? Does he come merely to watch the battle? Does he plan to offer his allegiance only to the victor? Your vision is no good, Darkcloak. Show me Averon. I must know more."

There was a moan and all the lights faded away. Darkcloak sat with his head bent forward. "That — that is all I can see now. I must rest my eyes, my mind."

"Very well then. If Gaspaar's whole army has come, then Randrew must have intended to invade me all along. *He* has betrayed the peace I would have offered him for the release of his sons. Now we must attack before he arrives. We must take the town at dawn and capture Derek for our ransom!" The king strode out of the chamber, calling for the captain of the guard.

Gerald sat with his head in his hands. How could the whole army of Gaspaar have come so soon? A mile-long army must surely be hundreds of men. It was not possible, yet the vision had been there to see. It was clear to him now he must find Max. Only the ransom of Randrew's favorite son would provide a way to avoid ruin. Max was somewhere in the fortress and Gerald must find him even if it took spells he had not dared to master. He was tired, but he must not rest. There was no time for rest.

CHAPTER 29

A CHALLENGING CHANCE

The princess and the prince sat in the corner of the palace stable as Leon and Caroline kept watch near the entrance. In the last darkness of the night the fugitives had managed to avoid being seen when at last they had crept from the main castle keep. The dawn was lighting the central courtyard of the castle outside.

Rhena stared into Max's eyes. "Are you certain this is the only way?"

"I am certain of nothing, Rhena, except that if we only

keep trying to hide, we shall be caught. And if we hold out somehow until the fighting is done, then almost certainly Garm will be king of Leorna . . . and who would want to live in that world?"

Rhena took Max's hands in hers. "Our friendship is all I have, Max. If we die today, then I will tell you that I have never had a friend like you in all my life."

Max swallowed then tried to laugh. "I am glad poor Malvern did not hear that."

Rhena chuckled. "He is not such a bad sort either. I misjudged him, I fear."

Max's smile was a lie. "Well — if all goes as we plan, we'll have plenty of time to settle with our friends later. I just wish Malvern and Jippit were here with us now."

Rhena nodded. "And I would kiss them too," she said and leaned forward to kiss Max on his lips for just a brief moment which passed before he had realized it.

Max felt his heart beating faster. His thoughts and feelings were too mixed up to understand. He swallowed. "There is so much happening today, Rhena. All of life seems to fall on us at once." It was true, yet with all that happened that day, he would always remember that first kiss.

Leon whispered from the entrance. "*They bring Jippit and Malvern now.*"

Max scrambled on his hands and knees to join Leon and Caroline. Rhena was right beside him. They looked where Leon pointed.

King Lull and Garm stood together as the prisoners were marched into the square. Darkcloak stood a little away. The king looked grim, his arms folded across his chest. He wore his armor with his great sword and scabbard. Garm swaggered with his hands on his hips as the elf and Malvern were brought before them. Beyond them all, a team of horses were straining at harness to pull down the throwing arm of the catapult. The loaded arm of the counterweight was rising upward. Men stood ranked around the square, the king's guards and the mercenaries in separate rows. Sunlight brightened the battle banners of Leorna that flapped atop the walls.

Caroline looked to Max and Rhena. "*Remember, as we said,*" she whispered, "*do not look back at either of us.*"

Max and Rhena nodded, each thinking of the plan they must soon follow and not fail.

In the square Garm greeted the elf with an evil grin. "Well, well, Jumpjilter, we meet again. Sadly, this will be a short visit. We are releasing you and your young friend from our walls. I should say releasing part of you, at least."

Jippit stared at the gloating chieftain but Malvern fell into the arms of the nearest guard.

Garm motioned to one of his men who held a large battle ax. "Dirkin, be sure your stroke is clean. We don't want the elf's friends in town unable to recognize his pretty face."

Jippit looked at the king. "King Lull, there is no reason to behead the boy. He has no friends outside these walls. This is beneath you, surely."

Lull shook his head. "The traitor is right, Garm. We want no part of a boy's death."

There was laughter among the ranks of mercenaries when this was said and an uneasy look passed among the king's men. At that moment there was a call from the stable and everyone turned to see Kenelm stride forward tugging Max and Rhena along, each gripped firmly by his hands.

"Sire. I have found them. I have both your daughter and the young Prince of Gaspaar. They were fugitives within the walls."

"Rhena!" King Lull's face was ashen, and he turned to stare at his daughter as the captain of the guard brought the young royals into the square. "What — what has happened? Why have you hidden from me?"

The princess stared at her father. "Why was I imprisoned? Why was Max nearly killed? Why do you hold Jumpjilter who was my friend? What have *you* done, Father?"

Lull turned to Darkcloak. "What of this? How is it he is here? What *else* goes on behind my back?"

Garm clapped. "This is an omen of the gods, Lull. Now we can do what has been my dream from the first. The young prince's head will sail high and wide. The nerve of his brother will be broken as well as his heart. We'll carve these rebels, so they'll beg to be our slaves."

Darkcloak stepped forward. "No, King Lull. We must keep Max to make the *peace*. We can force a treaty now. Gaspaar will never make war with us while we hold their crown prince."

"Rubbish!" Garm shouted so that all could hear. "I am sick of your cowardly ways. You will gain *nothing* more than what you had and *lose* the power you can win. You've already begun a war. Now we must finish it."

There were cheers raised all around the courtyard though the guards were not so certain of the cry. Lull looked from Darkcloak to Garm and back in stunned amazement.

"Soldiers of Leorna," Garm shouted again turning to Lull's soldiers. "Lull looks to one advisor and then another. He does not know his mind. He cannot lead. In the name of conquest, I take this charge as my own. Bring the prince of Gaspaar to the block."

Kenelm stepped forward, dragging Max who was glancing from his captor to the two silent guards who marched on either side of him. These two wore the long capes of the infantry with the collars up around their ears in the cool morning breeze. Rhena scrambled past the trio rushing to her father and crying for him to stop the horrible order.

Lull looked down into his daughter's stricken face as she reached up to grab his arms and shook him.

"Father. Father. *Stop* this. Stop this war!"

Lull's face twisted with doubt and anger. "You don't know what you are asking."

"Do *you*, Father? You *cannot* do this."

"Take the prince to the steps," Garm ordered.

Kenelm and the two soldiers in capes brought Max to the flat stone base of the entrance of the keep where Dirkin stood waiting with his ax.

"The catapult is set, sire." Beasley shouted from the machine where a wide hemp net waited for the round stones to be loaded. "The weight is locked. We have the horses switched to pull the firing pin on your command."

Garm lifted a hand to Dirkin who raised his ax above his head.

"*No!*" Lull commanded. "We do not slay *boys!*"

Though Max knew that the hands that held him would never let Dirkin's ax fall on his neck, he strained not to scream with the tension inside his body. Turning his head to stare at Lull, he noticed that Darkcloak had stepped back and fallen to his knees against the wall of the keep. The hooded counselor brought his hands upward as if lifting some invisible weight above his bowed head. Max knew all eyes were on the executioner before him or many would have seen Gerald's actions and wondered at their meaning as did he.

A high ringing horn note sounded from above them and everyone stopped to stare up at the highest tower. The lookout was waving from the top battlement. "Armies! Armies are riding into the town!"

A loud commotion broke out among the soldiers and mercenaries in the square.

Lull shouted up at the tower lookout. "What army is it? Gaspaar or Wotterham?"

The lookout called back. "I — I see two banners side by side. It is Wotterham *and* Gaspaar . . . riding together. The largest army ever — a, a *thousand* men, sire — a thousand men!"

Lull was dumbfounded. "*Together?* Gaspaar, Averon, and Wotterham against us . . . Then all is lost."

"No Father. We have *won* — there is no *war!*" Rhena was shouting to be heard over the cries.

"Rhena is right, my brother." One of the soldiers beside Max turned from the steps and threw off his helmet, drawing his sword. "End this war now before it begins."

"*Leon,*" Lull gasped.

Garm screamed his rage, "Take the prince's head!"

The executioner began his high two-handed stroke, but as the disguised Caroline pulled Max to the side, Kenelm brought his own blade to block Dirkin's blow with his own and finished the man with his next then turned to guard Max from the rush of Garm's men. Leon and Caroline braced ready beside him with blades drawn. In that same frozen moment of surprise, Jippit Jumpjilter shoved his distracted guard to the ground. Before the fellow could regain his feet, the elf bounded to the others and tore the battle ax from the dead executioner's grasp.

As planned, Max and Rhena started to run for the rope sling of the trebuchet, calling for Jippit to follow them.

Jippit Jumpjilter started to follow but instead headed back to the forgotten Malvern, who was slowly rising from the ground where he had been dropped. Jippit's guard, realizing Jippit's aim moved to head him off. Not stopping, the elf's ax rang loudly on the soldier's shield as he fought to get past. Hearing this, Max ran to help his friend, and threw himself into the man's knees. The surprised soldier tumbled and struck the stone steps with a sharp cry.

Garm was scarlet with anger. "Fools! Take them! We have them *all. Leon* — the *prince of Gaspaar* — *kill* them and we have *won*."

"Hold *back* men of Leorna!" Lull held up his arm. "It is finished. I will not lead my army into such a cursed and bloody day."

"Perhaps not *your* army any longer." Garm beckoned the warriors with a raised sword. "Soldiers of Leorna, join *me* now and my matchless fighters. *Your* king has given in without so much as a strike. Slay your weak leaders and follow me to victory and riches. Join with us or perish. There can be *no* going back."

The soldiers and barbarians had drawn forward and mixed together so that it was hard to say who was shouting what, but Max knew that battle was coming as sure as flint sparks on dry straw. Pulling Malvern with them, Jippit, Max and Rhena had reached the sling of the catapult. "My Lady," Max shouted and Caroline, with a glance to Leon, dropped her raised sword arm and ran for the others.

Lull took a step toward Garm with his sword drawn. "Cease this madness, Garm."

Garm shouted a savage battle cry and lunged at Lull

with his sword and the king only warded off the deadly blow by the narrowest parry, his own blade rising to meet the downward swing of the barbarian's weapon. The ringing blow as the King of Leorna and the mercenary chieftain clashed, was the beginning Max had dreaded, and from it battle broke loose like a forest fire with circling duels, rushes, screams of anger and shrieks of pain. The courtyard was fast becoming a vicious, seething killing ground.

As Caroline reached the others at the catapult, she saw that Malvern was in the net and stopped, turning just in time to block an over-eager mercenary's thrust with a downward cut laying open his forearm. The lady glanced back to the four figures on the net. "I cannot go with you," she called. "I had not figured *Malvern's* weight. We might not clear the *wall*."

Before anyone could answer, Jippit leaped from the netting and rushed toward the harnessed horses. "You go, Catterline," he shouted. In the next moment, reaching the team, he slapped the haunches of the lead horse which jerked forward. Seeing the elf's action, Beasley the armorer rushed to cut the heavy line to the firing pin to stop the launch, but Jumpjilter tackled him, spilling onto the cobblestones of the courtyard in a tangle with the armorer. The heavy rope pulled the great pin free.

Caroline shouted to the others. "Hold tight together — do not tangle in the netting!"

Then, amid all the shouting and ringing of blades, over the clatter of the hooves, Max heard and felt the rattle of wood and board beneath them as the catapult's sling net began to slide pulling them into its swing. Holding to each other with all their arms and legs in a bundle, they were dragged slowly backward then up, up, up, with a sickening, unearthly pull as if they were being mashed into the netting by a giant's heavy hand. Max thought for a moment he would be pressed through the ropes themselves. Then they were free of the sling. High up and higher — no rope — no net — just sailing upward and away. Keeping his eyes open, Max watched the castle fall away from them and then could only see the sky and moat turning over and over and then the far bank and gatehouse rushing fast toward them.

With a scream that Max did not realize was his own, he hit the water, and all was darkness. The prince felt himself going down and down but could see nothing. He remembered he was not alone and wondered when he had let go of the others. Had he died? Were they all dead? He felt his skin stinging with the impact now and something was wrong with his shoulder. But he was rising. There was light above him and then everything was dark again.

CHAPTER 30

SURRENDER

"He's alive!" Derek was looking into Max's face, grinning, and shaking his head with wonder. There were a lot of faces in a circle around his brother. "Max, can you talk?"

Max choked and spat out water before he could speak. "The . . . the others. Rhena? Caroline? Malvern? Are they . . ."?

"We're fine, Max." Rhena's dripping face pushed past the others. "We are all right. Even silly Malvern. It is a miracle."

"Close enough, my prince," he heard Caroline's voice as the lady in her soaked jerkin kneeled down beside Derek. "Do not try to move too quickly. Your arm seems to be out of joint. I'm afraid you came off worst. We hit just shy of the gatehouse. You were knocked out on the bottom."

Malvern shook his curly wet hair beside Caroline. "Bad luck on you, old man."

Max blinked and tried to rise from the grass. "My arm hurts, but what of Jippit? What of Leon?"

Caroline frowned. "Hold still. Of the others we are uncertain, but your father —"

"Is *here*, my son." A voice boomed from behind the crowd around Max.

Everyone turned and moved aside as Max was helped to his unsteady feet to greet the King of Gaspaar. A column of mounted riders had moved to the edge of the landing, amid the shouts of the townspeople and rebels. King Randrew swung from his saddle to dismount and stepped toward them, his arms open to his youngest son.

There were cheers as the king embraced Max.

There were more cheers as Prince Linus climbed down from his saddle to join the others. "No greater joy can I know than that we have arrived in time to save the princes of Gaspaar and Averon. Forgive our tardiness, sires."

Prince Galen chuckled. "We feared your return might be for other purposes, Linus." he said.

"Forgive us our doubts," Derek added.

Linus nodded. "I had my own as well. Yet I see we still face a strong castle and I have but only my twenty to add."

King Randrew frowned. "And my hundred are not fighters and are tired from the trail, though they will not run."

Rhena shook her head. "But what of the '*thousand*?' The sentry cried that there were a thousand riders approaching. He was certain."

"Ten times our number, my princess," Linus said. "Their sentry must have been drinking strong wine."

Max felt a pain sweep up his arm and grimaced. "He — he was under a magic spell — I saw Darkcloak casting it."

"Darkcloak? Why would that villain make such a charm *against* King Lull?" Derek asked.

Max closed his eyes with pain. "I will speak of it later, with you and with Father."

Galen stepped near to Max. "Perhaps your injury has addled your thoughts, Max. I know injuries. Your shoulder can be wrenched back right, and the sooner, the better. Lay down and let me pull it straight. Quick pain now is better than waiting.”

Max lay down and felt the Prince of Averon reach to take his hand and place a heel solidly on him near his shoulder. There was a sudden jerk and he shouted again with the shooting jagged fire in his nerves, but then he felt better. He could feel his shoulder was in the right place again though still aching.

There was a horn blast over the water and much scrambling as men at arms rushed to the battlements. General Goosell shook his head. “We can try launching the catapult now, sire. We must hurry if they attack.”

Derek looked to King Randrew.

The king nodded. “This is your battle, Derek. You order it as you think.”

Derek held his sword up. “Everyone to places. Prepare the fire wagon. We will not destroy the drawbridge if Leon still lives. We shall prepare a charge across the bridge.” He shouted for the men gathered around them. “Knights of Gaspaar to the front.”

“Averon beside them.” Galen ordered.

Linus held his hand up and called back. “Follow me, knights of Wotterham.”

“Sires! Sires!” A cry came from the gatehouse scouts. “The banner! They raise the white banner!”

Everyone rushed forward and climbed on logs or stones to gain a better look. High atop the tallest turret of Leorna, a white banner was beating in the wind. The sign of surrender.

“The drawbridge is lowering.” Galen said. “I hear the chains.”

“Steady men.” Derek commanded. “Stand ready. This may be a trick.”

They watched as the long wood and metal bridge slowly lowered out over the moat and fell with a hard thud onto the pier before the gatehouse. At the other end of the bridge, the iron portcullis was raised, and a column of men walked out from underneath the gate. A white banner like the one above the castle was held over them. The dark figure in front held a hand up as they moved into the daylight on the bridge. Beside Sir Leon walked a small companion, the elf, Jippit Jumpjilter. Behind them a line of bound prisoners, the mercenaries of Garm, moved at the direction of the castle guards who held their spears upright. As they neared the gatehouse Leon motioned for silence, though little had been said as the solemn band had marched toward them.

"People of Leorna, leaders of Averon, Wotterham, and Gaspaar, the battle has ended. The king's castle and army is surrendered. The leader of the mercenaries is dead, killed by your King Lull in the last good fight of his life. He died saving the life of his daughter and his brother. Too late he saw the evil of his ways — but not too late to face it. He leaves you with a new peace. A new peace among the friends of Leorna who have come to rescue you."

Max heard crying and turned to see Rhena leaning against Caroline, the lady holding the princess' face against her side. He did not know what to do.

Malvern put a hand on Max's shoulder. "Thank you for saving my life, Prince Max."

Max coughed. "It was Jippit that did that, Malvern. And you have served your princess as well as any knight could hope."

"I wish I could be happy," Malvern replied. "But I guess it's not a day for that, with the king dead . . . and others too."

Randrew was standing by his son watching the surrendering band march across the drawbridge but nodded slightly at the words of the young noble. *"And others too,"* he agreed in a whisper.

Though the castle was searched, there was never a sign of Darkcloak found.

***

Leorna

The next day in the great field of the tournament, with everyone in the town and all the attending visitors watching, the new king of Leorna was crowned. Princess Rhena held her father's gold crown in her hands above the bowed head of Leon who knelt on one knee before her. Banners of all the kingdoms flapped above them as the princess, dressed in the beautiful green and gold silks of Leorna, spoke for all to hear. Behind her, Lady Caroline, King Randrew, Prince Galen, Derek, Goosell and Jippit Jumpjilter, all draped in fine cloaks and capes, stood solemnly.

"People of Leorna . . . I, the daughter of Lull, the last King of Leorna, do place his crown on his brother's head, Prince Leon, calling him to kingship of our land. I call on all who live within Leorna from the smallest to the greatest to support his reign as sovereign. I ask you to join me as I swear my fealty first to his keeping. Rise King Leon of Leorna."

Leon, his hair now cleaned and combed, his beard trimmed, the grime of battle washed from the creases of his skin, cloaked in king's purple, rose with the golden crown upon his head. He took Rhena's hands in his and bent to kiss her cheek. The crowd cheered but drew silent as he straightened and turned to speak.

"People of Leorna, we have been through a very hard lesson. I pray we learn all we are taught. I pledge myself and the peace of our land to both you and the friends who have suffered with us, risking much to set right what was wrong. Leorna will be a land where fear is a memory. Where trust will be valued above all our treasures. The weak, the poor, the hungry . . . I ask you to trust your king. Today there is roof and fire and food for all honest folk. I ask you, judge the highest among us by how we shall treat the least among us. This is my pledge to you."

CHAPTER 31

NEW DAYS

There was much celebrating as the day wore into evening. On the morning of the next day the royal parties of the neighboring kingdoms were departing. Princes, knights and squires were starting their journeys home. Max was tying his pack on the back of Blueberry in the stable and Jippit was chiding him about losing his elfin bow.

"Leon may treasure noble thoughts, Prince Max, but I would think you would take some care with gifts an elf bestows on you. Few tall ones are ever entrusted with such valuables."

Max laughed. "Jippit, I have no idea where that bow is

now. I'm lucky to have not lost far more than that." He sighed. "But I must ask you, now that we are alone this morning . . . tell me what you know of Gerald, for you have seen more than I and little escapes you. Please, Jippit . . . I must know what happened inside the castle walls . . . what of the fight inside?"

The elf shook his head. "A terrible scene, Max. It is better that you and Rhena were spared such sights."

"But we both must know, elf friend," a soft voice spoke from behind them. Rhena had entered the stable and now stepped close as they turned. "I came to see you off," she said quietly, "but like Max, I wish to know all that happened from one who has never failed to be honest with me."

Jippit bowed slightly. "I hate to speak of such things that will wound your heart, dear princess. There is no kind way to speak of fighting with swords and axes. Blood is only glorious in tapestries and tales. It is awful when it bursts and slings with curses and cries. That was the way of the courtyard as you flew from us and I thanked Izmah that you both were taken clean away."

Rhena held her arms and took a breath. "Is it true? Did Father . . . change his mind?"

Jippit studied the princess' face before he answered. "He fought Garm with a passion. When Leon was knocked down near them, the villain saw his chance to sever his head. Leon's sword was free on the ground and I thought he was surely to be killed for I was fully pressed with a foul barbarian trying to hit me with a mallet and could do nothing. At that instant, Lull leaped across Leon, crying, 'Save Leorna!' and swung his sword with such force that it drove Garm's blade back. The two of them went down grabbing each other tightly. Leon scrambled to his feet to help but both Lull and Garm had ended their fight. Garm had stabbed the king with his dagger but Lull had pulled it free and finished Garm with it as well. The fight between the king's men and the barbarians turned with this fatal struggle and many joined Kenelm in forcing the wild men back against the walls. Princess, you know I was never a true admirer of King Lull, but in his last fight, I saw a life in him I had never seen. He looked as one who gave all for something beyond himself."

Rhena's tears shown on her cheeks. "Thank you, Jester."

Jippit smiled. "I wish I could raise your heart as a true jester should."

Max swallowed. "And Gerald? Did you see what happened with Gerald, Jippit?"

The elf nodded. "For a time . . . I am certain now the trance that fell upon him was some great spell that made the men upon the walls see ten times the armies that marched against them. To control the minds of men in broad day sun must have cost him much, for he fell as one stricken. When I saw him last, the battle was ending and he was hobbling past the wall of the keep, a hand braced against the stones as he moved in pain around the edge of the wall. I followed him, uncertain of what I should do, but as I turned the corner, I saw him disappear. At first, I thought he had entered a shadow beneath the turret, but when I moved there, there was nothing but stone. When at last I turned to go back I heard a voice trail after me, weak but clear.

Max blinked. "What did he say? What did you hear?"

Jippit frowned. "*Max wins . . . and I am lost. Protect him, elf.*"

Rhena put a hand on Max's bandaged shoulder. "There is hope for him, Max."

Jippit shook his head. "King Randrew has banned him from ever returning to Gaspaar. He had no choice. Evil sorcery is an offense and must be punished."

"Others died." Max said.

"But . . . he is your brother," Rhena said.

Max nodded. "Yes. Always. He is my brother."

***

Autry

In a barn outside the village walls, a little girl set a beaten tin water cup on the barrel beside the owl with a bandaged wing. She stroked his smooth feathers with the tip

249

of her finger as he dipped his beak into the water. "There Mister Fletcher," she said. "You drink good. I get you a bacon from the feast."

A new voice spoke from just beyond them.

"My, my, you find friends wherever you go, old one." A fox head appeared over a low half door in the wall.

The girl spun to stare at the visitor with the bright golden green eyes and wide toothy smile. "Fox!"

"Do not fear, child," the owl said as it rose to its full height. "It is my oldest friend. Prince Fanzig of Dumbwillow Forest, this is Lady Autry, who has saved me and perhaps all. The bravest and kindest heart we have met in Leorna."

Fanzig, who had leaped down inside the barn, bowed to the girl. "I am honored, my lady. I should never have spoken had I not seen the kindness in your face. Accept our thanks for all."

Autry stared at the fox and stepped slowly to him. She held out a hand. "Can I pet you, Master Fanzig?"

The Fox sat down on his haunches as the human child ran her hand over his red fur.

Autry shook her head as she felt the pointed black ears. "Nobody will b'lieve Autry if I say I done this."

Fanzig grinned. "Lass, it is not so important what others say or think about you, if your heart holds what is true."

***

And so, the princes and armies left Leorna with its new king and a peace was forged between that land and Gaspaar, Averon and Wotterham. It was a new beginning for that time, but few supposed that even greater dangers would rise again to threaten all that land and more. It would be a test and a legend and a tale of heroes, magic, and courage, but all the mighty deeds could never have made more joy than filled Autry's heart that day when she made friends of the speaking beasts of Izmah.

THE END

The Tales of Gaspaar continue in...

Book 4 -
The Return of Fears

(A brief selection from the fourth book follows.)

Maude felt her throat tighten. "And what have you seen?"

The man licked his lips again. "Seven days ago, I lit my fire and the Duke's men came to me. 'What is it?' they asked. 'Why have you set the beacon ablaze?'"

Maude waited, dreading what might be uttered, yet transfixed.

"I told them what I had seen. Yet no other beacons were fired. No other watcher spoke. I was called a fool . . . and sent on my way. Since then I have journeyed south to Gaspaar, whose king last met this danger himself in years past."

Maude reached across and gripped the old man's shoulder. "Speak, sir! What did you see? Giants? Sea monsters? Do the dragons return?"

"Vikings," the old man croaked. "Vikings."

Maude felt the warmth draining from the afternoon. "Vikings . . . " she whispered and heard herself ask, "And . . . where are they now? What have they done? Is the North afire again?"